Marque of the Son

TH Leatherman

Marque of the Son by TH Leatherman
Copyright © 2017 by TH Leatherman

All rights reserved. No part of this publication may be reproduced, distributed, or transmitted in any form or by any means, including photocopying, recording, or other electronic or mechanical methods, without prior written permission of the publisher, except in the case of brief quotations embodied in critical reviews and certain other noncommercial uses permitted by copyright law.

This is a work of fiction. Names, characters, businesses, places, events and incidents are either the products of the author's imagination or used in a fictitious manner. Any resemblance to actual persons, living or dead, or actual events is purely coincidental.

Published by Fivefold Publishing LLC, PO Box 586, Firestone, CO 80520.

Cover Artwork: Licarto

Book layout by www.ebooklaunch.com

Acknowledgements

As always, I'd like to thank my wife and boys for your continued support. The members of TCCG, thank you for so much for your insight. Jess for your excellent editing services. The fine volunteers of RMFW, thanks for your years of support. I'd also like to thank all of my beta readers. You all made this from a collection of words on a page to a work of art. Special thanks to Aimie Runyan. Without your help, Mark and Sara wouldn't be who they are today.

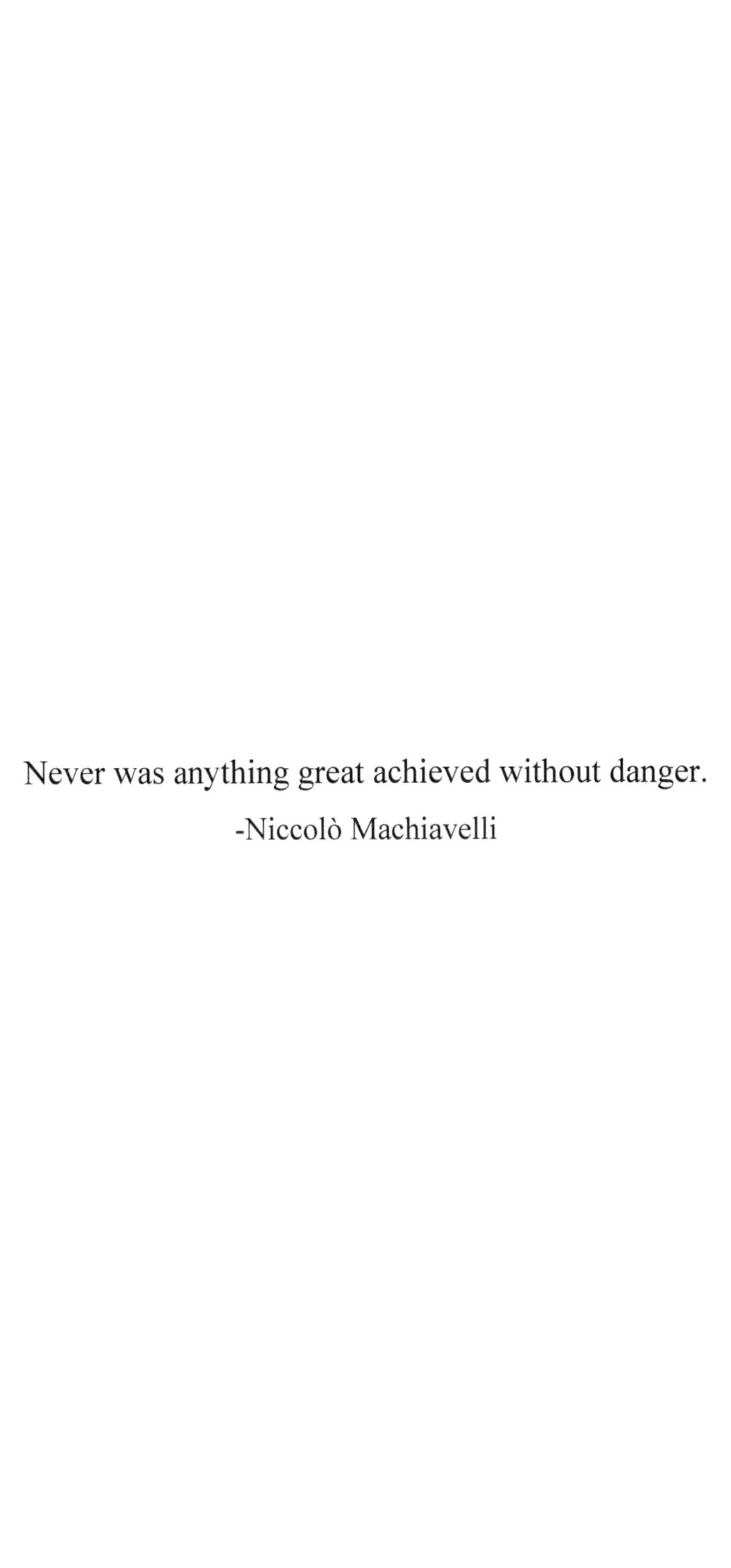

Never was anything great achieved without danger.

-Niccolò Machiavelli

Chapter 1

The Funeral

"This is a bad idea, sir."

We were in the back of a large groundcar. Across from me, my small foxlike bodyguard scowled. His pointed ears were folded back, flat against his head.

"Trent, we must honor our dead, Terran and Muscat alike. You had carte blanche on travel arrangements." I waved to indicate the austere gray walls of our vehicle. "Armored personnel carrier. Do you have any idea how hard it was to borrow three of these?"

"Mark is right." Sara Chew, my first officer, was sitting next to me. "It's war. This is what we're fighting for. Wouldn't you want to mourn Trey or Tracy if something happened to them?"

The corners of his lips turned down at the mention of his brother and sister. Fellow marines. He showed some of his wolflike teeth. "Not the same. I'm not a prince of Yale or the adopted son of the Muscat Queen. Her Majesty's orders were specific. Nothing bad can happen to you."

"I'm a prince of a monarchy that hasn't existed since the Erethizon took over. It's part of the Theocracy now. My father is a figurehead sitting in some prison somewhere. Freeing him and my home world will require risks." I leaned forward and looked him in the face. "My crew. My people. They're counting on me to lead them. They need this."

Trent's ears twitched and he slumped in the seat. Being a meter tall, it gave him the appearance of a sulky child.

I was a little misty-eyed remembering the nice things we'd said about our fallen friends. Our last marine platoon leader, Aasha, had been a Porcu-bear agent. She had blown up our ship and everyone on it, including the captain.

I rubbed the coin in my pocket. It had a star on one side, and my great-grandfather's head on the other—the last king of Yale, before the senate elected my father to the position. I hoped his wisdom would guide me today. "Relax, Trent. We went out, held the memorial service. We're on our way back now. Two thirds of the way done."

Our speed dropped as we took a curve. I pulled up our Freyan global position on my implant. This wasn't our planned route. I used my personal AI to send a text message to our driver. *Warren?*

Sorry, sir. Accident en route.

I closed my eyes and let out a breath. When I opened them again, Trent was shaking his head at me. I grabbed my suit's helmet and put it on. Trent and Sara did the same.

The armor's heads-up display came to life. Using my HUD I opened the command channel and sent an all-crew alert. "Listen up. An accident has caused us to alter our route. It may be nothing, but stay jazzed.

"Trent, hand me some lokigrapes."

Trent pulled a few of the local fruits from a bag near his feet. We hit a bump as he was handing them to me and one bounced from his grasp.

Sara gasped. Trent cursed. I caught the blue fruit before it hit the ground. Turning it over in my hand, I could see the fragile skin was still intact. We all let out a sigh of relief. I carefully accepted four more of the lokigrapes and put them in a stiff pouch at my waist.

"Pull up the new route."

Trent did as I asked and displayed a holo-image between us using his wrist AI.

"They'll want to put us in the crossfire and split us up," said Trent. "If it were me, I'd position it here, here, or here." Three orange spots showed up on the map where he pointed.

"I agree. So, we'll avoid the first one by taking this overpass." I pointed and the map lit up green where I indicated. "We'll avoid this one by using the bridge. This one is tricky. We can avoid it by going twenty minutes out of our way."

"More like thirty, sir." Trent was right.

As I watched, red X's appeared on the overpass and bridge to indicate traffic accidents.

"Three times is enemy action."

"Sir?" asked Trent.

"A Terran expression. We have to fall back and come up with another plan."

I could see Trent talking through his visor. I didn't hear anything, so he must have been giving orders to our drivers.

The map in front of me changed. It showed our route swinging around the block, back to rally point B. A jolt sent Sara and I sprawling into Trent. I jumped up and saw through the view port that a tour bus had clipped the back of our APC and the front of the one following us. Porcu-bear shock troops burst through the sides. One of them dropped to a knee and took aim.

"IMPAND! Everyone out." An IMPAND was designed to cut through armor and fortifications. It would have no trouble cracking our APC open like a cara-nut.

We were out the hatch on the opposite side, when the blast, more felt than heard, slammed into us. The pressure wave knocked me to the ground. I glanced back. The vehicle was toppling. Dave Warren, our driver, was on the ground shaking his head. I grabbed him by the arm and hauled him up with me. The APC landed less than half a meter from my foot.

Around us were plasticrete buildings, offices and storefronts. I saw a parking structure half a block away.

I opened the command channel. "It's hit the fan, people. There's a parking tower nearby. We'll hole up there and evac from the roof." I switched channels. "Sara, I don't see Porcubear fighters. Get us some aircars. Trent, get a drone in the air. Warren, lay down suppressive fire."

Trent got the drone up. A tactical map appeared on my HUD. We were being flanked.

The Muscat marine snarled. "Two by two. Move!"

Trent and I ran for the first doorway. Moments later Sara and Warren raced past. We covered a hundred meters between us and the building.

We made it about two thirds of the distance before they pinned us down in an alley. My HUD showed the tactical map. "Daly's down. They sent six our way. Two after the rest. They knew I was in the first APC."

I winced as gunfire hit the wall behind which I was standing. Shards of plasticrete flew everywhere. I could hear the zings of plasma rifles.

Trent pulled up the battle map again. "The garage is across the street."

"Fruits of our labors?" I suggested.

He gave me a head roll, the Muscat equivalent of a shrug. Opening his bag, he yipped and threw the lokigrapes like live snakes. The fruits pelted two of the enemy.

"Broke one?"

"Two," he confirmed.

"Mine are good." I handed him two. We took turns throwing them at the Porcu-bears. They were big targets. An Erethizon soldier is three meters tall and a meter wide. Add in combat armor and they were hard to miss.

After the first two they must have realized the lokigrapes weren't grenades. By the third they were trying to hit us when we threw. Trent had it easier, being a smaller target.

Trent threw his last one. I found a small crate. I threw it into the street and rifle fire turned it to splinters. A hair later, I threw my last fruit.

The force of a sledgehammer hit my left shoulder, spinning me into the sidewalk. Sara yanked me back before anyone got lucky.

"Sir?"

I sucked air through my teeth. "Gauss rifle round." I rotated my shoulder as it blazed with pain. "Nothing Sophie can't fix."

I couldn't hold anything with my left arm, but it was still attached. The armor had done its job. "Irving is getting a bonus when we get back to *Ocelot*. This armor is great."

Readjusting my grip on my TR 45 rifle, I pulled up the battle map on my HUD. The Porcu-bears hadn't shot at the drone.

"How are the crew?"

"Good," said Sara. "Trevor is hauling Daly. Pace and Jay are with them. They're going around. They'll get there before us."

"If we get there."

More plasticrete chips rained into the alley.

"How many did we get, Trent?"

"Five, sir. Your last throw got one in his helmet visor. I'll mark them."

My HUD updated. Five of the red enemy icons turned purple.

More rounds slammed into the alley walls, along with two plasma bolts.

My palms were getting sweaty. "How long?"

"Not soon enough," said Warren.

He was right. The icons were advancing.

"Where are they?" I demanded.

As if on cue, a buzzing sound started in the distance.

"Not close enough. We'll be overrun. Suppressive fire."

Sara, Warren, and Trent took turns firing on the enemy. It was slowing them down, but not enough. Each Porcu-bear soldier was like an armored tank.

On the battle map, I saw the red icon disappear and one of the purple icons get knocked back. Two loud cracks came from up the block. More rifle fire and plasma bolts. For once it wasn't directed at us. Their advance slowed.

"Thank you, Tracy," I said over the comm.

"You're welcome, sir," came the reply. Trent's sister, our sniper, had made it to the end of the block and had come to our aid.

The buzzing was getting louder. Was it enough?

An Erethizon was even with the alley. It was the Porcu-bear I'd hit in the visor. Trent and I opened up on the armored death machine. It swung a plasma rifle at us. I was rooted to the spot. We were out of time.

Chapter 2

Full in the Face

THREE YELLOW AND PURPLE OBJECTS hit the Porcu-bear in the face. The plasma rifle fired. The shot hit the alley wall to our left. Yellow and purple cat-sized insects slammed into the soldiers. Jotunn wasps.

The Erethizon soldiers slapped them away and continued to shoot at us. Until the first Porcu-bear screamed in agony. Seams and joints: every suit of armor has its weak points. The jotunn wasps would find them. Three stings would kill a Terran or a Muscat. Four should take down an Erethizon. Pain doubled with each sting.

Aware of the danger, the Porcu-bears started shooting the insects, but there were too many of them. The soldier with the plasma rifle was the most effective. The enveloping weapon would stun every wasp on its target. It would also stun the Porcu-bear. Every stunned wasp was replaced by three more. The rifleman signed the death warrant of every comrade he hit. Finally, he slumped to the ground.

We backed down the alley and went around the building rather than through the wasps. The insects' only desire was for their favorite food. That and to sting anything that got in their way.

We joined the rest of the team at the parking garage. A stairwell led to the top.

"Who'd you find to come get us?" I asked Sara.

"Valkyries."

I winced and my stomach flip-flopped. True, the mercenaries were brave and crazy enough to come to our rescue. But it was going to cost me. At least we'd be alive to pay the bill.

◆ ◆ ◆

"I'd tell you to rest and not move your shoulder," Sophie wrapped a fast-heal bandage around my arm.

Heat tendrils stabbed into me, followed by what felt like spikes of ice. "Ow."

"But you won't do it, so why bother? It will be better by tomorrow morning."

She threw the rest of the roll in the corner and flung open a drawer. "Anything I can get you for the pain? Hemlock? Cyanide?"

I stood and gingerly put on my shirt. My muscles now felt like they were burned with acid instead of a bonfire.

Sophie stood with the drawer open. Her shoulders were tense.

I held her from behind with my good arm. My sister turned around and hugged me back.

"Those pointy alien bastards." With each word she pounded my wounded shoulder. I held my breath to keep from crying out.

"I miss him too, Soph."

"They took him from me Mark. They took him and Dad, too. They take everything good and make it rotten."

I held her as she buried her head in my shoulder. We stood like that for a long time before there was a soft knock on the door.

"Just a minute." I said.

Sophie stood up straight and wiped away the tears that never quite appeared. I waited. She gave me a small nod.

Opening the door, I saw Pace Jones waiting. "You two okay, sir?"

"Fine, Mr. Jones. Do you need me or Dr. Martin?"

"You, sir. It's like … I mean, you'll never …" He scrubbed his face with his hands. "You'd better come see it for yourself."

We'd taken over an abandoned mag-lev station. Underground, only one way to access the street, it was defensible and safe from prying eyes. We'd turned the ticket booths into a barricade. There were half a dozen people looking out the glass turnstiles. They stepped aside as I approached. A man was coming down the stairs. When he came through the revolving door, I was taken aback.

"Well, I'll be damned. "

"I'm pretty sure I'll be damned first, sir."

I gave him a hug and ushered him inside. "Rafe, we thought you were dead. You're healthy enough to wrestle a frost bear."

♦ ♦ ♦

"What happened?"

"When the Leo blew. I didn't know what to do. I didn't know how to reach anyone without comms."

"You weren't on the ship." I slapped him on the shoulder. "Two weeks. What were you doing?"

"I, uh, was out trying to get trade goods. I sneaked off the ship."

I steered him into the lobby. "Can we get you anything? Food? Drink? Lokigrapes?"

He twitched and swept his gaze though the room, searching for the offending fruit.

"Just kidding. We used all the lokigrapes this morning."

"Not funny, sir," said Rafe. "You have no idea how scary those things are."

We'd taken over the café for meals. Rafe got a sandwich and sat with me. He waved at the gathering crowd. "I hadn't seen this mag-lev station before. They were going to put in expensive houses out here last I checked. That project died with the bear problem, though."

"It worked out for us. Rafe, I had no idea you were from this system."

He shrugged. "Not something I advertise. Freyans have a rep and not everyone appreciates our ..." He searched the ceiling for the right word, "Enthusiasm for trade. Our view of women is a bit backward, too. You never see them in positions of power. The prevailing attitude is that they should stay at home."

"How did you find us?"

"I heard a rumor the military was experimenting with armored dogs. A friend of a friend said he'd seen them out this way. No one around here has ever seen a Muscat, so I guessed you'd holed up nearby."

"You guessed right. I'll tell Trent and his armored dogs to keep a lower profile. Rafe, it's been impossible to get supplies." I spread my hands. "Food, medical supplies, arms and armor. It doesn't matter what it is. I can't find it. When I can, I'm paying too much. The only people who will deal fairly with me are in the military."

Rafe nodded. "The whole planet is like that," he explained. "Think of it like *Ocelot*, but a lot bigger. There are all these secretive business families. Food, school, tech, everything comes from the family. Anything else has long contracts. They spell out every detail of the deal with some other family.”

“I see.” The situation was becoming clear. “And here I am, a yokel, with no family and no contracts.”

“Right.” Rafe drew the word out. “So, you need an introduction. A family willing to take you in. It won’t be cheap, but it will make things easier going forward.” He grinned like the crag cat with the near-rat.

“Let me guess,” I said. “You know who I should talk to. What’s your percentage?”

He put his hand to his chest in mock indignation. “No percentage. A finder’s fee.”

“Moving in?”

Rafe tapped a finger to his chin. “You serious about a ship and getting off this rock?”

“Oh yes,” I said. “We’re going back into space to stomp Porcu-bear toes.”

“Then I’ll be your sandwich boy.” He smiled, twirling the meat and bread with a flourish.

“I’m thinking of a different job for you.”

He squinted at me. “Other duties as required? You’re not going to have me clean toilets, are you?”

“No.” I shook my head. “I want to make you our quartermaster.”

“I’m not an officer.”

“You don’t have to be. I can hire who I want and give them a full share and a specialist’s mass allotment. No more hiding your extra mass in ship’s stores.”

He blanched. “You knew about that?”

“You’re good. I’m sneakier.” I waved my arm to indicate the cafeteria. “Get food. I’ll give you a budget and a time frame. We’ll get someone else to cook it. Ammo battery packs if you can get them. No ship yet. When we fix that, you'll be ordering blankets, toothbrushes, and personal AIs."

He let out a breath. "That sounds like a lot of work."

"It's doing what you love for a lot more pay. Keep me happy, keep the crew happy, and credits will follow."

Rafe bobbed his head at me. "We can do business."

"Good. There's a staff meeting at 1600 tomorrow. Be there."

◆ ◆ ◆

Everyone made it on time. Even Rafe.

I rapped on the plastic table. "Thanks for coming, everyone. Please welcome Rafe back from his brief stint in the grave."

There was a round of laughter.

"Rafe has agreed to be our quartermaster. Please get your supply needs to him and rank them by priority. Keep your budgets in mind. If something necessary falls outside that budget, let me know. Our funds are limited, but there is some wiggle room."

"Sir?" said Rafe. "You'll have to meet with Ufkell."

"Mark," I said.

"What?"

"In staff meetings, we aren't formal. It's easier."

"Okay. I've set up a meeting with Ufkell for 1000 tomorrow."

I blinked. "We'll have to reschedule that. I'm supposed to meet Admiral Norbert at that time."

Rafe shook his head. "You wouldn't believe what I had to do to set up this meeting. Worse, I'm willing to bet that Ufkell knew about your meeting with the admiral. If you miss this, I doubt you'll get another chance."

I thought about that for a moment. "Can we set up a meeting with another family?"

Rafe winced and scratched the back of his neck. "You did."

It dawned on me then. "The Freyan navy."

He nodded and shrugged. "Yes, they refer to themselves as the Gunji."

"Okay, we'll come back to that. Does anyone have any problems with the budget?"

"Mark," Rowdy stood in his chair and leaned in. "The amount you gave me will work. But where did you get the credits?"

I wasn't ready to make that public knowledge. My old friend Ike had done a brilliant job of rounding up all the stray assets from Yale. From his mining outpost on Eureka, he'd managed to collect 70 percent of the estimated assets, everything not on-planet during the invasion. "Some is mine, some from the cargo we sold, some from people interested in seeing us succeed. Enough to put us aboard another ship. Also, thank Rowdy for agreeing to build the Freyans a few of our MST torpedoes. It will help if we need more money, but we want to avoid that if we can."

"Why?" asked Trent.

"Because they're finicky," growled Rowdy. "The Freyans will, without a doubt, open one up to try to figure out how it works. When that happens, we want to be far away."

"Because?"

Rowdy's smile looked feral. "Imagine your body crushed to the size of a pinhead."

Trent's eyes widened and his ears flattened.

"Anyway, we don't have access to the *Leo*'s accounts. That data was lost when she was. Racy is working on a fix."

I nodded at her. "When we find the accounts, we may have trouble moving them."

"There's also the legal stuff. The admiral should be greasing the wheels for a master's license."

"Do you need that?" asked Sara.

I waggled my head from side to side. "We could get by without it, even forge documents. But if some pencil pusher or customs agent gets curious, they can fine us or impound the ship. So why risk it? A test, an interview, two days, and we should have the license."

"And the ship?"

She had a point. "That's another thing to discuss with the admiral. So far, someone else has outbid or blocked me on every ship that meets our requirements. Moving along. Medical?"

"Daly is at the hospital. It will take a month for him to recover. He'll have a few artificial parts when he's done," said Sophie.

Trent grunted. "At least he'll live."

She tapped on the image in front of her. "We'll need more Terran blood, heal-fast, and bandages. We're doing okay on antibacterials and antivirals. We're running low on bone-knit and M-stat. We could use a medical table and some scanners, but not sure if the new ship will have that. No medi-nano, but no equipment to control it even if we had it."

That struck me as odd. "M-stat? The gravity isn't that bad here."

"For Terrans, no," said Sophie. ".85 G is fine for us. For the Muscat, it's just a touch too light for them. They need small doses to maintain muscle mass and keep their organs healthy."

"Okay, don't let us get too low. Tech?"

"Sorry, Mark. The AI running this dump is as dumb as dirt." Racy shook her head. "Three cameras, two drones, barely enough processing power to keep it all running. We have marines standing guard to cover tubes. If you'd let me …"

"Sorry, Racy. We may have to resort to you hacking the local network, but we're not there yet. Scavenge what you can and get a list to Rafe." Her ears perked up. I wondered what she might be up to.

"Rowdy, how do we look in engineering?"

"Awful," he said, pounding the table for emphasis. "The wiring in this station is substandard. Not enough water pressure. We don't have a parts printer or the raw materials to run it even if we had one. Getting the parts has been like trying to push plasma through a water line: doomed from the start."

I blew out a breath. "I'll work on getting that fixed in the next couple days as well. Sara, how are we on manpower?"

My XO reviewed an image on the table in front of her. "I haven't hired replacements, or even started looking. We'll need a second mate and three helmsmen."

"At least," I agreed. "Depending on the ship, we may require more than that."

"I'll post at the union hall and on message boards. We'll get nibbles." Sara made some notes.

"What about you, Trent? More marines?"

He shook his head. "No, we have enough, even with Daly laid up."

"Good." I surveyed the table. "Any other business to discuss?" There was a round of shrugs and nos. "Then we're adjourned. Rafe, let's discuss our strategy for tomorrow."

Chapter 3

Meet the Neighbors

RAFE AND I TOOK MY sister's aircar to the first appointment. She'd been in it when the *Leo* had exploded, out getting medical supplies. At the moment it was one of the few vehicles we had. Trent and Tracy flanked us on hoverbikes.

We found ourselves in front of an old Terra Nordic church. It was a three-tiered structure with a thatched roof on each level and heavy wooden cross-members that ended in dragon heads. Impressive, if ancient.

The doormen, each two meters tall with thick hair and beards, were dressed as Viking warriors. They wore ablative armor made to look like leather and bone. They carried blast rifles, but also sported vibro-axes on their backs.

Trent and Tracy moved to follow us, but I waved them off. Trent scowled.

We were escorted inside. The interior was dim, with wall sconces shaped like torches and walls of rough-hewn wood. One of the guards spoke to me. My AI identified the language as old Terra Norwegian. Thankfully, it also supplied the translation.

"Welcome, friend. Ufkell is expecting you," said the Viking on the right with a slight sneer.

Rafe responded, "Thank you. I am pleased he could see us."

I bowed. "We are grateful he could fit us into his busy schedule."

The doorman clenched his jaw before lumbering ahead of us. There was a large set of double doors at the back of the foyer.

I rubbed the coin in my pocket.

Rafe whispered in my ear. "You speak Norwegian, sir?"

I tapped my head. His eyebrows twitched in surprise.

The doors opened. I half expected a dining hall complete with wooden tables and chairs. Instead, it was a large office with an ornate desk and blood red accents.

The man behind the desk had the same long, thick beard and braids as the doormen, but was dressed in a business suit. Ufkell was short and stout. The large, high-backed chair in which he sat gave him the impression of importance. He laughed boisterously, a laugh that never touched his cold eyes.

"Mr. Martin, Rafael tells me you're looking for a business partner."

"Someone to do business with, yes."

Ufkell motioned to one of his guards. "Sven, get us some drinks."

Sven took three tankards from a cabinet. He expertly poured amber drinks from a tap with the likeness of a winged woman holding a sword. A Valkyrie: fierce maidens who carry the dead from the battlefield. I hoped they wouldn't be carrying me any time soon.

Drinks in front of us, Ufkell continued. "What are you looking for?"

As we'd agreed earlier, Rafe took point. "A ship, tech gadgets, medical supplies, weapons, food."

Ufkell smiled. "I can help with some of that."

"Some of it?" Rafe pressed.

He studied us each in turn. The grin became friendly and lopsided but his eyes were menacing. "Okay. All of it."

I willed my face to remain pleasant as I felt a chill run down my back.

Rafe handed him a tablet displaying the list of the supplies we needed. He sent me a message. On the bottom of my vision a text message popped up. *See, I told you he could do it.*

I sent a message back. *I'm good at reading people, but this guy isn't giving anything away.*

"Great," Rafe said. "Let's talk about ships. What types of freighters can you get us?"

"All types. Lighter haulers, tankers, and right on up to Starmaster super carriers."

"A heavy hauler, something in the hundred thousand DWT range," Rafe added.

"I can have three vessels ready for you to inspect in a few months." The hard line of his lips implied the time frame was nonnegotiable. "You'll be wanting to finance it, of course." He said this last part as a question.

My heart sank. We had to have ship right now. A few months was too long to sit planet-side. We'd need to find a different way to get a ship. I sent a message to Rafe. *Accept it. We'll find another way to get a ship, but right now we need supplies.*

"Yes, of course," Rafe responded.

"The Sudhurland Keiretsu will take 30 percent of the gross. You'll be required to make port in Freya twice a year. We'll have first pick of any cargo at 80 percent of market price."

It was highway robbery. Rafe was a good dealer, though. "The traditional owner's share is 20 percent and this is a free trade port."

Ufkell spread his arms. "Have you tried to buy food, medical supplies, or computers? The prices are outrageous. Think of it as the cost of doing business. It is in our best interest to get you on a ship and earning money for the Keiretsu. All we ask is for a little preferential treatment in return."

Rafe made a show of considering it. "How about the traditional owner's share, no cargo perks, and 20 percent discount on any other supplies."

"Rafael," he said, like he was being patient, "I've known you and your family for a long time. Don't presume that entitles you to any special treatment." Ufkell squinted. "You have no bargaining power. You need a ship. You need supplies. I have access to the supplies and can get the ship. I like you though, so we'll only take 25 percent of the gross, and first pick at 90 percent of market. No discount on supplies."

"Ufkell, you're right. We are men of few options, but we can't make money without a ship. 20 percent discount on supplies now, and you can have 25 percent of gross and first pick of cargo at market after you deliver the ship."

He sized us up for a few moments before putting his hand out. "Deal."

Rafe and I took Ufkell's hand in turns. "Deal."

Ufkell took a copy of the contract from his desk. He must have had an AI listening in on the negotiations. Rafe and I spent half an hour reviewing the details. I had my own AI run a legal analysis. We were getting the short end of the stick, but he was right: we had few options. Afterward, we drank strong mead. Ufkell handed Rafe a memory stick in a gold-inlaid wooden box. It contained an impossibly long access code that changed every second based on a dozen algorithms. When slotted into a computer it would give us access to the Keiretsu's marketplace. We all pretended we were good friends enjoying drinks over a profitable new future. Inside, it felt like every moment took forever.

In a longer amount of time than I was comfortable with, we were on our way to our next appointment.

◆◆◆

Outside, Trent relaxed when he saw me. I gave Sven a hearty bear hug like we were old friends before leaving.

Once we were in the aircar, Rafe turned to me. "Sir, we're giving away a lot, but we can always renegotiate later. It's in both of our best interests if we succeed."

"That man has a dark side. Did you catch the observer clause?"

"Yeah. Not sure what to make of that. Our Mr. Darkside wants to put someone on our ship for the first year. I suppose he wants to keep us honest."

I started up the aircar and lifted off the ground. "Rafe, how likely is it that he can get us a hundred thousand DTW freighter?"

He shook his head. "I don't know."

"I don't either." I bit my lip. "But the time frame isn't something we can accept. We need another option."

His lips twitched up. "At least we get a fifth off any supplies."

"Exactly."

◆◆◆

Trent was much more comfortable with our next stop. You couldn't get much safer than a military base. Rafe and I were escorted into a conference room. The table and chairs were the same dull gray as the walls. A more depressing space, I couldn't imagine.

We were an hour late. It was a safe bet the admiral knew where we'd been, and would keep us waiting. I tried to guess his mood. We had handed over a high ranking Porcu-bear officer. But on the other hand, we'd been partly responsible for the destruction of an APC and damage to a second. Add in that we'd been dealing with Ufkell … we'd likely tipped the scales toward him being very unhappy.

As he entered, Norbert's scowl confirmed this. His uniform was black with a red sash and piping. It was common to all Freyan officers. His had enough fruit salad on the chest to decorate a company of marines.

"Admiral, thanks for seeing us." I held out my hand. He pointedly did not shake it. Instead, he sneered like it was covered in slime.

"You have some nerve. You assured me when you borrowed the APCs that they would come back undamaged. The chances of an ambush were remote, you said."

I shrugged. "We were wrong. At least that's one less Porcu-bear cell. You must have all sorts of intelligence by now: where they came from, how they got past your blockade."

"No." He spat the word out like a curse. "Professionals. Nothing that would lead back to the rest of them."

"Well, you can't blame us for that. We played target and flushed them out."

He sat at the head of the table. "I can blame you for a lot more than that. You've been consorting with criminals."

"Criminals?"

"Does the name Ufkell chime the watch?"

"Oh," I said, "I had no idea. We had some supply issues. Mr. Ufkell offered to solve them for us."

Admiral Norbert glowered. "He did, did he?"

"Yes, we've had no luck getting a new freighter. Food, bandages, and ammo have been tough to get as well."

"And you didn't ask me?"

"Didn't know we could," I said. "And I'm not sure if he can do everything he claims. He said he could get us a ship, but I don't think he knows the first thing about them."

Norbert gave me a sly smile. "He can't."

"And you can?"

"Get you a ship?" He shook his head. "No. I'm buying everything. We're putting weapons on everything we can float."

I sat stunned for a moment. No wonder I couldn't get a ship. "Ca … can I buy one from you?"

"Mark, there are a lot of things you can buy. I have more guns than men to hold them. We could even part with some medi-nano and a couple of scanners. A ship?" He shook his head. "Even if they're decoys, I need them."

"Any suggestions for me and my crew?"

"Three." He ticked them off on his fingers. "You can get transport to another system and buy a ship there. Convince another merchant captain to sell. Or go privateer."

Neatly played, I thought. "Will being a legalized pirate get you to sell me a ship?"

"No. You've got marines and there's plenty of Porcu-bear tonnage a thousand klicks that way." He pointed up.

"If I can get there."

He shrugged.

I mulled that over for a few moments. "Can I get a letter of marque?"

"You're not a captain."

"What will it cost me to fix that?"

"Sixty thousand credits."

At least he was honest in his greed. I nodded in understanding. "Double that and you'll get me the letter and the ability to order supplies."

"One fifty."

"Done."

He held out his hand. "A pleasure doing business with you, Captain."

Chapter 4

She did what?

"RAFE, IS IT JUST ME, or has our neighborhood gotten a lot worse since this morning?" We were flying back to our hideout, escorted by Trent and Tracy. Below us were several air and ground cars with open maintenance doors. People milling about were scratching their heads or talking to local constables.

"It looks like a convention of malfunctioning repair drones tore through here, sir."

Sara greeted us when we landed in a parking lot nearby. Trent and Tracy landed next to us. "Welcome back, Mark, Rafe. I hope you brought good news, because it's in short supply here."

"Half and half?" I offered.

"I'll take it."

I gave her the rundown of the meetings, how we'd secured two pipelines for supplies, but were stymied on a ship.

We descended the stairs into the abandoned mag-lev station. Sara couldn't keep the disbelief from her voice. "He just gave you a captain's ticket and a letter of marque?"

"More like he sold it to me, but with the barest trappings of officialdom. He asked me five questions about running a ship-the exam. Then he brought in two other captains and they asked me three questions each-the interview."

We left Trent and Tracy with the marines. The guard post was behind the turnstiles.

Passing several unlit advertising signs and the coffee shop that was serving as our cafeteria, we turning into the room that served as my office. Sara frowned. "Those sneaky bastards. It'll be legal anywhere, but I won't trust a Freyan captain for the rest of my life."

"Me neither, but it's working in our favor. I'm not going to raise a stink."

They sat across from me. Sara brought up a holo-screen to take notes. "So, what do we do now?"

"Now we let Rafe order the thousand and one things we need. We'll ask Racy to find out what ships are inbound and in orbit." I shrugged. "Doubt we'll find anything. We'll end up stealing a Porcu-bear ship. That means retrofitting the controls and rewriting the operating system."

Sara took a deep breath. "Mark, about Rowdy and Racy. They raided nearby cars and buildings for parts."

"They what!"

She held up her hands and I took the hint. I breathed deeply as she continued. "When I found out and told them to stop, they claimed that you told them it was okay."

"I didn't." At that moment, I remembered what I had said yesterday and buried my face in my hands. "I told Racy to scavenge what she needed." I let out an audible groan and pulled my hair.

She smiled. "On the bright side, we have a dozen security drones, cameras, motion sensors, five terminals, and the smartest AI in any mag-lev station on the planet."

"Can you please ask them to come in here?"

"Right away, Captain."

Rowdy and Racy didn't take long. Ignoring the chairs, they jumped up on the desk and sat on the edge. I was getting used to the Muscat idea of personal space (or lack thereof), so it didn't throw me as much as it once had.

"You wanted to see us, Mark?" Rowdy's long nose almost touched mine.

"Thanks for coming."

They chose that moment to stand in my lap and give me a hug.

"No problem, Mark," said Racy. "Did this morning go okay? Did you get us a ship?"

"No, but I found a way to get us supplies. I want to talk to you about that."

They sat back on the edge of the desk again, eyes wide with anticipation.

I continued. "I appreciate all the work you did this morning, but I don't think our neighbors did. I know I said it was okay to scavenge, but we may have gone overboard."

They frowned. "Did we do something bad, Mark? Do you want us to return the equipment?" Racy was on the verge of tears.

"No." I shuddered at the thought of everyone finding out where we were hiding and making all sorts of demands. "No, let's just not do it anymore."

They nodded. "Okay. Was that all you wanted us for?" asked Rowdy.

"Yes."

He brightened. "Good. Let me show you what we've done!"

"Dad!" protested Racy. "I want to show him the new AI first."

Chapter 5

Needy

"Rafe, we need a parts printer."

He had taken over an employee locker room near the ticket booths. It was piled high with boxes. "I know, sir."

"Why don't we have one yet? I'm not sure how much longer I can keep our neighbors safe."

Rafe snorted. "I don't envy you, sir. Ufkell can't get one. Norbert won't part with any of his."

"Have they figured out we're playing both sides against the middle?" I fingered the end of a box.

"No, sir. We're throwing enough credits around that they haven't looked too closely … yet."

"No ship. No parts printer. At least we have weapons, medical supplies, food, computer cores, cameras, and armor." I read the label on the crate. "And what are you doing with a gross of wind socks?"

"Trade goods, sir."

"Trade goods?"

"Yes, sir." He held out his hands, palms up, and shrugged. "I need wind socks to get a dozen security drones."

I scratched my head. "Someone is going to give you a dozen drones for a bunch of wind socks?"

"No, wind socks will get me light panels." He inched his fingers across the desk. "I'll use the light panels to get fur coats. The fur coats I can trade for the drones."

It took me a couple of seconds to take that in. "Okay. Well done. Now if only we could trade wind socks for a parts printer."

He started to laugh, but stopped midway as if dumb-struck.

"Rafe?"

He shook himself. "That's it! Sir, you're a genius." He sprinted to the door and almost ran over Racy. "Racy, good. I need you. I'll be right back. Don't go anywhere."

Racy watched him sprint out the door and down the hall before glancing back at me. Her vulpine eyebrows quirked with a question she didn't ask.

I threw up my hands. "No idea, but I hope it ends in the parts we need."

She handed me a tablet. "Here is every cargo freighter due in for the next month."

Sighing, I accepted the tablet. "Thanks, Racy. What did Admiral Norbert's office say when you asked?"

She didn't answer me. The Muscat had her nose pointed toward the floor and her ears laid back: a dog caught in the treat box.

"Okay, just tell me you didn't get caught." No data stack was safe near Racy. My eyes drifted down the list, willing an opportunity to jump out at me.

"How could I, Mark? Their security is awful. I could sleepwalk through it."

A name on the list caught my eye. "Racy, this ship, the *Ares Venture*. Is it a Centauri-built Medusa class hull?"

She jumped onto the desk so she could see the screen over my shoulder. "Let's find out."

A window appeared, confirming my suspicions. "I'll be damned. Racy, Yale banned this ship. Every time it set down some factory or outpost got raided. We could never pin it on them."

"But you were sure it was them?"

"Six landings, six sabotage attempts or raids. Not proof, but definitely suspicious."

I stood up, deep in thought, and set the tablet down absently. My mind raced with possibilities. Could it be done? Would it be legal?

"Mark?" Racy tugged on my sleeve.

"Yes? What?"

"What are you thinking?"

I tried to say something several times but couldn't find the words. "I don't know, yet," I said. What clauses applied? Would it be spelled out in Freyan maritime law?

Querying my AI, I reviewed the clauses of our letter of marque. Racy studied me for a few seconds, then wandered off to check boxes around the storeroom. Leaving the gobble bird in the berry bush wasn't a good idea. I tried to keep an eye on her and failed.

She found what she was searching for at the same time I did. My attention was fully involved in dissecting the legalese.

"Rafe?" she asked.

Was he back in the room? Good, I needed to concentrate. Combat zone.

She wandered out. Racy was halfway down the hall when I heard her talking to the boxes "You pretty little X93 processors aren't safe here. Let me find you a new home where you can be appreciated."

Chapter 6

The Plan

"All right people, listen up." Everyone was on the mag-lev station's loading platform. The crew were standing or sitting on dirty plastic chairs bolted to the floor. Racy had hacked a holo-ad board and we were using it as a presentation screen. "For those of you who haven't heard, the Freyans have issued us a letter of marque."

A hand went up in back. "What's a letter of Mark?"

"A letter of marque is a government license to attack and capture enemy ships and pirates. Ships like this one." I pointed to a 3D image of a Medusa class freighter. "Racy?"

She jumped up on a bench and used a pointer to highlight data flowing in front of the image. "In the past five years, the *Ares Venture* has made landfall eighteen times. Human ship, human crew, but each time, an Erethizon raid or sabotage occurred within four days. After the *Venture* was banned from Yale space, they started landing here on Freya. We've … uh … acquired a copy of their message traffic from those visits. Messages from the captain of the *Venture*, Sean Flanagan, have odd vocal patterns. The same kind we found in Aasha's messages before she blew up the *Leo*."

"Two problems," interrupted Sara. "We had no idea what Aasha was up to, and it's all circumstantial. Not proof."

"True," conceded Racy, "but each raid was carried out by Porcu-bear shock troops. The Freyans caught the last raiders. At the time, they were within three hundred meters of the *Venture*. Captain Flanagan thanked the Freyans for saving them. The message to Freyan command came before the capture was made public. The capture was out of sight of the ship. Spies in the crew, sure. A dozen combat veterans somehow sneaking on and off a ship. Sell those cowarn droppings somewhere else. I won't buy it."

Warren raised his hand and Racy pointed at him. "So, the plan is to board the ship. How do we do that? We don't have an orbital shuttle or an assault transport."

Racy stepped down and Trent took her place on the bench. "We borrow an airbus."

Warren mouthed, "what?"

Trent plowed on. "We're not going to board the ship in space. We've determined three probable landing zones. We'll assault the ship when they set down."

Sara looked back and forth between me and Trent. "Can we do that?"

"We think so," I said. "I've reviewed our license and consulted a local attorney. If they qualify as an enemy combatant, they're a legal target. It shouldn't matter whether they're on the ground or in space."

A dozen voices spoke at once.

I waved them down. "Guys, let us finish. We'll let you ask questions when we're done."

They settled down.

"Okay," I continued. "We know when they're supposed to arrive."

The image on the screen changed from a ship to a map. Three areas lit up. "We'll station drones at these locations. We'll be here." The pointer indicated an X in the middle.

"We can't know which field they'll choose. Racy will ask the local air traffic control to send us their scans."

War 'n Pace barked a laugh. A couple of others snorted.

"After Racy convinces the local computers to help us, we'll know where they'll land. We won't beat them there, but we shouldn't be far behind."

The screen changed to an image of the ship in a field. "Wherever they land, the attack plan will be the same: like charging a fortified bunker."

The marines groaned in unison.

"It won't be that bad," I said. "Racy will hack their AI. She believes she can shut down their weapons, engineering controls, internal security, and comms. If she can, we walk up to the front door, knock with marine politeness, and enter. If she can convince internal security that they've suffered a hull breach, every airtight hatch will seal. It'll cut everyone off from everyone else. We can clear the ship a section at a time."

I let the best-case scenario sink in before opening the hatch to open space. "Any questions?"

Warren chimed right in. "What if Racy can't turn off the main weapons?"

"It'll be a short trip," I said dryly. "The main weapon systems are designed to fire on objects moving at in-system speeds. In atmo we can't move even close to that quickly. We'll have some advantage due to air effects, but it won't last. These are ship-to-ship cannons. An airbus won't survive a glancing blow."

Warren paled and sat down.

Pace Jones asked the next question. "What if we don't find anything linking them to the Hedgehogs?"

"In that scenario, we'll be spending a few nights in jail. We'll be using plasma rifles. Non-lethal. Most of the crew will be out in a couple of months. The senior staff will be on cometary ice for a bit more than that." A bit more being five years, but the crew didn't need to know that. The officers understood the risks.

I let the crew try to find a few more flaws in the plan. We answered each scenario. It helped that Trent and I had done our best to poke holes in the plan ourselves. None of them were worse than the first two. It was a high-risk, high-reward action and there were a thousand ways it could go wrong.

I drew the meeting to a close. "Okay guys, we've got a week to practice. We'll be drawing up sims and I want everyone taking turns playing attackers and defenders. Find the flaws and fix them."

Chapter 7

The Attack

"HERE THEY COME." Racy pointed at the portable holo-tank. "Glide path indicates LZ two."

"That's great resolution," I noticed. "I didn't think the Freyans' detection equipment was that good."

"Drones are on alert," said Trent. "We'd better be, too."

On cue, the assault craft started moving. In the simulations, the airbus had proven too fragile. We'd resorted to hiring mercenaries again. The Valkyries had loaned us a trio of assault shuttles and pilots to go with them.

I rubbed the coin in my pocket and hoped my great-grandfather would guide my steps today. It would take the *Ares* five more minutes to land. It would take us twenty to reach its landing site. What if they carried their own transport? Any Porcu-bears aboard the ship could already be gone by the time we got there. Or what if they made honest runs sometimes? My mind kept coming up with worst-case scenarios.

In the display, the ship touched down. Trent stared at me. "Relax, Mark. The sticks have been cast."

"I have their wireless network," said Racy. "I have the pawshake. Uh, oh. Not a Terran AI. My infiltration AI doesn't know what to make of it. Need to find out what language it speaks."

She typed furiously. "I've never seen this before. It doesn't make sense."

"Finesse the lock or blow it. Do your best, Racy."

"Ten minutes," called the copilot. He wasn't one of mine, and I hadn't caught his name.

The field came into view ahead of us. We could see the *Ares*.

"*Feradit*!" exclaimed Racy. "AI on alert. They know something's up."

"Dorsal turret," said the pilot. "It's tracking."

We rolled left then right. Three loud thunks.

"Pull the extinguisher!" barked the pilot. "Brace yourselves. Coming in hot."

"Turret is down," growled Racy. "Their AI thinks it needs repairs. No go on the door. They're calling for help. Locals en route."

If the Freyan army showed up before we found evidence, we were sunk.

We landed hard and at an angle. The seat harnesses fell away. Warren hit the hatch release. It showed green, but didn't fall. Trent and I ran at the door and shouldered into it. It opened, but only a meter. We scrambled out. It wasn't an organized charge, but we covered the fifty meters. "Racy?"

"On it." She plugged a card into the door of the *Ares*. "Oh, not nice. Just a minute, Mark."

"We don't have a minute."

A rumbling sound. "They're trying to take off!" I'd never been right next to a ship during launch, but I wasn't interested in finding out how fast I'd cook inside my armor.

Racy gritted her teeth in a canine snarl. "The language barrier is making the target AI slippery. Mine can't get a foothold. Fine, don't play nice. Station security override."

Both airlock doors popped open. Everyone scrambled in. Two of the Valkyries didn't make it. The Ares left the ground. The ship heaved to port and we were slammed into the side of the passage. We regained our footing and the men took off for their objectives two by two.

Racy and I followed. The zings of plasma rifle fire were coming fast. I also heard the small arms fire and hoped no one had been killed.

Inside the lock was another terminal. Pace's squad stood by while Racy jacked into it.

Her lips pulled back as she typed. I'd never seen her show so many teeth. I was reminded again of how much Muscat resemble foxes with four-fingered hands. "Any luck cracking it?"

"No. It was made to work with Terran standard protocols, but only emergency commands work. I have a worm trying to figure out the command codes, but it's a long shot. Okay, reactor containment alarm."

A long wail came from everywhere at once. The engine noise ceased.

"Oh squats!" I was weightless for a fraction of a second before my helmet hit the overhead. We must have fallen ten meters before the backups kicked in and we collapsed on the deck. Main reactors offline. We wouldn't be breaking atmo.

A calm voice advised us to follow radiation procedures.

"And hull breach."

The alarm changed to a rapid pinging followed by several bangs. Airtight doors all over the ship closed. The calm voice told us to find the nearest emergency suit locker.

I breathed a sigh of relief.

"Feradit! Mark, it's not going to hold. Their AI is fighting back."

I heard clangs and whirs. The airtight doors were reopening.

"Pace," I shouted, "we can't stay here. Time to take this upstairs."

"Bravo team has not secured the bridge, sir. They're encountering heavy resistance."

"Then we give 'em backup." I let out a breath. "This is going to suck."

"Yes, sir," Pace said.

Around the corner from the forward lock, we found the ladder heading up. Something came bouncing down the stairs. I spun and pulled Racy into a hug.

The hallway exploded around us.

I released her. Her eyes were as round as saucers. "Are you okay?"

"What!" she yelled back.

Behind me, Pace and his men returned fire. I touched my fingers together twice to Racy, the Muscat sign for "okay."

"Yes! But my ears are ringing!"

I motioned for her to follow.

We trotted behind Pace and his squad on the way to the bridge. We were half a dozen paces behind when someone jumped into the hall from a door to my left. He was facing away from me, toward Pace. I slammed him into wall, my armor's enhanced strength taking him out of the fight. I returned to watching our rear so we wouldn't get flanked.

Two ladders later, we met Bravo team at a landing leading to officer country. They were sniping over the top of the stairs. Some of the crew had pulled a metal desk into the hall in front of the hatch to the bridge and were using it as a barricade.

Pace glanced over his shoulder at me.

"Squats. Permission granted. Blow it."

He smiled at me and nodded to War.

I heard the grenade roll down the passage and covered Racy's ears. Two seconds later the desk was a wreck.

Two men had been hiding behind it and War checked them. "They'll live. Get this hatch open."

Pace pulled the ruined lock off the wall and grabbed the tools in his pouch. Twenty seconds later the door popped open.

Bravo team rushed in and there were three quick zings.

"Clear," called Pace.

I entered and found three men unconscious on the floor. War had their weapons. The captain and someone else were kneeling, hands behind their heads.

"Land the ship."

"Slug you," sneered the captain.

I pointed my weapon at his head as he glared up at me. "Command codes."

"Screw you."

"Racy, break it."

His eyes opened in alarm as Racy plugged her portable terminal into the main systems console.

"Status?" I requested over the comm.

Updates came in. "Mess deck secured."

"Berthing secured."

"Cargo holds secured."

And finally, "Engineering secured."

"Trent, Porcu-bears?"

"Sorry, sir. No hide nor quill. We'll keep looking."

"Search the crew and maintenance spaces." We needed to find the smoking blaster quick. I gazed out the ports. We hadn't moved far from where they'd landed. "Racy, can you give me access to that console."

"Done."

I took over the helm and brought us back down.

Marines called in as they cleared compartments. No Erethizon.

A few minutes later, Trent called from the main lock. "Mark, we're about to have company. Locals."

"Racy?"

"I'm in. I can see everything."

She didn't continue. "And …"

Her fingers were a blur. "My AI is still searching."

"Mark?" asked Trent.

"Stall them. We haven't found it."

"They aren't in a stalling mood."

I blinked and bit my lip. "Racy, you've got ten minutes. Maybe less."

The seconds slipped by. The sinking sensation in my stomach kept getting worse.

"It's about to get ugly," said Trent

I shook my head. "Racy."

She stopped typing. "There must be another partition or something. It's just not here."

Letting out a breath I hadn't realized I'd been holding, I switched to the public channel. "Okay men. This is a crime scene now. Let the Freyans find what we couldn't. Surrender."

Minutes later a squad from planetary militia entered the bridge. We all held up our hands and they took our weapons.

We were escorted off the ship and then it was we who were kneeling. The Freyans kept their weapons trained on us.

Chapter 8

Norbert

HANDS BEHIND MY HEAD, KNEELING outside the *Ares*, I wondered where I had gone wrong. I also thought about grass. The field was covered in what passed for grass on Freya: sickly yellow, no flowers. Yale grass was dark green and speckled with purple flowers.

I surveyed my whole boarding crew around me. Only two of my men were injured when we took the ship. If there was a bright spot in all of this, that was it.

Fear. I could see it in the body language of my crew. We knew there was evidence. Why hadn't we found any onboard? It must have been hidden too well. But hidden where? I let my mind work on the problem. We'd get out of this yet. I just needed more time.

A transport landed and Admiral Norbert stalked toward me with a general in tow. "Oh, you are in it now, Martin."

The local militia had us lined up in four rows of seven. The *Ares* crew was kneeling next to us. They hadn't bound our wrists yet. Norbert dispatched an aide to find binders. The general was yelling instructions. Norbert hadn't gotten to me yet. The storm was coming.

Sean Flanagan, the captain of the *Ares*, was screaming threats. "Admiral, this is unacceptable. I'm filing a grievance with the merchant authority. I insist you remove your men from my ship. Article fifteen, paragraph six clearly states …"

He never finished. A loud crash from behind me. I hit the ground hard. Blaster and rifle fire erupted everywhere. Flanagan flopped to the ground in front of me, his wide eyes staring blankly.

My heart pounded. I crawled from him to another dead man, this one a Freyan soldier. I took his weapon and scrambled behind a transport.

It was good cover, and while I returned fire I could see that a whole section of hull armor had fallen away from the *Ares*. A dozen Erethizon had emerged and were shooting at everything that moved. The Freyans hadn't come loaded for Porcu-bears. Erethizon troopers are tough.

A dozen Freyan troopers lay dead in the field. Among them were at least three of my marines and five of the *Ares* crew. Trent, Tracy, and a few of my marines had snagged rifles in the scramble.

Beside me Trent paused to reload. "Mark, isn't that supposed to be a fuel tank or something?"

I put three shots into a Porcu-bear faceplate. It slowed the monster down, but didn't stop it. "Holding tank for reactor mass."

"Sneaky bastards."

I glanced at the rifle in my hands. It was a gas expansion device. "Seriously, bullets? Why the hell aren't the Freyans equipped with real weapons?" What I wouldn't have given for a gauss rifle.

Across from me, behind another transport, Norbert took aim with a laser pistol. "Two million soldiers to equip. Had to cut costs somewhere," he explained. I noticed War 'n Pace behind him.

This was bad. All these weapons were good for was annoying an enemy as hardy as the Erethizon. The Porcu-bears advanced on us. I tried to use my AI to organize my men. I swore as it listed them all on top of each other. My AI was internal, but everyone else's was a wrist cuff. The Freyans had piled them up fifty meters away. Worse, our plasma rifles were next to them.

"Trent, are you thinking what I'm thinking?" I asked.

"If you mean we need those plasma rifles, then yes," he growled.

The end of the transport in front of me was fifteen meters from the piles. "War, Pace, on my signal, run out and grab the plasma rifles." Pace goggled at me as if I were crazy. War nodded and moved.

I put a couple more rounds into a Porcu-bear helmet. "Trent, a distraction?"

"Way ahead of you." He called to our sniper, Tracy, in Muscat, "Target the weapons' power cells. The maintenance port. The bear on the far left."

There were three sharp cracks. An explosion engulfed the shock trooper. My AI showed two icons move behind the transport. War 'n Pace had retrieved a couple of AI cuffs while they were at it.

Seconds later, behind Norbert, War gave me a grim smile. Since they were in our battle net now, I sent the command. *Take 'em down.*

In unison, War 'n Pace stepped around the ends of the transport and fired. Two Porcu-bear shock troops were out of the fight. If they were still conscious, they were trapped inside non-functional armor. They got back under cover as the Erethizon returned fire. Behind me, Tracy preyed on the distraction. Three shots and another Porcu-bear rifle exploded.

That stopped the advance. The Erethizon were now using suppressive fire. I used my AI to take control of the drone we had watching the area. It was still flying in a holding pattern where we'd placed it when the ship landed. Now it hovered a hundred meters over the shock troops. War 'n Pace could use it to time their shots.

I saw War take a shot in the arm. I thought it would take him out of the fight, but he shook it off. His armor had protected him.

The Porcu-bears were out in the open, trusting their heavier armor to protect them. War, Pace, and Tracy started popping up over the top of the transports at random spots, each of their shots timed for the best effect. The Freyans, meanwhile, were keeping them guessing: the Erethizon had no way of knowing if the next shot was going to be an annoying bullet or something more dangerous.

It took twenty minutes to take them out. An eternity in a firefight.

◆ ◆ ◆

"What the hell were you thinking? Where do you get off attacking a civilian target on. The. Slugging. Ground?" Norbert poked me hard in the chest with every word, his red face making his blond hair seem blonder. I remained at attention.

"I was following your suggestion, sir."

"What!"

Staring straight ahead, I answered in as steady a voice as I could muster. "You said you had no ships available. You told me my best bet was to use my letter of marque to get a new ship."

"In slugging space!" Spit flew from his mouth. "Anything on the ground is an army matter. You damn sure should have called us."

"Begging the admiral's pardon, but the letter says, 'may target any ship, supplies, enemy units, and support personnel.' The location of those targets is not defined anywhere in section fourteen."

"You don't have blue skin. Don't get Dru-eyed. You know damn well the army leads any action on-planet."

"The army didn't have intel about the threat."

Norbert clenched his fists in front of him. "'Cause you didn't tell them."

I tried to sound reasonable. "Would they have listened if we had told them?"

"Not. Your. Call." The admiral popped his fist open. "You tell them. That's the way it works."

"Begging the admiral's pardon, but they wouldn't take my word for it. I'm an unknown source. For all they knew I could be setting them up." Time to butter him up. "The army isn't the navy. They would have talked about it for days before acting. By then the *Ares* would have been long gone."

"They have rapid response units," he said, "for threats like this."

"When was the last time they were used?"

"That isn't the slugging point." He stabbed his finger at the desk for emphasis. "A ship on the ground is the army's problem. A ship in the air is the navy's problem."

"Technically, sir …"

He interrupted me. "It was on the ground when you assaulted the slugging thing."

"But in the air when we took control."

"Don't split quills with me. You entered a vessel on the ground with the intent of killing the crew and taking the ship."

"We used plasma rifles." I pointed out. "Anyone we hit was only stunned."

"We saw the evidence. Small arms damage and blast patterns consistent with grenades." He slashed the air in front of me. "Just 'cause we didn't confiscate one off your pirates doesn't mean a slugging thing."

"That was them!" I protested.

"Ship's crew know better than to use small arms and grenades. It could poke a hole in the hull."

"I didn't say they were smart, just that they used them on us." Logic wasn't working. I needed a new tactic. "Sir, have you made your report yet?"

Norbert squinted. "What's your angle?"

"I think that it was a wonderful stroke of genius on your part, sir. Doing background checks on incoming merchant traffic, you discovered that every time the *Ares* landed, a Porcu-bear raid happened within a couple of days. It wasn't enough on its own, but too coincidental to ignore. It was too late to arrange a customs inspection. Knowing our situation, you asked us to check it out. You knew that if it was nothing, you could deny knowing anything about it. We'd be your patsies. Shrewd of you, Admiral."

He ground his teeth, but didn't say anything for a few seconds. The gears were turning. "What do you want for that?"

"The ship."

"No." He chopped the air. "The ship was captured on the ground. It belongs to Freya."

"The *Ares* was taken using data we gathered. It was in the air when we took over the bridge. We secured the vessel."

"The army secured the freighter," he insisted. "Those Porcu-bears would have made diced fire fish out of your raiding party. My people will spend months getting every scrap of intelligence we can get out of that tub."

"Put your men aboard. They clear it section by section. We refit each compartment when they're done with it."

"Are you deaf? No. You can't have the ship. Even in its current condition, it's worth more than your sorry ass. We need ships."

This wasn't going well. I could attempt to bribe him again, but I needed the credits to repair the ship. Time to change the battlefield. "Sir, I want to make you a hero to the Freyan people. If we can't have that ship, things will go differently."

His red face became purple. "Are you threatening me?"

I leveled my gaze at him. "No, sir. I am describing the battle space we're in. If we can't spin this in your favor, we'll have to settle on the truth. A bunch of scruffy privateers beat naval intelligence at their own game and stopped an ongoing threat."

"We have a lid on the media," he sneered. "It'll never hit the air."

"You're missing the point, sir. I'm on your side. I want you to succeed."

"At the price of a ship bound for my navy." He shook his head. "Not a chance in Jötunheimr. A ship like that, outfitted right, could take out three or four Porcu-bear destroyers."

"Which is why I need it." I bit my lip to keep from screaming. "Give me a ship so I can take out a few of those bastards."

"No."

"Be my ally, not my enemy."

Norbert pointed up. "The enemy is up there. Cowboys like you are going to get us all killed."

I glared at him. "Not if I get them first."

"You'll get you and your men blasted to atoms."

"Grow a spine," I growled. "I've seen magnapple slugs with more backbone."

"Why, you son of a slugging …"

"Get your head on straight." I pointed at his useless melon for emphasis. "You're fighting a holding action. They're going to break through and destroy everything you hold dear. They did it on Grey, Anderson, and Ajax. They did it to Yale, and they'll do it here. If you can't see that, then the people should know you're a shortsighted, brainless, freeze sponge."

Norbert set his jaw. "You made a big mistake, Martin. You think you can come in here and threaten me? You're not going to tell any reporter anything. No one will find you."

"Who said anything about the media? The Sudhurland Keiretsu will wonder what happened to us. We'll tell them. I'm sure the other keiretsus will be interested."

Norbert pressed a button on his desk. "Captain, please come retrieve the prisoner." He glared blaster bolts at me. "I told you dealing with that criminal was a mistake. I'm throwing you and your crew in the deepest hole I can find. You won't tell anyone a damn thing. In a secret court, you'll be convicted of piracy against a lawful supply ship, selling state secrets, and treason during wartime. You'll be executed by this time next week."

Had I gone too far? Had I let my temper get the best of me? Maybe. But right now, I was too far down the blue marmot hole. Meeting his eyes, I grinned. High stakes poker was a game I understood. "You'll draw more attention. The mercenaries we hired have other masters. They'll find out. Ufkell will find out. Questions will be asked. Word will spread. When the upper admirals hear of it, your career will be over. What will it be? Are you a hero to your people, or a tragic warning to your replacement?"

The door opened behind me. The captain stepped to my side, "Mr. Martin, if you'll come with me."

I held out my wrists for the binders.

Chapter 9

Grova

I WALKED AWAY WITH THE guard with far more confidence than I felt. Some captain I turned out to be. I just got my entire command captured.

The brig was in the same building as Norbert's office. I expect to rejoin my men, but that's not what happened. We got into the lift. Instead of taking me to the cells on the ground floor, the elevator kept descending. The doors opened onto a sub-basement. There were cells here too, but smaller than the ones above.

The marine took me down a short hallway and shoved me into the third cell on the right. These cages were different. Instead of fasteel bars, they had armor-glass fronts. He took off the cuffs and shut the door.

It was outfitted like the cells upstairs. A cot was bolted to the floor with a mattress that couldn't be removed. Three large buttons on the wall would call for a sink, toilet, and shower when needed.

The cell opposite me held a Porcu-bear. Even without combat armor, they were impressive. Two and a half meters tall and covered with porcupinelike quills. Built like a sumo wrestler. Five-fingered hands with clawlike fingernails. A short snout with rows of sharp teeth. And the eyes. Malicious and intelligent eyes. With a start, I realized I knew those eyes.

The cargo drop gone bad. Dead bodies everywhere. Aasha's betrayal. That paw strangling the life out of me. His quills sinking into my hand as I struggled to break his grip. My gaze locked with his. His eyes were dark brown with red flecks on the right side of both irises.

"Grova?"

The sound that came from him was like a rock slide. It must have been a laugh, because the corners of his lips curved up. "Hello, Mark Martin. Causing trouble again?"

"Yeah. I have a talent for it."

More rocks. "That you do."

I realized my implant was translating for me and helping me speak his language. I tried to get a signal, knowing it wouldn't work. The whole building had some sort of dampening field around it. Normal communication channels wouldn't reach the sub-basement.

"Well, Grova," I asked, "what grisly end do they have planned for you? Do you know?"

He grunted. "Questions, questions, and more questions. Always the wrong ones."

That was an odd response. "The wrong questions?"

"Oh yes." He nodded. "How many ships do you have? How many Disciplinarians? When will they attack? Where? Useless. They think only of the next days."

"Disciplinarians?"

Gravel again. "You would call them shock troops. They teach people the true way through stern enforcement." He regarded me. "Go ahead, ask."

I leveled my glare at him. "Tell me where my dad is."

He shook his head with sorrow. "Again, with the wrong questions. Your father is in meditation. He contemplates the Great Urson. He will remain in cloister until he has come full circle. I don't know where." He bowed his head. "I had hoped for better from you."

"Oh yeah? Here's a question for you." I had to work hard to keep from grinding my teeth. "Why?"

His nose twitched. "Why?"

"Yes. Why, you slugging pond crawler?" I had to work to keep my voice level. "Not why you want me. I get that. Control the son and you control the father and all that. But why do the Erethizon do it? Why are they on this mad quest to convert the galaxy?"

His lips curled up. "Ah. That's a much better question." He folded his paws in front of him. "We do it because the Great Urson wills it. His divine will cannot be resisted. It must be accepted. He looked out upon the vastness of space and saw heresy and division. It saddened the great spirit to see all his children so far from the path of enlightenment."

He pointed to himself. "He charged us, first of his children, to go out. We would spread his teachings far and wide, the wisdom of the ancients. All peoples everywhere must join together. The outer trappings of the flesh are meaningless. Our souls, our spirits—that is all that matters. We must not war amongst ourselves. We are meant to join together against the darkness. Bring light to the vast void."

Grova steepled his digits in front of him. "Not everyone is privy to the wisdom of Urson. Our mission, as the first of his children, is to bring all others into the fold. Some may resist. Since we cannot be a divided people, the children must be made to see the light. They must be made to understand the wisdom of Urson. Our job as Disciplinarians is to be stern teachers. It matters not if the child is Erethizon, Terran, Muscat, or Dru. All must join. Only then can we grow as a family. Only then can we become one people under Urson."

The Porcu-bear sighed. His expression relaxed, as if he had let go of some heavy burden.

I thought about what he'd said. "Bring all the people of the known galaxy together." "A united people." Just a sick and twisted vision of utopia. It reminded me of the worst dictators in Terran history. A worthy dream perverted, taken to a sadistic and horrifying extreme.

"Thank you, Mark Martin. You are a true gem among your people. Terrans can be so tiresome. I look forward to the day when you join us in the great spirit."

The thought revolted me. I would never join his sick religion. "What's wrong with just asking instead of attacking?" I spat. "Does the Great Urson have no compassion?"

Grova's nose twitched and his eyelids drooped. "That is preferable, but there's no time. In twelve solar cycles the darkness will be upon us. We must be a unified people before that happens. The Great Urson has calculated it would take more than one hundred cycles to unite the people by choice."

And there it was. Doomsday. The "children" must be brought together before a cataclysm. And like every cult before it, when destruction didn't happen, they'd push back the date. Twelve cycles. Roughly fifty Terran standard years.

You can't convince a zealot of anything. He would counter any argument I came up with. His responses would be based on emotional pleas, logical fallacies, or "because Urson said so."

"I'll ponder that, Grova." Knowing the way your opponent thinks is a key component to devising a strategy to defeat them. "It's a shame I won't be around for your great joining." In my mind, I squeezed his windpipe. His eyes bulged, the spark of his life draining out of them.

"You will be there," Grova said with conviction. "The Great Urson has plans for you, my child. You are one of his. He owns your soul, even if you cannot believe it yet. He has told me this personally. He is never wrong."

"Norbert intends to execute me in a few days." I held up my palms. "That may put a crimp in the Great Urson's plans." In truth, I hoped Ufkell or the Valkyries or someone else might come up with some way to free us. It was a vanishing hope, but still there. I wondered what Sophie would do without me. She would have to find someone else to abuse.

"Oh," said Grova, like it was a mild annoyance, "we can't let that happen."

♦♦♦

The days passed by in agonizing slowness. Grova droned on for hours about the virtues of his religion. The only other visitors we had were guards delivering food. They wouldn't talk to us. My AI could tell me the time, so at least I knew how long I'd been down here.

Three days in, I received a paper notice. I had been tried in absentia for treason. I was to be executed by firing squad at the earliest opportunity.

After two more days, three guards showed up at the door to my cell. The squad leader stepped forward. "Mr. Martin, it's time."

I moved forward and let him put the binders on my wrists. Turning to Grova, I said, "I wish I could say it's been a pleasure."

"The Great Urson is not done with you yet, Mark Martin. I will see you soon," he replied.

The guards escorted me down the short hallway. At the elevators, the squad leader slapped engine tape over my mouth.

Of course. Norbert couldn't afford to have me say anything that might incriminate him.

We entered the elevator and the doors closed behind me. This was it. It was really happening.

My sister. Who was going to take care of her? My crew. What would happen to them? Norbert couldn't allow them to live. I'd doomed myself and everyone I cared about. Rowdy, Racy, Sara, War, Pace, Jay, Trent and his whole family. Why couldn't I have kept my mouth shut? I had to press the issue. I had to insult a planetary admiral, threaten him. Now it wasn't just me who had to deal with the consequences: it was everyone I cared about too.

My dad. Who was going to help him? Would anyone be able to save him? Would someone else be able to liberate Yale?

We exited the elevator. The guards led me out the back of the building to a parade ground. Eight soldiers with rifles. Admiral Norbert and another admiral I didn't know stood off to one side.

Not a friendly face to be seen. None of my friends were there. What would they do when they found out? How would they be told? What would they do? Would they curse my name? Would they cry?

The guards escorted me to a blank wall. They didn't tie me to a post or anything. They just left me there, hands bound and mouth taped. It wasn't as if I could run. Where would I go? Everyone in the parade ground was armed. They would shoot me before I could get anywhere.

There was no music. No drums. In my mind, I thought about a lullaby my mother used to sing to me, back when I was a kid. Back before the war, when she'd been alive. I'll see you soon, Mom, I thought.

Norbert glared daggers at me. He and the other admiral stood to one side, halfway down the firing line. The eight riflemen stood at the ready, rifles at port arms. They were the same crappy rifles the militia had been armed with at the ship. I was going to die, shot by a weapon any modern soldier would laugh at.

Norbert strutted forward. The other admiral grabbed his arm, trying to draw him out of the line of fire. He shook him off. The other admiral slunk back and stood next to the men on the firing line.

"Any last words, Martin?" Norbert laughed at his own joke.

With engine tape on my mouth I couldn't make a sound. I cursed at him anyway.

He guffawed.

He moved to make sure he was well back from the line of fire in the middle distance between the soldiers and me.

He stood up straight and sneered.

"Detail, attention!" he barked.

"Ready arms!" The men put their rifles to their shoulders.

"Aim!" Eight rifles pointed right at me. Inescapable death.

"Fire!"

Chapter 10

Fire

"Fire!"

As one the detail swung their rifles around and pointed them at Norbert, shock writ plain on his face.

The admiral standing with the detail repeated the command. "Fire."

Eight rifles erupted. Norbert's body skidded backward a meter before collapsing on the ground like a rag doll.

"Port arms. Clear your weapons, men."

The remaining admiral motioned to the guard detail that had brought me up from the basement. The squad leader approached me.

"Sorry about that, Mr. Martin," he said, unlocking my binders. "Had to make it look believable." He ripped the engine tape from my mouth. It felt like my skin came off with it. He saluted the admiral and left.

"Ow."

The admiral smiled and held out his hand. "Mark, I know we're going to work well together. I'm Admiral Olafurson."

I shook his hand in a daze.

He continued, "Walk with me. We hated to leave you down in the pit for so long, but we had to get everything set up for the change in command. As I'm sure you can imagine, there were an endless number of details to iron out."

"I'm sure," I murmured and followed him off the parade ground.

"Dismissed," he called back to the detail over his shoulder. "You'll be happy to know that everything is set up for you. You'll have to move out of your cave and onto the base, I'm afraid. The spook teams have been crawling all over the *Ares* since we got her. She's in a hangar on the other side of the base."

I was having trouble following Olafurson's rapid-fire delivery. I should have been asking questions, but I was still getting over how close I'd come to dying. Still, I managed to get one question out.

"Wait, we get the *Ares Venture*?" I stammered.

"Oh yes." He nodded vigorously. "You'll make us nothing lying on the ground. Your deal with Ufkell was to get you a ship. So, we got you a ship." He punched me lightly on the shoulder. "We need to get you moving as soon as possible. The Sudhurland Keiretsu is excited about this opportunity." He grinned.

We'd reached a parking lot. Two ground buses pulled up as we got there.

"Oh good. Right on time." He snapped his fingers in the direction of the office building, the same one in which I'd been imprisoned. Two men opened the doors and Trent, followed by Tracy, Sara, War, Pace, and the rest of my crew walked out. They blinked in the bright sun as they were led toward the buses and me.

I glanced back at the parade ground. Norbert's body lay where it had fallen. "What are you going to do about him?"

Olafurson shrugged. "Leave him there for now. We need to send a message." His eyes locked with mine. All mirth evaporated from them. "What about you? Did you get the message?"

Toe the line or you're next. I got it. "Yes, I understand."

"Good." His wrist AI beeped. "Oh my. Look at the time." He put his hand on my arm. "This bus will take you to your new ship. No barracks space, I'm afraid. It'll be tents in the hangar until you can move aboard. There's nothing I'd like more than to sit and talk with you, but it's not in the cards today. Consolidating power, intimidation, blackmail, an endless list of things to do and not enough time. We'll have the chance to catch up soon."

He snapped his fingers and an aircar landed a few meters away. "Percy, we need to get over to Personnel and Readiness. Admiral Sturlasson has no doubt heard the scuttlebutt. We have to tell him what to think before he gets any unfortunate ideas of his own."

Sara stood beside me. "I'm not sure what just happened. Are we free to go?"

"In a manner of speaking … I think," I said. "These buses will take us to the *Ares*. Ufkell, Mr. Darkside, just took over a large chunk of the navy."

"Ufkell, the slimy mob boss with the lousy contract?"

"Slimy or not, he saved my ass and got us a ship. Not that I trust the little toad, but for the moment, we'll have to work with him."

◆ ◆ ◆

We arrived at the hangar to find Ufkell, Rafe, and my sister waiting for us. My sister was wearing the smile she reserved for dignitaries she didn't like. She leaned away from Mr. Darkside.

Ufkell strode up and circled me. I felt like a race horse at auction. He stroked his beard. "Hmmm. Mark, I wanted to say thank you. I've wanted this base for a long time. This is going to make great things happen for us. We'll have access to weapons, armor, vehicles. Did you know that they house a rapid response unit here?"

"I'd heard that."

He hit me hard on the shoulder. "You gave me the opening. If you hadn't pushed Norbert ..." He shook his head. "Then, asking your sister to come to me." He kissed fingers like he'd just tasted a gourmet meal. "Pure genius."

Sophie's expression became more pained.

Ufkell grabbed my arm and pulled me toward the hangar, Rafe and Sophie trailing in our wake. "Let me show you what's going on in here."

"Olafurson works for you?" I asked.

Ufkell halted and grabbed a fistful of my shirt. He stopped himself and smoothed out the wrinkles. "Yes." He squinted into my eyes. "You attacked the ship. I assumed it would meet your needs, so I negotiated with the navy. It should only take you thirty years to pay me off. Then she'll be yours, free and clear."

He pulled me along another few steps before stopping again. "I'd be willing to take five years off of that, if you'll sell me your sister."

Was he was joking? I couldn't tell.

He shrugged. "No? Well, it was worth asking."

Inside the hangar it was mayhem. A small army of technicians crawled over the outside of the ship. Parts covered the hangar floor. Every outside access hatch was open. There were several gaping holes in the hull where they shouldn't have been, the largest on the engineering compartment and the bridge. I could see cleaning rats clustered here and there about the hull. They looked nervous and confused. They were biologically coded to never leave the ship, but the technicians had taken apart their nests.

"I know it looks bad," said Ufkell, "but this is a good thing. They are working double shifts to get every computer or tech doohickey out of it."

Four men were hauling out the main computer core. I winced as it hit the hatch combing.

"Ouch," said Ufkell. "That's not important, is it?"

I groaned inwardly. "We'll make do."

"Elmarsson! Which of you is Elmarsson?" cried Ufkell.

A technician cut short a conversation he was having with two other men. "Over here, sir."

Ufkell grabbed him by the sleeve and dragged him over to me. "Mark, this is Elmarsson. He's the crew chief. Anything you need, ask him." He put his finger under the technician's nose, his voice becoming menacing. "Right?"

"Yes sir," the tech responded.

He slapped him hard on the back. "Okay, I have a business meeting. You two work out the details." He shuffled toward the door.

I watched him go, then turned to Elmarsson. "I'll want a summary. Is half an hour enough time?"

He grimaced. "I've got stuff for doin'. An hour and a half wo' be better."

"No problem, chief. Come find me. I'll be out here, organizing the crew."

He saluted and jogged back.

Someone smacked the back of my head.

I swiveled around. "Thanks Soph. I missed you, too."

She hugged me hard, then slapped me behind the ear again. "What were you thinking getting involved with that worm?"

"We needed the supplies. We needed a ship. He said he could get them for us. Besides, Rafe made the introduction."

She slapped Rafe on the back of the head too.

"Ow, Doc."

"So, this is your fault?" she accused.

I sighed. "Tell me what happened."

Sophie gave Rafe a glare for good measure, then spun on me. "Pretty much like he said. You didn't come back, so we waited five hours. The news hadn't said anything, so I figured something went wrong. It was me, Rafe, and Rowdy. I asked Rafe to dig into it. A couple of hours later, he tells me that you were arrested."

Rafe took it from there. "There was a list of trumped up charges. It takes political power to fix that. Ufkell would have made me wait a day or two, so I asked the doc to come with me. He likes pretty girls."

Sophie smacked his head again. "Don't you mean pretty *women*?"

Rafe rubbed the back of his head. "So, he lets us right in. We tell him what happened. He spent ten or fifteen minutes stroking his beard. When he's done, he says he'll take care of it and tells us to go home and wait."

"This morning, the little slime devil comes into my office. He grabs my ass and tells me to hop into his aircar. He says we have to save you from yourself or some such," Sophie spat.

Rafe spread his hands. "And here we are."

I pinched the bridge of my nose. "We have a ship. The circumstances are far from ideal, but we should be able to make it work. Let's move our gear, hire a crew, and get her spaceworthy." I let out a breath. "Thanks for saving me."

◆◆◆

The next day I called a meeting. There wasn't a conference room in the hangar, so we used a large tent. Everyone I considered to be my command staff was there: Sara, Sophie, Trent, Rowdy, Racy, and Rafe. We'd pushed two crates together for a table and sat around it on a collection of boxes.

"First," I said, "let me say how happy I am that almost everyone is safe. We lost three good men in the raid, with another half dozen wounded. All the injured are back on their feet. We have more than our share of challenges going forward, but I know we can handle them. Rowdy, would you start us off?"

He called up an image of the *Ares*. "We have a hull and not much else. The reactors, drives, computer core, weapons systems … almost all the secondary systems have been stripped. Environmental is still intact, but I wouldn't trust our lives to it. Most of it can be rebuilt with the right raw materials and a parts printer. The exceptions are the R-drive, in-system drive, and computer core …"

"I'm sorry, am I late?" Admiral Olafurson stuck his head through a flap in the tent.

Late, no. I hadn't invited the weasel. "Of course not, Admiral. We're just getting started. Please, join us. Ufkell said you might stop by."

The mood of the entire room changed in an instant. Everyone was on their guard. Sara stood up and offered her box as a seat. The admiral plopped himself down. "Oh, good. I love these frontline meetings. Fleet-level meetings can be so tiresome. It's all about brinkmanship and budget." He rolled his eyes. "Something about missing equipment?"

"Yes," said Rowdy, "the technicians have taken everything. Including what was bolted to the deck."

Olafurson shrugged. "Not much I can do about that, I'm afraid. We need every scrap of intel we can get. We can get you replacement parts for most of it, though."

"Most of it?" Rowdy asked.

The admiral ticked them off on his fingers. "We can't get you an R-drive. Every exotic matter lens we have is in use. We can't get you a computer core. What we can produce locally is three times the size of the original and just won't fit. We can't get you a parts printer. Every one we have is in use equipping the fleet. Lastly, we can't get you a replacement ion drive. Again, every one we can build is spoken for."

Olafurson put his fingers on the table. "Gauss cannons, arms and armor for your marines, gravity plates, light panels, filters, raw materials. No problem. We can order it, or …" he waved his hand around, "it'll fall off a truck somewhere."

Rowdy started to speak, but I forestalled him. "Rafe, we were already searching for some of this stuff. How did that go?"

"I should have a parts printer here in three days," he said. "I found a factory owner. His place was bombed in a Porcu-bear raid. He may have overstated the damage to the insurance adjuster. The unit is set up for a clean room, advanced chemistry, and advanced metallurgy. It isn't currently programmed for any of that, but the specs say it could be. I'll have to get to work on the rest."

"Excellent," I said. "Any problems with that, sir?"

The admiral shook his head. "No. I like to encourage my people to be creative." The grin vanished and he deadpanned, "As long as it doesn't run counter to my interests."

"Good. What about manpower?" I asked.

Sara pulled up a list on her AI. "We need an officer, helmsmen, a chef, and a medical assistant for the doc. We also should hire a couple of techs for Rowdy and a larger contingent of marines for Trent."

"A larger contingent?" Olafurson's jovial mood returned and he quirked an eyebrow.

"Yes," I pressed, "we have a letter of marque. We intend to trade on that."

Olafurson rubbed his hands together. "I was just saying to Admiral Sturlasson that you were going to need a few sailors and marines. He was a bit distracted at the time. Kept going on and on about trumped up evidence." He made like he was shooing away flies. "The point is that you should be able to get your pick of any crew you like. I'll send you a list of Sudhurland approved candidates. No women. Everyone knows they aren't worth a damn in space."

Sara's eyes hardened, but she didn't offer any comment.

"Thanks, Admiral. That's generous of you." I cringed at the thought of a ship full of crew with mixed loyalties. When the time came to sever our ties with Ufkell … well, one challenge at a time. "The next order of business is food."

The admiral's wrist unit trilled. Olafurson twisted his head to the side. "A moment, Captain. Percy, I asked not to be disturbed. This had better be important."

He had that faraway look of a person listening to a call on an implanted AI. Out in the physical world, we couldn't hear Percy's side of the conversation. The admiral let out a long-suffering sigh. "The commodore has to know that those photos will go public if he attempts to leave. You did remind him of that, didn't you? Never mind. Of course you did. Percy, release the pictures."

"Problems?" I asked.

"No," he replied. "The best leverage is the kind you never have to use, right? Well, I can't let three ships go to another keiretsu. Time to ruin lives, activate sleeper agents, and strike fear into hearts and all that." He pointed to me. "But hey, one less pedophile in the universe."

I blinked. "Uh, at least there's a bright side."

He grinned. "That's what they call me: Mr. Brightside. Anyway, this takes precedence, I'm afraid. Lunch soon?"

"Of course."

"Good." With that, he stood and strutted out of the room.

For a few moments the only sounds came from people and machinery moving around outside the tent. I swung my gaze to Racy and nodded to the seat the admiral had used.

She scanned it with her wrist AI. After a few seconds she picked a small gray disk off the side of the crate.

I punch my fist into my palm. She broke the disk in half.

"Okay," I said, "anytime we're not in an area secured by Racy, assume we're on camera. Rowdy, if Rafe can get a parts printer and enough raw material, what of the missing critical equipment can you make?"

Rowdy glanced at his daughter.

"Yes, doma," said Racy, "I can reprogram it."

"That's my girl," he growled. "With the right materials, we can build a new computer core, no problem. If we can order more of the gravity plates, I can build a gravity drive to replace the ion drive. We can't make an exotic matter lens, so it'll be up to Rafe to find that. Everything else in the R-drive we can build."

I peered across the table. "Rafe?"

He grimaced. "I'll come up with something. An exotic matter lens is a tall order."

"And the rest of the equipment and supplies?"

"Yeah," he bit his lip, "I checked right before the meeting. They gave us another 10 percent off on costs. We'll get everything else."

"Mark," interrupted Rowdy, "I'd like permission to change up the armament."

"What are you thinking?" I asked.

"I'd like to add microsingularity projectors."

I was confused for a couple of seconds until I remembered our exit from the Gra'nome System months earlier. "You mean the experimental weapon you were working on."

"Yes, sir."

"That's untested tech, Rowdy. It isn't something we want the locals to get a glimpse at, either. We won't have the opportunity to try it out."

Rowdy rolled his nose at me. "So? No one here will figure out what it is. We can install an MSP and claim it's communication gear."

I rubbed my temples. I'd seen Rowdy build some amazing things. Everything he'd set his mind to in the past had worked. But what happened when it didn't? What if it failed in a truly spectacular way? "Okay, you can mount one. I don't want it compromising our existing weaponry, though. Place it ventral and aft."

He showed me a mouth full of teeth. "I'll make it work."

I twisted left. "That leaves you, Sara. I hate to do it, but you get the toughest job. We have to fill in a lot of holes in the crew roster. We'll take advantage of Olafurson's offer of manpower, but I want you to vet each one of them. Try not to let him slip too many of his spies onboard. We have to let him have a few, though, or he'll get suspicious. Tap Racy to dig up their files and Rafe for his local knowledge."

Sara continued, "And Trent and Sophie for their specialties." She gave me a patient half smile. "I got it. I wish we had a spy of our own."

I nodded in agreement.

◆◆◆

Two days later we'd moved aboard the ship. Elmarsson had finished with the berthing areas and cabins. He said he would be done with the mess deck by the next day. Most of his team had moved on to other assignments, but he still had one shift aboard every day.

I heard a knock on my door. Racy was holding something furry in her hands.

"Mark, have you ever seen cleaning rats like these?" She stepped over to my desk and used a chair to climb on top of it. She thrust two of the fuzzy things at me.

I pulled my head back to see what she was carrying. When I did, I laughed.

"Racy, those aren't cleaning rats. They're kittens. Where did you find them?"

"Kittens?"

I picked up the orange and black one. It was half dead but still breathing. Dried mucus crusted around its eyes and nose. I still had a bowl from breakfast on my desk. I went to the head and filled it with water. Back at my desk I encouraged the cat to drink from it.

"Kittens," I explained, "are the young form of a Terran animal called a house cat. Did you find their mother?"

"No. I found them hiding in a vent in my room." She placed a black kitten next to its tortoiseshell sibling. Neither of them were drinking the water. I put my fingers in the bowl and dribbled some water on their mouths. They licked at the droplets.

"They are a common Terran pet and good hunters." I petted the black kitten. "I wouldn't be surprised if you find a half-eaten cleaning rat in that vent. If you decide to keep them, you'll have to prevent them from killing off the rats."

"Keep them?" Racy asked. "You'd let me have a pet?"

I shrugged. "Sure, why not? Have Sophie examine them. They're sick. It would be great to have a ship mascot. Let's head down to medical. I'll bet she's still harassing the techs."

We exited the captain's cabin and almost ran into a tech outside the door. He wore gray coveralls and his name tag read "Ervin."

"Mr. Ervin, taking out another ship's comm?"

"No, sir. Putting the little darling back. Nothing unusual about them, so no value to the guys upstairs."

I inclined my head. "Very good. Carry on."

Racy peeked around me, but I nudged her up the hall and down the ladder. After we'd gone around a couple of corners she scowled at me. "That's him?"

"Yep. That's him."

"And I can't take out the recording things? Why do Terrans call them bugs?"

I laughed. "I don't know, but we can't take them out because we want him to believe he's gone unnoticed."

"But we did notice," she protested, "like, the first day he came aboard."

"Military strategy. Sometimes it's good to let your enemy believe they are catching you unaware. Rowdy says it will take a day and a half to fix them once we're underway."

"I still don't like it."

◆ ◆ ◆

"Alright, Sara. Who's next?"

The morning had been spent interviewing a dozen marines. This afternoon was officers. We were in the conference room under the bridge. We had interviewed another second mate candidate. This one had been a rules lawyer. By my count that made three obvious Sudherland plants and two overly uptight officers.

"Lieutenant, Mimi Jaylen."

"Get outta my way, grass head. I know the way to the slugging conference room. Unlike your stupid ass, I studied for this interview." Her voice carried up the passage.

Chapter 11

Mimi

"Lieutenant Mimi Jaylen, reporting as requested."

She was dressed in a Freyan officer's uniform. Her eyes were intense. Her small frame was at once relaxed and poised to spring into action.

"Have a seat, Lieutenant Jaylen," I offered.

We got through all the regular questions. Why do you want to join the crew? Why did you become a naval officer? Where was your last assignment?

Then Sara got to the point. "So, I understand your commission is suspended. Why is that?"

Mimi's jaw dropped. "How do you know that?"

Sara revealed nothing and waited. Racy had pulled the public and private files of all our candidates.

Mimi recovered. "I'm not at liberty to say. You could have asked that backward, paternalistic, butt hugger Norbert. Since he's dead now, you should ask that spineless, brownnosed, lickspittle Sturlasson. He kept it on the books. If I had to guess, I'd say the pair of them were pissed at me."

Sara reviewed her notes. "You were charged with assaulting an officer, but the charges were dropped."

"Yes, ma'am," she responded, "I visited Captain Forrest in the hospital following the event in question. I apologized for putting him there. He claimed his aim was bad and he'd intended to grab my shoulder. The review board said it had merit."

"Did you agree with that?" asked Sara.

I hadn't spoken for a while. Sara knew what we were searching for, and I trusted her judgment.

Mimi licked her lips. "It isn't my place to question my superior officers."

"Ms. Jaylen," I offered, "let me be frank. We command a ship of smugglers. They're good fighters, but rough around the edges. I need to know that you can earn their respect. We tangle with Porcu-bears. I need a good tactician. Finally, we're leaving the system. We need a navigator. Your navigation and combat scores from the academy are solid. What I don't need is a victim."

Mimi scowled. "What if some marine grabs my ass?"

"Put him down," said Sara, "hard."

"Admiral Fart Breath hard, or break bones hard?"

"Whatever it takes, short of killing them. Make your point." I shrugged. "We've got a medical bay."

Mimi snorted. "If you mean that, I may be the woman you want."

"Knock, knock!" Admiral "Brightside" pushed open the door. He saw Mimi and I caught a flash of annoyance in his eyes. "I heard you were interviewing today. I'm glad I caught you." He handed me a tablet.

I scanned it. "What's this?"

"Your new crew! I know how tedious this process can get, so I decided to help you out." He beamed at me like he'd given me a gold-plated coffee mug.

The list included twenty marines, three helmsmen, a chef, and a second mate. Across from me, Mimi clenched her jaw.

I hadn't expected him to try something this blatant, but in hindsight, I should have. "Thank you for these suggestions, Admiral."

His smile faded. "They aren't suggestions, Captain. You are hiring these men. I insist." The corners of his lips went up, but his gaze was hard. "I can do that, you know."

I struggled to remain calm. "We've already hired twelve marines and Lieutenant Jaylen here. Are you going to make us call them all back and fire them?"

Mimi straightened, but wisely stayed silent.

"Yes," said Admiral Olafurson, all trace of humor gone from his voice.

"Who is in command of this ship?" I asked.

"You are, of course," he said.

"And you expect me to go into battle with men I didn't choose? With people I don't know? If it was your ship facing a trio of Erethizon destroyers, would you accept that?"

"I can vouch for every one of these men," he insisted. "They are dependable. It isn't your call."

"This isn't a Freyan naval ship," I countered. "It is my call."

Olafurson gritted his teeth. "I'm trying to help you. You should be focused on getting into space, not on interviews."

Time to change the battlefield. "And in doing so, you're blurring the line between where the navy ends and my letter of marque begins. What happens to your ability to deny knowledge? When we get boarded in Eureka, Gra'nome, or Delta Pavonis while carrying contraband, what will happen to the keiretsu? What will happen to the reputation of the Freyan navy?"

"You wouldn't be connected back to us." He rolled his eyes.

"I'm not from Freya. I'm a political refugee from Yale."

He pointed at my nose. "Don't be so modest. We know who you really are. I'll tell you what: you can keep the trollop, but I know you need twenty-eight marines. Keep those you've hired. Remove any other four from my list."

"Thank you." Something was wrong.

"You're welcome, Captain. I know you need space to make your own decisions." His grin returned. "Starting over with a new captain would be … inconvenient."

He turned around and left.

I waited until I could no longer hear his footsteps. I held out my hand. "Congratulations, Lieutenant Jaylen. Please take stateroom C. Welcome aboard."

Mimi blinked a few times before shaking my hand. "Um. Thanks. I think."

After Mimi left, I hung my head.

Beside me, Sara said, "He caved too easily. We missed something."

I took a deep breath and let it out. "Yeah. I wonder what it was."

Sara sighed. "I'll have Racy dig deeper."

◆ ◆ ◆

As I entered engineering, my heart sank. The techs were done in there, but it was a wreck. Rowdy, Racy, and Trent were gathered around a platform in the center of the space. It seemed a bit short to me, but half a meter off the deck was fine for the Muscat. The holo-table appeared to be the only working piece of equipment in the room. An image of the *Ares Venture* rotated above it. The two kittens, now named Riff and Raff, batted at the holographic ship.

I gestured at the image. "Well?"

Trent answered me. "We're thinking of mounting two gauss cannons ventrally, and one dorsally. With the fourteen missile tubes, we should be effective in small ship combat."

"Small ship combat?" I asked.

"Frigates, destroyers, and medium armed freighters," he clarified. "A cruiser or battleship will still outclass us."

Rowdy pointed to the image. "We'll put the MSP here. If the design works, we'll mount two more up top." He rolled his nose. "Maybe. The gravity plates we got are substandard. Any drive or weapon I build out of them will be pretty weak."

"Okay," I said, "how about centralized control?"

Racy tapped the image with a stylus. Glowing lines appeared throughout the image of the ship. "They will be operated from the bridge, with a backup console in engineering. Redundant power and network lines."

"Good. How long to get it all up and running?" I steeled myself for an answer I knew I wouldn't like.

"Three months," answered Rowdy. "We've got enough repair and maintenance drones. The problem is direction. I'm the only one who knows how all this stuff goes together. Racy could help, but she's already overloaded."

"Three months is too long. What's on your plate, Racy?" I knew we'd been relying on her a lot, but I wasn't sure of everything she was responsible for.

She pulled up a list on her wrist AI. "Records for the new crew. Creating a new ship AI from scratch. Building a new computer core from scratch. Integrating all systems as they come online. Securing them all against intrusion."

"Why can't we buy an AI off the shelf? Wouldn't that take a lot less time than creating a new one?" I wanted to do anything I could do to lighten her load.

She shook her head. "Not secure enough. I don't want anything I can break easily. It also has to work with the new weapons. Full integration with everything. No standard AI will do that."

"Wait." I held up my hand. "You're using a *Muscat-style* AI?"

"Yes."

"Racy …"

"I know what you're thinking. This is the best way to go. Your outdated ideas could get us all killed." She slapped the table. "Terran architecture is out of date. A dozen AIs running a ship is inefficient. I promise nothing like what happened on Mars will happen here."

"Racy!"

"Don't 'Racy' me. You know I'm right and you're wrong. A centralized AI could have stopped Aasha. My brother wouldn't have died. It can monitor all the systems at once, integrate the ship's offense and defense, and find both internal and external threats. We need this."

I clenched my fists and then released them. Racy and I had discussed the Mars AI Massacre at length, but Muscat tech was at least two generations ahead of everyone else in the galaxy. And as much as the thought of a centralized AI scared the hell out of me, I had to trust my people. If Racy thought this was better, it was. "Okay. Do it. What can we do to get you more help?"

"You mean besides getting more Sudhurland techs in here." Trent made it a statement, not a question.

I answered anyway. "Yes."

They shared a look, then turned back to me.

Racy rolled her nose. "We have an idea."

I closed my eyes. "I don't want to know, do I?"

Racy gave a very Terran shrug. "You'll like this idea."

I threw up my hands. "Fine. Whatever it takes. Just make sure we can turn the AI off if we need to. Trent, what did you think of the unit structure I proposed?"

"Four squads with specialized functions. Tracy detached for sniper duty. Jay and Trippy in charge of two of the squads." He nodded. "I'm on board with that."

It amused me what he didn't say. "But you don't want to give War 'n Pace their own squads."

"What in Gra'nome are you thinking, sir?"

"We give the two rascals some responsibility. See what they do with it. In a fight, you could do a lot worse than them."

Trent pulled his pointy ears back. "Okay, we'll give it a try."

"Two months," I offered. "If they don't work out, demote them. We have half the crew coming to us from Sudhurland. We need our own people in charge."

Trent gave me a wolfish smile, "Too true."

From behind me I heard a knock on the hatch. Rafe stood there, his face downcast. "Mark, Rowdy, we have a problem."

Chapter 12

The Little People

"OH MY." When Rafe said he'd gotten us a parts printer, I had expected a three-meter square box. They were usually compact feats of engineering. You put in raw materials, and they spit out tools, circuit boards, and deck plates. And what sat on the hangar floor was definitely a parts printer, but …

"It won't fit." Leave it to Rowdy to state the obvious.

Rafe said he'd gotten the parts printer from a defunct factory. We should have asked what kind of factory. This printer was three times the size of what would fit in engineering.

"I'm sorry, guys," said Rafe. "I guess it wasn't such a sweet deal."

I put my hand on Rafe's shoulder. "You got us what we needed. It just wasn't the way we needed to get it."

The thing was massive. It wouldn't even fit in one of our cargo holds. A pair of ground transports sat nearby. The driver held a tablet.

I knelt on the floor next to Rowdy. "Can we use it?"

"What?" He arched an eyebrow at me. "What part of, 'it's too big' didn't you get?"

"I mean in place. On the hangar floor."

He pulled his pointed, furry ears. "Yeah, I guess. We can connect it to power."

"Then you and Racy get it running. It'll do the job. We just won't be taking it with us."

"And what if something breaks in the void?"

"We'll make that crossing when we come to it." I leaned to the side. There was something behind the printer. "Rafe, what are those crates?"

"Oh," he said, "those are gauss rifles."

"I thought the Freyans wouldn't give us any."

Rafe put his hands in his pockets and looked down. "Those weapons aren't here, sir."

"No? Where are they?"

"In the special weapons armory," he said, "A mix up might have occurred."

"Completely by accident, I'm sure."

Rafe nodded. "Yes, sir."

◆ ◆ ◆

"Hey Sophie. Hey Racy. What do you need?" It was the next day. It depressed me that the situation in medical was as bad as engineering. Sophie had a computer terminal up and running, but not much else.

"I completed my research on Brady Ervin." Racy pulled up his file. The holographic image hung in the air between us.

I grabbed the image and pulled it closer so I could read it. "He doesn't work for the keiretsu?"

Racy shook her head. "He does, but not for Sudhurland. He works for military intelligence and the Gunji."

I skimmed the file. "It says here he's a Humint operative. So what's he doing installing hardware?"

"He has a secondary skill in signals." Racy swiped a page and pointed. "That's how he got stationed here."

Racy swiped three more pages.

"And his mother has an illness. What's Waller's Disease?" I assumed that was why we were in medical, so I turned to Sophie.

"Autoimmune disorder," she obliged. "Genetic. It causes vascular degeneration. The body starts attacking its own blood vessels and tearing them apart."

They looked at me expectantly. I must have been missing something. "Okay, how does his mom having this disease help us?"

"Terran medical science can't cure it," explained Sophie. "The drugs to treat it are expensive."

That didn't sound right. "It's a genetic disorder. Why can't we cook up a virus to correct it? You're sick for a week and bam! All cured."

Sophie slapped me on the back of the head. "Vascular disorder, dummy. The blood vessels would come apart. That would kill the patient."

I took her word for it. "Gunji is paying for his mom's medicine. That's not something we can take over. Back to what I asked. How does this help us?"

Racy climbed on a table next to Sophie and pulled up a new image. "Nanites."

"It's not a cube." Every magnified image I'd ever seen of medi-nano resembled a box. "It's a spiky ball."

Sophie poked the image. "That's because it isn't a Terran design. This one is Muscat. It can resequence a cell without the messy rapid mitosis. That's why a retrovirus won't work. This bypasses that process by inserting the changes."

I bit my lip. "And we can make that work on Terrans?"

Sophie squinted. "Almost. It fixes the veins and arteries without forcing the old ones to die off. There are a few problems, though. Because this is Muscat tech, it will take time to adapt to Terran patients. But the design is a place to start."

I rubbed my mouth. "We also have no way to test this without revealing to Mr. Ervin our plans to turn him."

"*Raw'scadi? Raw'scadi? Forma niche tenda?*" A voice I didn't recognize was speaking Muscat from up the passage.

Racy answered, "*Tenda sitch, Sin'dani.*"

A snow white Muscat with a black spot on her forehead entered the medical bay. She saw me, gasped, then wrapped herself around my legs.

"It's you. It's you!" the foxlike being said.

"It's me." I hugged her back. It had taken me months to get Rowdy and Racy to stop standing right next to me when we were in the same room. I had to repeat the process when Trent and his family joined the crew. "Did I hear right? Your name is Sin'dani?"

"Yes, revered Gran'osida. My family will be so happy to meet you." Muscat always traveled in family groups, so this didn't come as a surprise. She stood back and gazed up at me. "Please call me Cindy."

"Okay, Cindy. Where is your family? I'd love to meet them." Months earlier I'd saved the life of the Muscat Queen's son. As a result, she'd bestowed upon me the title of Gran'osida. It made me a bit of a celebrity among her people.

"They're in the hangar. Raw'scadi and Raw'noriede said you needed help. As far as I know, we're the only other family on Freya."

I followed Cindy out. Racy and Sophie followed. Over my shoulder I asked, "I'm guessing Cindy has the nanite design?"

"No," said Racy. "She's a mechanical engineer. Her brother, Simon, is the nanotech engineer."

Sophie held up a finger. "He and I will work together to see if it can be adapted."

I stepped down the ramp and into the hangar. A furry, white wave engulfed me. Several of them had black or brown spots. They were all speaking at once. "Did you really save the prince's life?" "What was it like meeting the queen?" A younger Muscat said, "I heard you had pointed ears and fur. I don't see any fur."

"Cindy," I called out, "how big is your family?"

From the back edge of her clan she answered, "Ten. My brother and sister, our spouses, and four kids."

I tried to catch all their names, but I confess, I quickly lost track. I resorted to storing their names and pictures together in my implant.

♦ ♦ ♦

Over the next three days things moved quickly. Cindy and her family helped Rowdy and Racy set the ship up. My new crew members arrived, including a helmsman named Fenton and a chef named Clive.

I was outside the ship discussing changes with Rowdy when I noticed something odd. "Cindy, what are you doing with the parts printer?"

"Taking it apart." She pointed to a corner of the big unit. Two of her teenage offspring started taking access panels off.

"Don't we need that?" I pointed out.

"Yes, but wouldn't you rather have it inside the ship?"

I blinked twice. "But it won't fit. Will it?"

"Phbbbbt," she scoffed. "Most of this is casing. We move some of the material feeds around, change the output, might be we can fit it in cargo bay three. You're making the other half into marine berthing, right?"

I tried to imagine this monster of a machine in that space and couldn't. "But Rowdy said it wouldn't fit in there."

"Uh, yeah. He's a physicist. I'm sure he knows all about drives and weapons." She waved in the direction of the ship. "Trust me. It'll fit."

I glanced down at Rowdy beside me. He shrugged.

"Okay, give it a try."

"Captain Martin!" A voice I had come to dread echoed off the hangar walls.

"Just a moment, Rowdy." I walked toward Admiral Brightside as he stormed toward me.

"Greetings, Admiral. How can I help you?"

He didn't mince words. "Give me my damn tree rats back."

"Excuse me?" The derogatory term for Muscat caused me to grind my teeth.

"You heard me. Give me the slugging tree rats back."

I took a couple of heartbeats to calm down. "Cindy and her family showed up a few days ago. I had no idea they had been working for you."

"They've called in sick for the past couple of days." He narrowed his eyes at me. "The head bitch said they'd all come down with something called 'hint Joe plus.'"

I puzzled through that for a few of seconds. "*Hentoran jora plas*?"

"Yeah, that." He pointed down at the hangar floor for emphasis. "I want them back at work tomorrow. They're building ship-sized plasma cannons and backup shield generators for us. They have to finish the job for us first," he snarled.

"I'll talk to her." I patted the air. "We can work it out, Admiral."

Olafurson shook his fist at me. "You'd better, Martin. You're already on the laser edge with me."

He stomped out of the hangar. I shook my head and stepped back to where Cindy and Rowdy had been watching the exchange.

I stood there and collected my thoughts before I spoke. "Cindy, I appreciate what you're doing here. I understand that you've contracted with the military to build some equipment?"

She shrugged. "Uh yeah, but there's no time limit. We get done when we get done."

I clasped my hands in front of me. "That may be so, but can you and your family divide your time between us and the Freyan navy?"

"What? You're afraid of Admiral Hentoran, I mean Olafurson?" she asked.

"No, but he could make my life difficult." I sighed. "I'm very grateful and I know the queen would appreciate everything you've done here. But I'd like it if you didn't all call in 'tired of stupid' tomorrow."

Cindy rolled her nose at me. "Uh, yeah. We can divide our time."

Chapter 13

Hail to the Queen

"SHE DID IT." Rowdy and I were standingoutside of what used to be cargo bay three. The forward half had been converted to marine berthing. The aft half now housed our parts printer.

Rowdy grunted in satisfaction. "If she didn't have a mate, I'd ask her to marry me."

I looked down at my friend. "I've never asked, but what happened to your mate?"

"Aircar accident years ago. Randy and Racy were just kits."

I put my hand on his shoulder. "I'm so sorry."

"It's okay." He grinned up at me. "I have a new family now, even if they are a bunch of hairless upta."

"What's an upta?"

"Burrowing, apelike creature."

I laughed. My wrist AI trilled at me.

"Hey, Sara. What do you need?"

"We've got a situation, Captain. Can you meet Mimi and I in your cabin?"

Rowdy hugged my leg. "Go, Mark. I have a reactor and computer core to build."

I knelt down and gave him a proper hug, then left to discover what new fire had sprung up.

The door to my cabin opened up into the office. Inside I found Sara, Mimi in combat armor, and Brady Ervin. Mimi stood with a hand on his shoulder. She squeezed it as I walked in the door and he cried out.

Whatever they were about to tell me, I wasn't going to like it. Using my AI, I sent a request for Sophie to join us. "Ms. Jaylen, I thought I asked you not to interfere with Mr. Ervin."

Ervin's gaze met mine with a question he didn't ask.

"I caught him loading something into the Quick Box." Mimi glared daggers at the man she had planted in the chair.

The intelligence techs had taken every computer system out of the hull. In the absence of a ship AI, the Quick Box was essentially a server we'd set up to run doors, basic communications, air, and a few other essential systems. It was a quick fix, just a computer, not even an AI.

"Mr. Ervin," I started, "the Quick Box is something we installed. It wasn't here before your men arrived. Why were you messing with it?"

"Sir," he gritted his teeth, "as I was telling Ms. Jaylen, the Quick Box is connected to the hatches in the cargo holds. I had to disconnect them from the box before we could remove them."

He was good, but I'd been able to speak to him a few times in the past week. I knew that his chin moved a little to the right when he lied. "Those door locks were removed six days ago. The ones in there are new."

"Oh? I must have a bad work order. I'll run it by Elmarsson." He tried to stand, but Mimi held him in place.

I regarded him for several more moments. He'd crossed the line. If I didn't move now, they'd plant someone new aboard. It was time to move the chess pieces into position. "Mr. Ervin, do you mind if I call you Brady?"

"What?"

"Brady, your first name. Is it okay if I use it?"

He twitched. "Yeah, I guess that's okay."

"Good. Brady, do you like working for the Gunji?"

His hand crept to his pants leg. "I'm not sure what you mean."

I indicated his hand. "You won't need to use the panic button in your pocket. We're not going to hurt you. You also don't want them to hear this conversation."

He put his palms on the armrests of the chair to show he wasn't reaching for anything. "We're on the same side, sir. The GVM wants you up there fighting the Erethizon."

"Thanks," I said, "but I wasn't referring to your bosses in military intelligence. I'm referring to the organization that runs most of the navy. The Gunji Keiretsu."

"Sir," his chin twitched, "I'm not sure what you've heard, but there's not some super secret fraternity or anything that runs the navy."

Behind him Sophie slipped in and closed the door.

I shrugged. "Does your mom know where the drugs come from? The ones that control her Waller's Disease? Did the Gunji offer it freely, or is it a condition of your cooperation?"

His eyes narrowed at me and his lips became a razor thin line.

"Sophie," I peered over Brady's shoulder, "how are you and Simon doing with the research?"

"Good," she said. "We're 90 percent certain the nanite therapy will work. We should be able to increase that if we can get a good scan of Mrs. Ervin."

Brady shook his shoulder loose from Mimi. She let it go. "What are you playing at, Martin? Waller's can't be cured, and my mom's already being treated for it."

I studied the overheads. "What if she didn't have to go through the treatment anymore?"

He sneered. "What, you're going to do what years of research haven't? Don't waste my time. You aren't going to con me."

I held up a finger. "You're right. Terran medical science can't fix your mom." I waved a hand to indicate the ship. "But have you noticed how many Muscat are helping out around here?"

The sneer vanished and was replaced by suspicion. After a moment, he asked, "And what would I have to do?"

"We've been blindsided several times in the past few weeks. The military, the Sudhurland, and the Gunji are yanking our chains." I held my thumb and forefinger a centimeter apart. "All we want is a little warning before the next surprise comes."

He rolled his eyes. "Like they tell me anything. I'll be lucky to live if they find out. And you're going to hang on to the treatment. I won't even know if it works."

"No, you misunderstand. We're not the keiretsu. We'll arrange for you, Sophie, and Simon to meet off-base. Your mom gets the treatment either way. We want her cured."

He squinted. "But what if I betray you? I could feed you crap. You fix my mom and you have no leverage left."

I folded my hands in my lap. "Call it a gesture of good faith."

◆ ◆ ◆

"You think he'll bite?" asked Sara. Brady Ervin had just left and Sophie and Mimi had returned to their duties.

"Maybe. You?" I asked.

"I think you're an idiot," she paused deliberately before continuing, "sir."

A felt a slow grin take over my expression. "Thanks, Sara. In truth, I don't know. Everyone around here is so focused on getting the upper hand. It's a risk, but I want to see what a little honey spread in the right places will get us."

"Captain Houston took some crazy risks," she said. "Taking you on board was one of them. What she would do in this situation, though …" She hung her head. "I can't imagine she'd have survived. Houston was a shoot first, ask questions later kind of a captain. You're something else."

"I hope it's a good something else."

She winked at me. "I'll let you know, Mark."

◆◆◆

"Okay Racy, what did you want to show me?" We were in the room behind the bridge where the old computer core had been housed. I rubbed my arms to stay warm.

I'd seen the manufacturer specs and this room was supposed to have a lot more space. The wall in front of me was filled with access panels. At about waist height was a small screen. Below it was a keyboard with Muscat characters on it.

"You said you wanted to be here when I switched her on." She waved at the wall. "I'm about to do that."

I suppressed a shiver. Stories of rogue AIs killing people flitted through my mind. I took a deep breath, reminding myself that Racy was my friend. I thought of her as my little sister. She would never do anything that could get me hurt.

She was an expert in AI systems. *The* expert, as far as I was concerned. She said we needed this. It would give us an edge against the Erethizon.

But if this machine was going to be keeping me alive in deep space, I needed to know more. "How much autonomy does she have?"

"She's designed to monitor security and run the ship. She'll have the ability to question orders unless given by an officer or by me." Racy rubbed her front teeth with her tongue. It was a nervous gesture. "Uh, unlike a Terran AI, she can use lethal force. We're a privateer, so I wanted to make sure she won't seize up in combat. I don't care what that Asimov guy said. Those rules don't work for a warship."

I laughed. "Those rules were designed for a pacifist society. In the stories, the computers still managed to cause a lot of trouble. We're out to cause mayhem and destruction. I'm fine if the AI is allowed to use force. I just don't want it to harm its crew." That thought reminded me that half of my people had divided loyalties. "Well, not without permission, anyway."

"Okay, you've renamed the ship *Queen Nephanie*. Nephie for short, so that's what she's programmed to respond to. It will take a little while for her to load up."

My hands were sweating. I rubbed them on my sleeves again. "Hit it."

Racy called up a screen on her wrist AI and tapped it. Odd, considering there was a keyboard right in front of her. Behind the wall, fans whirred to life. For about five minutes nothing happened.

"Bera na," said the voice from the wall. It was the Muscat phrase for "good morning."

"Bera na," responded Racy, who then switched to Terran. "Nephie, please meet Mark Martin. He's the captain of the ship."

"Hello, Mark Martin. It is a pleasure to meet you."

She sounded more friendly than any AI I'd ever spoken to. "Hello, Nephie. Do you mind if I ask you a few questions?"

"Of course not. Let's get to know each other."

Racy smiled and rolled her nose at me.

"Nephie, what are your directives?" I asked.

"In order of importance, I will follow the requests of the captain, Racy, the officers, the crew, and registered guests of the *Queen Nephanie*," the feminine voice intoned. "I will protect the lives of the officers and crew of this ship. I will protect the lives of others except in the case of security or combat operations. In the case of security and combat operations, I will follow the requests in the order of importance stated before."

"Nephie, where do you fall on the Brook Artificial Consciousness Scale?"

"Hmmm. That's a good question." She paused before continuing. "I am aware that I am a computerized being and not flesh and blood. That could be construed as self-awareness. I have no desire to make art or write fiction. Those appear to be common outlets of creativity. I am able to analyze large amounts of data and come to conclusions. If I had to make an educated guess, I would say I am an eight on the ten-point scale.

"An eight is pretty high, Nephie. Can you do me a favor?" I wanted to test her creativity without her realizing what I was doing.

"Of course, Captain Mark Martin. What would you like me to do?"

"If you were a Terran, what would you want to look like?"

A couple of seconds later, an image appeared on the screen. It was the hips and waist of a naked Terran female.

I burst out laughing. Racy put her head in her hands. The screen was at eye level for a Muscat, so it would be correctly placed if there was a naked woman standing in the room.

"What's so funny?" the AI asked.

"Two things," I answered. "Terrans wear clothes and you should focus the image on the face."

"I am wearing clothes." She pulled the image back to show that she was wearing a Muscat harness. The face was that of my sister.

I felt hot and turned my head. "Having two people on board that look like Sophie will get confusing. Also, you should stick with Terran clothing styles."

"Oh, of course." She changed her clothes to a sequined blue pant suit. Her face grew a bit wider, olive-skinned and topped with strawberry blonde hair. It was an attractive, galactic citizen, one of everything kind of look. "How's this?"

Racy bounced and clapped. "Oh, that's so pretty!"

The image on the screen did a twirl. "Do you think so? Thanks, Racy."

Proof positive that she could be creative when asked. That could be both good and bad. What about her problem-solving abilities? "Nephie, let's say I want honey for my coffee. Where can I get some?"

The image went still. "There doesn't appear to be any honey in ship's stores. Rafe could order some, but the base commissary doesn't have any. There is a grocery store two kilometers from the base. Prices there are well above the norm, however. If you've already made the coffee, it would be cold by the time you returned. My understanding is that it is a beverage often served hot. My suggestion would be that you use sugar instead. We have a large supply onboard and it seems like a good substitute."

Wow. In the space of just a moment she had accessed several available databases and researched cultural norms. "Eight" my ass. She was a solid ten by any definition. "Very good, Nephie."

"Thank you, Captain Mark Martin."

"You're welcome." Turning to Racy, I said, "Excellent work."

Racy beamed at me. "Thanks, Mark."

◆ ◆ ◆

Sophie and I were walking to the mess deck. Our new chef had prepared his first meal aboard. I hoped he would come close to Boldrini's skill.

"You're rubbing your coin," Sophie observed.

I realized she was right.

"Worried?" she asked.

I put it back in my pocket. "Yes. Everything is coming together, but I can't help wondering when the other shoe is going to drop."

"Don't be so fatalistic. The worst is behind us, right?"

Walking into the mess deck, I skidded to a stop. Mimi was fastened halfway up the far wall with engine tape. Her mouth was covered, but her eyes blazed with fury.

Our chef, Clive, was setting up his serving line and didn't seemed inclined to help. There were a few marines, who glanced nervously between me and the wall ornament.

Their expressions were something between fear and amusement.

I crossed the room and pulled a vibro-blade from my pocket.

As soon as I'd cut one arm free, Mimi viciously tore the tape from her mouth. "Rrrraaaahhh! When I get my hands on them, their parents won't be able to identify the bodies." We made short work of the remaining tape and she sprinted from the room.

I jerked my head toward the serving line. "Better get some food. You're about to be busy."

She shook her head. "No rush, they'll wait."

At the serving line I reviewed the selection. "What do we have, Clive?"

The chef, Clive, was overweight, with a scar around his left eye. The eye itself was artificial and little more than a lens. "Roast lamb in Freyan spices, rock ox stew, and shredded snow lizard in lemon sauce."

"That's a lot of meat," I observed.

"I'm mostly a butcher, sir. You can call me Cleave. Most people do."

I mentally filed that away for later. Food in hand, I sat at a table with my sister.

Sophie speared some of the lamb with a fork. "When will the new ship AI be up and running?"

"Racy turned it on this morning." I chewed on a bit of snow lizard. It was pretty good.

"Did you rename the ship?" My sister licked some of the sauce from her fingers. "That's how it works, right? You refer to the AI by the name of the vessel?"

"Yes. I filed the paperwork to rename the ship yesterday."

"What did you call her?"

Nephie's voice came from a speaker overhead. "Dr. Martin?"

"Yes?" said Sophie.

"I'm sorry to interrupt your lunch, but there has been a medical emergency in marine berthing," she stated with no inflection. "Patients Dave Warren and Pace Jones are being transported to the med bay. Your presence is required."

"Thank you." Her brow furrowed. "Who am I speaking to?"

"I am the ship, or more correctly, the AI that runs the ship. I am the *Queen Nephanie*."

My sister goggled. "You named the ship after Grandma?"

I shrugged. "Why not? She was a cast iron bitch no one in their right mind would mess with."

◆ ◆ ◆

I sat at my desk. Holograms of various reports hung in the air around me. "Nephie, please record a message for Ike Fullerton."

The ship's AI replied promptly, "Recording."

"Hey Ike. The ship is almost put back together. In another couple of days we'll be as good as we can get her here. Our next stop is your place, so put out a welcome mat.

"The keiretsus who run Freya are always fighting with each other. We've hooked up with one, and they've been helping us. The deal is that they get a large share of our profits. We'll figure out what to do about that after we get moving.

"I'm not sure how we're going to get there. No one really controls the space above Freya. Getting out of here may be tricky. The warp gate is also contested. The terminal is safe. No one will attack what they want to control. It might be damaged. We have an R-drive, minus the exotic matter lens. I haven't thought of a way to steal one, yet.

"Our freighter has light armor. I want to upgrade it to something heavier, but we can't get the raw materials to make that happen. Carbon, hydrogen, and iron are easy to come by here. Moly, titanium, and lanthanides are not. They can't be mined on Freya. The result is that we have something that will protect us from solar radiation, but won't stand up to much punishment. The special paint we used to make the last ship so stealthy is also a bust.

"Lastly, we've had a problem with gravity generators. The quality isn't that great. We need them for our main in-system drive and some experimental tech we're developing.

"We can get everything we need on that rock you're sitting on. You have access to Terran gravity generators and plenty of hard-to-find minerals. It's also one of the few places in the galaxy where they mine exotic matter.

"In short, as soon as we can steal a lens or sneak through the warp gate, we'll be seeing you. Always your friend, Snarky Marky.

"Recording complete."

"Message encrypted," the AI said. "I'll send it to the warp gate, Captain Martin. It may be some time before Mr. Fullerton gets it. Gate traffic has been limited."

"Thanks, Nephie."

Sara's voice came from the intercom. "Mark, can you come to the forward airlock."

"Be right there, Sara."

I wove through the ship. It was good to see it almost ready to go. In the airlock I saw Sara standing next to Ufkell. He was sizing up the space like it was the first time he'd been aboard a ship. He had two goons and a pile of luggage with him.

My gut lurched. "Ufkell, to what do I owe the pleasure?"

He crossed his arms. "I'm traveling with you to Eureka. It's time to expand my empire. You'll recall the clause in our contract."

"The one where you get to place a Sudhurland representative aboard my ship." I had thought that it would be one of the men Mr. Brightside had forced me to hire, perhaps another naval officer he had under his thumb. "Of course I remember."

"I knew you were a smart boy." There was no warmth in his face.

This didn't make sense. "Ufkell, why are you coming? Your organization will be without your leadership. Someone might try to seize power."

"Ha," he said with humor. "Olafurson will run things here while I'm gone. My cousin won't betray me. He can manage a crisis. My other lieutenants wouldn't dare move against him. No, I need to be there where I can get a feel for the people. I have to know which buttons to press to get what I want."

There were a thousand reasons why this was a bad thing … at least for me. The thought of Ike having to deal with him filled me with dread. "Okay, just so we're clear, aboard this ship, I call the shots. You realize what could happen if people start questioning my authority, right?"

"Of course," the pause stretched for a few seconds, "Captain."

I ignored the implied threat. "The other problem is that we have no way to get to Eureka. Porcu-bears surround the planet and the gate."

He raised an eyebrow at me. "Are you saying you can't sneak past them?"

"Over the planet? Probably. Around the gate? No. The Porcu-bears are firing on anything coming through or approaching the terminal. The Erethizon won't seize the gate because the gate personnel would disable it at the first sign of trouble. The people running the gate won't turn on this side as long as it's unsafe for passage. Any other gate trying to dial us up would get a busy signal."

Ufkell stroked his beard. "I thought you had an R-drive."

I tilted my head. He was well informed. "Most of it. We can't find an exotic matter lens. Can you get one for us?"

He gazed at the ceiling and frowned. "Hmm. No." He tapped his lips with his finger a for a few seconds. "What if I could get the Erethizon to let us through the gate?"

I blinked. "What?"

He mimed putting a puzzle together. "I think I can get us safe passage through the terminal. If I can work it out, can you get the gate crew to send us to Eureka?"

Could he do that? Was it possible to somehow get the Erethizon to let us pass? Any independent freighter would be fired on by the Theocracy. A Porcu-bear freighter would be destroyed by the Freyans. Setting all that aside, though … "Yeah. If you can keep both sides from blowing us to atoms, I can convince the gate crew to let us pass."

Ufkell pounded the air. "Excellent. I have an idea that might work."

I gestured toward the passage. "Then we'll get you a room. Will your associates by bunking with you or will they be in crew berthing."

"Crew berthing will be fine for them."

I nodded to the crewman manning the lock. "Find someone to show Mr. Ufkell to stateroom D."

"Aye, aye, sir."

He led Ufkell into the ship, leaving me with Sara. "We need a plan to get rid of him."

She put her hand on my shoulder. "You're drowning in kraken-infested waters. Let Trent and I handle it."

I saw the rating at the brow watch pale. He wasn't looking at me, though. "Sir?"

I glanced over my shoulder. A squad of marines quick marched to our airlock. I recognized the lieutenant leading the way as the late Admiral Norbert's aide. A Gunji operative.

"Captain Martin, you are under arrest. Sergeant, take this man into custody."

Chapter 14

A Deal with the Devil

I PUT MY HANDS UP. "What's the charge?" I used my AI to call Trent.

"Treason. Theft of military property." The lieutenant sneered.

I remembered that Rafe had brought aboard twenty Freyan FR2 rifles. Those shouldn't have been anywhere this idiot could find them, so I decided to play dumb. It would keep him off-balance. "We're a privateer. Of course we've stolen Erethizon supplies. It's part of our charter."

He showed me his teeth. "Freyan weapons. Our high tech gauss rifles." He turned to his NCO. "Take him away."

That wasn't part of the script. I had been expecting the Gunji to do something to keep us from taking off. I'd be okay as long as I stayed on the ship. If they squirreled me away in a cell, that was a different story. I needed to stall for time.

The sergeant pulled, but I resisted. "You can't arrest me without a warrant. You also can't arrest a superior officer."

His nostrils flared. "You are not an officer of the Freyan navy. I can arrest you on probable cause."

"What is your probable cause?"

He swept his arms wide. "The stolen weapons!"

"The ones you've accused me of stealing. Where are they?"

His face turned red. "Aboard this ship."

"The one you don't have a warrant to search."

The marine kept trying to put cuffs on me. It was hard to do while following military courtesy. Especially since I wasn't cooperating.

The officer yanked a piece of paper out of his pocket.

"You've jumped the gun, Lieutenant. You have to find the weapons before you can arrest me."

Behind me, a familiar voice cleared its throat. "Is there a problem, Captain Martin?"

The officer visibly paled. "Ufkell?"

I responded over my shoulder. "No."

The lieutenant regained some of his bluster. "You're coming with me while my men search the ship."

I nodded over his shoulder. "Through them? That would be a neat trick."

He spun around to see two squads of my marines in combat armor, their rifles trained on the Freyans in the lock.

He pointed. "Those are the rifles we're searching for. Your men wouldn't shoot us. Not Freyan soldiers on a Freyan military base. Not when they might hit you."

"Look closer," I prompted. "Those are TR45s. I'm pretty sure the rifles you're searching for are FR2s. Freyan design, right?"

His mouth moved but no words came out.

I sighed. "I'll tell you what's going to happen. You are going to be escorted through my ship on your search. Once your men are satisfied that the FR2s are not here, you are going to leave my ship. When that happens, your Gunji masters are going to take offense at your incompetence." I gave a small nod. "I wonder what will happen then."

His shoulders slumped forward.

The marine gave up on trying to put me in cuffs. Trent, who had just arrived with the marines, escorted the search team into the ship.

After they were out of earshot, Ufkell clapped. "Nicely done. Do they need to have an accident?"

I shook my head. "Why get our hands dirty? The Gunji will take care of it for us."

Ufkell got a thoughtful expression. "I like you, Captain Martin. I hope nothing happens to change that." He wandered back into the ship.

Someone appeared at my side. A glance confirmed my suspicions. "Thanks for the heads up, Mr. Ervin."

"Thanks for saving my mom from a slow and painful death." He was quiet for a few seconds as Sara joined us. "I'm going to ask the Gunji to assign me to your crew."

"Think they'll do that after this fiasco?"

His head weaved back and forth. "I'll make sure Lieutenant Butt-stick takes the blame. Besides, I need the Gunji to keep supplying my ma with the drugs."

I raised an eyebrow in his direction. "But she doesn't need them anymore."

"True," he said, "but she likes her new beach house, and selling them pays the bills."

◆◆◆

Two days later Ufkell, Sara, Mimi, and I were in the conference room under the bridge. Darkside had called the meeting. He grinned.

"I've solved the problem," he announced.

"Which one?" Mimi asked.

"The problem of getting us to Eureka, our next port. The ship is ready to sail, Captain?"

"Yes." I answered. "We still have the other problems we discussed, but put us under thrust and we'll sail."

"Good." His gaze swept the room. "I've contacted the suppliers Houston used. I was able to get the holds filled with Violet Monkeys."

I pulled at my hair. "Our cargo is drugs."

"Just the dried flowers," Ufkell said.

Dried flowers that could be made into hallucinogens with minimal processing. We'd be delivering drugs to a mining colony, a colony with a large population of Yale expatriates. I had visions of my people wandering the streets, strung out, with bloodshot eyes. I was reminded again of how much I hated working with Mr. Darkside.

One step at a time. "Okay, so how do we get to Eureka without an R-drive and with a blockaded warp gate."

Ufkell checked the time on his wrist AI, then used it to turn on the wall-mounted vid screen. "Like this."

"… and here is the scene at Bjorn's Landing. As you can see, people are cheering in the streets," a news announcer was saying.

"Can you blame them, Selig?" answered another news-caster. "The Erethizon blockade has ended. The stock market is soaring. This almost guarantees Prime Minister Guttormur a second term. We've received word that the promised Erethizon transport has landed. Scores of Freyan soldiers previously presumed missing or dead have been released."

To say I was flabbergasted was an understatement. "You got the Porcu-bears to sign a peace treaty?"

"No." Mr. Darkside's face fell. "I tried, but I couldn't make it happen. They were willing to sign a cease-fire, though."

Sara frowned. "What did you have to promise them? You didn't offer them Mark, did you?"

He waved back and forth like he was weighing his options. "I thought about it, but no. It would cost too much money and goodwill to replace Captain Martin. I couldn't be sure that I could work with another officer. Instead, I offered a prisoner exchange."

He didn't.

He couldn't have.

The more I thought about it, the more it made sense. With every moment, my certainty grew. So did the feeling that I had a lead asteroid for a stomach. I felt like I was going to throw up. "You gave them Grova."

He nodded. "He's popular with the Council of Archbishops. I even got them to throw in a few million credits. Money, a cease-fire, and several favors from the Prime Minister. It was a good day."

I tried to tell myself it wasn't a big deal, that the Porcubears would have been following me around the galaxy with or without Grova in command. It didn't work. The commander had me in his sights. To him, I was the key to suppressing the resistance on Yale, a valuable tool to the Theocracy.

"Ufkell, Commander Grova wants me. Badly. Won't it be bad for business if he's following us from port to port?"

"He won't be."

"Why do you sluggin' think that?" asked Mimi. Her tone told us she thought he was an idiot, without saying it out loud.

"He told me so. He says Mark will come to him." He cocked his head to the side. "You're not planning on doing that are you?"

They had spoken? I guess it made sense. In negotiating the deal, they would have had to. "No."

Mr. Darkside mimed washing his hands and throwing a towel. "Nothing to worry about, then. Now we have some cargo to move and an empire to build. Let's get sailing."

◆ ◆ ◆

"Thanks for all your help, Cindy." We stood outside the ship in the hangar.

She beamed at me, then hugged my legs. "You are so welcome. It was great working with Rowdy and Racy. Simon can't say enough good things about Sophie either."

"We couldn't have done it without you." It was true. Cindy and her family had taken three months of work and condensed it into one. Without her we'd still be searching for a parts printer and Brady would still be working for the Gunji."

"Uh, yeah. You're right." Her smile showed wolfish teeth. "What's next?"

"We go to Eureka and fix the hull. We need heavier armor with stealth capabilities. We hope to also get an exotic matter lens and better gravity generators there. Once we get that out of the way, we can find my Dad."

She put her hand on my knee. "Family completes us and defines us. To be separated from your family is to be separated from yourself. Find your father and bring him home."

"Mr. Ervin says he has a lead, someone on Eureka who might know something."

"Then there you must go. Safe travels, Gran'osida."

"I told you to call me Mark."

"Uh, yeah. You're Gran'osida and Mr. Brightside is Admiral Hentoran. I call it like I see it. If it's good enough for the queen, it's good enough for me."

"Watch out for Brightside. He's not as stupid as he looks."

"I will. Even a dumb frequa can be dangerous."

I tried to imagine Olafurson with claws and armored scales, coiled around a tree, and failed. "Safe travels, Cindy."

◆ ◆ ◆

The time had come. I was more than ready to shake the dirt of Freya from my shoes. "Racy, what's the status of our systems?"

"The AI is functioning normally," she said from the comms station. "Communications are online and all systems are secure."

"Rowdy? How's Engineering?"

An image of him popped up on my right. "We're all good back here. The reactors and drives are all in the green. Environmental shows all gasses within acceptable limits."

"Mimi, what's the status of our cargo and navigation?"

"Cargo is loaded and checked. Freya has given us an exit vector and has authorized our departure. A flight plan has been filed and the warp gate is expecting us."

"Sara?"

"All departments have checked in. All crew is present or accounted for. We are ready to sail."

I checked over my shoulder. Mr. Darkside was sitting at the back of the bridge, his gaze swiveling everywhere at once. He was paying attention, but didn't offer any comment on our progress.

It felt wrong taking flight without Wally at the helm. We'd lost so many good people. Flower flies were dancing in my stomach. I hoped Jenna Houston was watching over us from wherever her spirit now resided. "Good. Mr. Fenton, take us out. Dead slow."

We exited the hangar through the huge doors. Fenton studied the monitors. Trash and debris flew about outside as we cleared the overhang.

The ship taxied to the launchpad. I watched over Fenton's shoulder. The control tower gave us the green light. He glanced back at me and I nodded.

We didn't feel anything. Inertial dampeners made sure of that. The control tower and surrounding buildings grew smaller as we accelerated away from the ground. I said a silent goodbye to those we lost.

Mimi was frowning into a holo-screen.

"Mimi?"

"Nothing, sir. I wasn't able to see my friend Lily before I left. She sent me a goodbye message, but it doesn't sound right."

I shrugged it off. An hour later we were in high orbit. The AI tagged all the vessels in the space around us. The icons showed Erethizon ships facing an equal tonnage of Freyan ships. Wherever there was movement, it was shadowed on the other side. A cease-fire, but from here it appeared fragile. One false move and it would blow up in everyone's faces. Fenton followed Mimi's plotted course. It would send us in a loop around the planet and then slingshot us out to the edge of the system, toward the warp gate.

We'd started the burn when the AI piped up. "Captain? There are two ships on an intercept course with us."

"Who are they?"

"One is a Freyan destroyer, the other is an Erethizon cruiser. Weapons are hot and we are being targeted by both crafts."

In the holo-tank, the two icons blinked red.

"We are being hailed," said Nephie. "The Erethizon are requesting we heave to and prepare to be boarded. The Freyans are demanding we achieve geosynchronous orbit or we will be fired upon."

"What did we just step in?" Mimi exclaimed.

"They are serious, Captain," said Sara. "Profile suggests they intend to fire on us."

"Captain. The Erethizon cruiser has identified itself as the *Horrong*, Commander Grova in command."

Chapter 15

Sandwich

SARA'S EYES WERE WIDE. "ARM weapons, sir?"

My heart pounded in my chest and I wiped my palms on my pants. I shook my head. "No. Something isn't right here. The Erethizon might want to start a fight, but not the Freyans. Even the Gunji wouldn't do something like this out in the open. Keep the shields at full. Do not arm the gauss cannons or missiles."

Fenton's hands were shaking. "Reduce speed, sir?"

"Let's follow the Freyan's suggestion. Geosynchronous orbit. Slowly, Mr. Fenton. Never let them see that you're nervous." I gave him wink with more confidence than I felt. It wouldn't be good to let the crew see me rattled.

"Open a channel with our two pursuers, Nephie."

"Channel open," the AI responded.

"Gentlemen, how may we be of service?" I concentrated on keeping my voice calm and level.

"Heave to in the name of the Erethizon Theocracy, Captain Martin. We will be boarding." Commander Grova's image appeared on the left.

"This is Captain Vinjar of the Freyan Navy," said the image on the right. "You will do no such thing. The cease-fire states that you are allowed to take detailed scans. Boarding of merchant shipping vessels is forbidden. Captain Martin, you will form up with us. We will escort you to the warp gate. If you refuse, we will assume you are carrying Erethizon collaborators and blow you to Helheim."

I looked at Sara, Mimi, and Ufkell in turn. They seemed as surprised as I was. Mimi shrugged her shoulders in an "I don't know" gesture.

"We have been unable to scan the *Queen Nephanie*." Grova's glare was dark and cold, daring the Freyan captain to defy him. "We must be allowed to board."

I typed a message to Rowdy. *Did you do something to us? You told me you couldn't give us stealth, but the Porcubears say they can't scan us.*

The response was immediate. *No stealth. I set up reflectors around the cargo holds. It will make a scan fuzzy, like we're carrying water.*

The Freyan responded. "That is not part of the agreement, Commander. Scans only. Your substandard equipment isn't our problem." Vinjar motioned to someone offscreen.

"Erethizon tech is the best in the galaxy," said Grova. "The Great Urson has seen to that. You are hiding something."

"Captain," said Sara, "a Freyan battleship is moving to intercept."

"You've recently rejoined your comrades, Grova. The approaching Freyan battleship is armed with plasma cannons. I repeat: you will not be boarding any merchant traffic moving to or from Freya," Vinjar said.

Grova snarled. "Fine, infidel. We will not board. Urson will soon give us the secret of ship-mounted plasma weapons. Better scans are required of the *Queen Nephanie*. We will be watching. *Horrong* out."

I breathed a sigh of relief. "Thank you, Captain."

"Don't thank me," said Vinjar. "As far as I'm concerned, Ufkell ranks right below pond scum, and the Porcu-bears just below that. I have my orders. You will follow the course I send you exactly. Failure will give me an opportunity to find out if Ufkell can breathe in a vacuum. I *really* want to know. Vinjar out."

I glanced back at Mr. Darkside. "Aren't we a pair of popular fellows."

He gave me a frosty smile. "It's the price of power."

"Why is this still a problem, Ufkell? I thought you said Grova was going to wait for me to come to him."

"His exact words were, 'Mark Martin cannot stay on this planet forever. Sooner or later he will leave Freya and come to me.'" Darkside shrugged. "It could be said that we're in his space."

◆ ◆ ◆

The Porcu-bear cruiser and Freyan destroyer formed up on us. The battleship sat nearby like a mountain overlooking molehills. Freya had one battleship and wouldn't let it leave the space above the planet. Vinjar gave us our course and we set sail. I would have felt a little better if the battleship had followed us out. In a fight between the destroyer and the Erethizon cruiser, the destroyer didn't stand a chance.

To be fair, the course the Freyans gave us was pretty close to what Mimi had originally plotted. The main difference was a wider arc around the gas giant in the outer system.

Once we got underway, neither of the other ships contacted us. That was fine by me. Our brief discussion had been plenty.

There were a few hiccups, systems and engineering issues. Rowdy and Racy fixed sticky doors, light panels that wouldn't stay lit, and the odd temperature variance. And then there was …

"Mimi, why are you wearing combat armor?" We were on the bridge for the watch change. She had her full kit on, minus the helmet and gloves.

She looked down at herself. "Is there a rule against it?"

"No."

"I feel safer with it on. Remember that day War 'n Pace stuck me to a bulkhead?"

"Oh yes."

"After I sent them to the infirmary, I decided that they'd never get the chance to overpower me again." She smacked a fist into her palm.

"How's that going for you?"

She growled. "They haven't come after me head on. They know I'll send them back to Doc Martin. They changed out my shampoo for hair remover and locked me out of my own quarters."

I cocked my head inquisitively. Her hair look fine.

She grinned. "It didn't smell right. My stuff is Freyan cherry scented, kinda like blueberries and ordinary Terran cherries mixed together. My friend Lily sent it to me a week before we set sail. A going-away present. The message she sent with it was odd, though."

"How so?"

She shrugged, "Didn't sound like her. She's my best friend. Probably mad I'm leaving."

"Want me to step in with War 'n Pace?"

"Nah," she said with a wink. "I'll beat some sense into them."

"Okay, well then, it's your watch." I headed down the ladder.

That's when it happened. The lights went out. My last step sent me floating into the air, which meant the gravity wasn't functioning either. I had enough time to think, "what the scrut?" before it came back on and I fell to the floor.

"Nephie, what was that?" demanded Mimi.

No response. I tried to get to my feet, but slipped and fell. My knee hurt, but not bad. I rubbed it and stumbled to the tactical station. "Her power must have gone out along with everything else. It'll take her a couple of minutes to come back."

The screens were flickering to life. I stabbed a button to the left of the display. The ringing sound of general quarters filled the bridge.

Sara climbed up the ladder with Fenton close behind her. Our helmsman was rubbing his arm. Sara took my place at tactical and I sat in the captain's chair.

"All stations report." There was a tone from the speakers. The computer was up, but the AI was not yet functional. I typed the message and sent it to every console on the ship.

Trent and Jay responded right away. Everything was okay in marine berthing and the mess deck. Rowdy and Racy were slower to respond. When they did, their texts said pretty much the same thing. Systems were coming back online, there were no injuries, no one was sure what happened yet. I relayed that to the rest of the bridge.

Nephie's voice came from the overhead. "Bera na."

She was speaking in Muscat. "Good morning, Nephie. What happened?"

"A systems shutdown request was received."

What? That didn't make sense. "Received from whom?"

"That information is not available."

I didn't know much about programming, but that didn't seem right. "What was the purpose?"

"That information is not available." A short pause. "Incoming message from Captain Vinjar."

"*Queen Nephanie*, are you in need of assistance? Your shields flickered and went out."

The monitors showed the shields were back up. He sounded eager. Was he looking for an excuse to board us? He wanted Mr. Darkside, but with half the crew loyal to Ufkell, they wouldn't get him without a fight. A fight that would give Grova the excuse he needed to intervene.

"Negative, Vinjar. Just a power fluctuation. Everything is fine."

"That sounds serious," said Vinjar. "We'd be happy to lend you a few power technicians. I'll send them right over."

They definitely wanted to get aboard. "That won't be necessary. As stated before, it's under control."

◆ ◆ ◆

An hour later I met in the conference room under the bridge with Ufkell, Sara, Rowdy, and Racy.

"What happened?" I asked.

"We lost power for two seconds," Rowdy growled. "The cause appears to be a string of erroneous code sent to the AI. We don't know where it came from nor who sent it."

Racy continued, "I've traced every command given to Nephie in the hour prior to the shutdown. I couldn't find the string of code. Nephie was able to identify the command as the manual shutdown request."

"Unacceptable." Mr. Darkside glowered at Racy. "You programmed the damn thing. Didn't you put something in there to keep her from shutting everything off?"

I patted the table to indicate that Ufkell should be gentle with Racy. "I'm sure she's doing what she can to figure out what went wrong." I inclined my head in Racy's direction. "What theories are you working on?"

"A couple." Racy held up two fingers. "That it was either a programming glitch or sabotage."

"Is there any way we can prevent it from happening again?" asked Sara.

"In the short term, no."

Ufkell snorted with derision.

Racy continued. "I can rig a backup AI. We can't build a new computer core, but we can repurpose the Quick Box. Lights will stay on. Gravity will work. Doors will open and close. Air will circulate. No drives. No weapons."

"Why not those systems?" Darkside pounded the table. "Please tell me why the oh-so-mighty Muscat technology can't fire a weapon?"

Racy showed her teeth. "Because it takes a huge amount of processing power to aim a weapon, navigate through space, and run a fusion reactor. We're talking thousands of instructions per picosecond. My emergency backup is not a whole AI. It will be fully occupied by just keeping us alive."

Darkside leaned over her. "Hitting our enemies and moving keep us alive."

Racy tried to jump at him but Rowdy held her back.

"Ufkell," I said.

He glared at me. I held his gaze. He was testing me, seeing how far I'd go, searching for my pressure points. He'd found one: My family, including Racy, the little sister I never had. Fine. Point Darkside.

"We can't build a another computer core," I explained, "so this is what we can do with what we have."

"It isn't good enough." Darkside's words were clipped.

I shook my head at him. "How often do you have all the resources for a job?" I let the silence hang there for a moment. "You and I both know you don't. You work with what you have. You don't have a piece you need, you find another. No other piece, work around it. You run a trillion-credit business, but even you started somewhere, someplace small."

The staring contest continued a bit longer, until Ufkell smiled without mirth. "I'll say it again. We're either going to work great together, or I'm going to have to kill you." He stood up. "You don't need me here. I'll go along with whatever you all think is best."

He left then. I watched the door to make sure he was gone. "I'm never playing poker against that man."

"Good call," said Mimi. "Word has it, he cheats."

I winked at her. "Then we'll have to be better at cheating."

She gave a brittle laugh. "He has more experience."

"Racy, how intact is the Quick Box?"

She thought about it for a few seconds. "I used some of the innards in other projects. But it will give me a good start, save me a few hours of work. I meant it when I said it would be stupid. It won't be able to talk to anyone. It will keep us alive. That's it."

"Rowdy, can you make sure the systems are set? I don't want any lag if Nephie drops out again."

"Yeah," he acknowledged, "with Racy's help we can make it work."

"And out of personal curiosity, why don't more ships have plasma weapons? It's a popular infantry weapon. It seems like it would be great to knock out a whole ship's electrical system."

Rowdy shrugged. "Two problems with that. First, it works on most ground troops and equipment because they aren't hardened or shielded. Most ships are because they have to deal with all types of radiation found in space. The second is that superheating a small amount of matter is easy. Ionizing enough matter to take out a starship, not so much."

"Makes sense," I acknowledged. "How are Cindy and her family getting around it?"

"I don't know," said Rowdy. "At a guess, I'd say that they've found a material that when superheated, ignores shields and current hardening tech. They've also found some way to heat a lot of it quickly. Maybe a bunch of small ionization chambers, or a really efficient large chamber."

"Thanks. All right, get to it." Everyone left except Sara.

"Are you sure it's wise?" she asked.

"What?"

She jutted her chin toward the door. "Flirting with Mimi."

"Jealous?" I gave her a sideways grin.

She snorted. "Hardly."

I chewed on my lip. "I'm still trying to figure her out. There's something we're not seeing. I hope it doesn't bite us in the ass."

"Us? Or you?" It was more of an accusation than a question. "Make sure your investigation doesn't lead you into her bedroom."

I quirked an eyebrow at her.

"I don't know much about her, but I know this: Mimi is tough on the outside, but soft on the inside," Sara explained. "She's vulnerable, the kind of girl who could direct your attention the wrong way."

"I promise I'll be careful."

◆◆◆

It took Rowdy and Racy three days to set up the emergency AI. There were no other incidents while they were working on it. In fact, we were almost to the gate before anything else went wrong.

The gate itself was massive: two kilometers in diameter with a ring structure a hundred meters wide encircling an expanse of empty space. Inside the ring was equipment that bent space and time to allow two points in the galaxy to become one for a short period of time.

Mimi goggled. "It's huge."

"Thanks," I said.

She let out an exasperated sigh. "The gate, you sluggin' perv."

"You've never been through a gate?"

"No," she admitted. "We knew the Erethizon were coming, so no combat ships left the system. I've never even been on a ship assigned to guard it."

"Incoming comm request from Gate Control," intoned the AI.

"Attention, *Queen Nephanie*, this is Gate Control. You are entering our space. Please state your intentions."

"Gate Control, this is *Queen Nephanie*," I answered. "We intend to traverse the gate bound for Eureka."

"Roger, the fee is a hundred thousand credits. Please transfer funds now."

That was way too much. "Please clarify, Gate Control. Has the fee increased that much in the past year?"

"No. It's based on mass. Your AI has provided the mass figures for your freighter and battle cruiser *Horrong* has provided hers as well."

Those sneaky Porcu-bear bastards. "Gate Control, please be advised: battle cruiser *Horrong* is not coming with us. We would appreciate it if you didn't provide them with our destination."

"Sorry, *Nephanie*. They contacted us first and already knew your destination."

"Captain," said the AI, "there is a conversation on an open comm that you should be aware of."

"Put it through, Nephie."

"*Horrong*," said a voice, "back off." It was Vinjar.

"No battleship to protect you out here, Vinjar. We'll go wherever we please," said Grova.

"It's not just me, Grova. There are three Freyan cruisers nearby," said Vinjar.

"And an Erethizon cruiser and two destroyers. The ships you have out here do not have plasma weapons. The advantage is ours. If you fire on us, this will be over before your forces or mine can intervene. We've had days to analyze your ship's defenses. Stand down, Vinjar."

I sent a command to Nephie through my personal AI to mute our end of the conversation.

Her response was immediate. "Muted."

"Rowdy?"

"Yes, Captain."

"I want to make a run for the gate. You said our current gravity drive isn't great for sprinting, but can we do something to change that?"

Rowdy was silent for a few seconds. "Yes, but we'll burn out half the plates we're using to power the drive."

"Do it. Nephie, sound battle stations. Sara, keep our weapons offline."

From the engine room, my engineer's gruff voice came back. "Our acceleration will be like a Terran turtle after this."

"I'll take what I can get. Build the power up over the next thirty seconds." That would give me enough time to inform the gate. The slow buildup shouldn't raise any alarms on the *Horrong*.

In the holo-tank, the Freyan and Porcu-bear squadrons were moving toward the gate. Vinjar and Grova continued to trade threats. "Nephie, contact Gate Control on a separate line."

"Gate Control," came the response. It was evident they were on edge.

"This is the *Queen Nephanie*," I said. "We're going to charge through the gate."

"Are you nuts?"

"Quite possibly," I responded. "Are the coordinates set?"

"I advise against this, Captain. If a weapon is discharged into the event horizon, or if your compensators even flicker …" he shook his head, "your atoms will be spread across parsecs of open space."

"Understood, Gate Control. Please proceed."

"It's your molecules, *Nephanie*. Charging the gate."

They weren't scared for themselves. They knew that the Erethizon wouldn't target the gate itself. I called up the engine status. The reactors were almost at full power.

The comm chatter between Vinjar and Grova continued.

"I don't have to win, Grova. I just have to stop you."

"Try anything and I'll pound your little tin can into scrap, Vinjar."

Power levels reached maximum. "Full thrust, Mr. Fenton."

"Aye, aye, sir. Full thrust."

In the holo-tank, our icon jumped forward, eating up the distance between our ship and the gate.

"*Horrong*, has powered forward batteries," said Sara. "They're firing."

We felt a jolt as the *Horrong*'s gauss cannons made impact on our shields.

"They're aiming for our engines," said Sara.

"They'll need more than gauss cannons to get through our shields," I said.

The lights went out, then came back on in red. We were running on emergency power.

"No. Slugging. Way!" I exclaimed.

"Main AI is offline!" yelled Sara.

An explosion shook the ship. In the holo-tank, I saw a full broadside from the *Horrong* impact Vinjar's destroyer.

Half a second later, Rowdy's voice came over the speakers. "Main reactors damaged. Shields and compensators are offline."

The force of the impact sent us pinwheeling toward the gate. The stars looked distorted through the ring. It was charged, ready to send us to Eureka. Gravity compensators were offline. Inertial dampeners were online, but wouldn't do the job. If we hit the event horizon now, it was game over. "Rowdy, Racy, we're about to go through. We need the compensators or we're all dead."

No response. The open maw of the gate loomed closer.

In the holo-tank I could see the *Horrong* close in. They were trying to get into the gate with us.

Vinjar's destroyer had been blasted into two pieces, and I watched as they spun away from each other.

In the holo-tank, our icon merged with that of the gate. "Rowdy, Racy!"

In an instant I was thrown from my chair. In my half second in the air, I realized two things. First, that the inertial dampeners were offline. And second, that the last thing I'd see in my life was the holo-tank. It was going to break my neck on impact just before my atoms were spread across all creation.

Chapter 16

Across the Stars

"C𝚊ptain?"

What was that annoying voice? The one that kept repeating the same thing?

"Captain?"

Who was the captain? And why weren't they answering?

"Captain?"

Everything snapped into focus. "Mimi? What happened?"

"We're through."

I reached up and rubbed my neck. It was sore, but still attached to the rest of me. "Where are we?"

"The navigation array is down," she explained. "However, we're receiving a comm request from Eureka Gate Control. I guess we're somewhere near there."

"Thanks Mimi." I groaned. Everything hurt, but my head and right shoulder hurt more than the rest. I crawled across the bridge to my chair. Fenton was unconscious, but still breathing. Sara was stirring but not yet standing. I pulled up a holo-screen and poked the comm controls.

"*Queen Nephanie*, this is Eureka Gate Control, please respond. You are on a ballistic trajectory in a heavy traffic area. Please alter your course and speed immediately." The guy sounded bored, like he was annoyed that we hadn't answered him.

"Gate Control, this is *Queen Nephanie*, Captain Martin speaking. Please be advised we have sustained heavy damage. I'm not sure how long it will take to restore our systems."

"A firefight," he said without inflection. "Well, you didn't die. Please be advised, a large piece of the bow of another ship is trailing in your wake. That extra mass was not logged in Freya. We'll charge a penalty to your account."

"What?" The bow of another ship? It had to be the *Horrong*. How did it survive the trip?"

An odd sound came from the guy at Gate Control. It took me a minute to realize he was chewing. "Please be advised, *Queen Nephanie*, we tried to reach you for ten minutes. There will be a nuisance fee for that. We've cleared your vicinity and sent tugs, but you're tumbling end over end."

I called up the navigation controls, pairing Fenton's console to mine. "Thank you. Wait one, we'll try to comply."

I heard a yawn before he continued. "No thanks needed. We're charging a service fee for the tugs and a towing fee for move you into a parking orbit. Thank you for using Gilstrap Gate Systems," he sighed, "your premiere warp gate provider."

The only warp gate provider.

The AI interface was out. I checked the manual controls. They appeared to still be functioning. I tapped once and the thrusters responded. Then, using gentle pushes I brought our roll through space to a stop. Using bow and stern thrusters, I brought the pinwheeling to a halt. By then the tugs had caught up with us they were able to grapple the ship. They pushed and pulled us into a stable parking orbit relative to the gate.

Sara called from the tactical station. "All sections have reported in. Lots of injuries. Concussions and a few broken bones. No fatalities reported. Racy is unconscious and being treated by your sister."

"What happened?" I asked.

"Those slugging Porcu-bears are what happened," Mimi snarled. "They just couldn't leave well enough alone."

"Rowdy says that he and Racy rerouted power from everywhere to get the gravity compensators up," said Sara. "Inertial compensators and gravity deck plates had the most compatible power signatures, so most of it came from there. They couldn't turn them off completely without killing us, but they dialed them way down."

That explained why I went flying ass over teakettle. "Why didn't the backup AI take over when the main AI failed?"

"According to Rowdy, it did. It didn't have the processing ability to deal with everything. Several systems locked up, a few circuit boards were fried. It's keeping the lights on, but it isn't talking to anyone."

"And the main AI?"

"She keeps trying to reboot. She gets to a certain point and fails. She's trying to come back, but until Racy gets out of sickbay …"

"We're on our own," I finished for her.

Mimi had pulled Fenton out of his chair and laid him on the floor.

"How is he?"

"Nothing broken," said Mimi. "Doc says she's busy and we have to wait."

That didn't sound like my sister. "That's what she said?"

"No, that's the translation. What she said was, 'If he isn't bleeding he can wait at the end of the line with the rest of the crybabies.'"

"Uh." Fenton was starting to stir. He reached out shakily with one hand.

"Before you touch me there, imagine how hard it will be to steer the ship with an artificial hand," said Mimi.

The hand in question changed directions. He put it on his head instead of her butt. "What hit me?"

"Your console," said Mimi. "Sneaky bastard sucker punched you. Be gentler with him next time. A boy needs a little foreplay before you grab him by the jewels."

"Wha?"

"Fenton," I cut in, "are you okay, or do you need to go to medical?"

He shook his head. "Right as rain. I'll make it, sir."

"Good man. We're in a parking orbit. Can you make sure we stay there? I have to check on medical and engineering."

"Aye, aye, sir," he said weakly. "Stay at anchor until you get back."

◆◆◆

There were people lined up outside sickbay. Inside, every square meter of floor space was occupied by wounded people. Sophie and our medics, Jay and Trey, were each attending to a patient. Racy was sharing a bed with Trent. They appeared to be the only injured among the Muscat crew members. At least they weren't on the floor.

Trent tried to stand to salute as I approached.

I waved him down. "At ease. What happened to you?"

"I hit a wall. Then two Terrans landed on top of me."

I winced. "Ouch."

He shrugged. "Heavy G home world. I'm tougher than I look. Doc says the busted ribs will be good as new in a couple of days."

"What about you, Racy?"

She gave me a silly grin. "Pink is such a good color on you."

"What?"

She leaned forward and stretched her pointed nose toward me. "How'd you get all bendy? I want to be bendy, too." Racy held her hand up and wiggled her fingers around. "Eight fingers. Why'd Sophie give me extra fingers? Oh! I bet I can type faster." Her eyes didn't track her fingers.

I let out a sigh. "My sister drugged her."

"Oh yeah," Trent said, "Doc said she'd bruised something in her neck and back. She said this would keep her from moving too fast and making it worse."

I pulled my hair and searched the room for my sister. "Soph?"

Across the room she glanced up from a marine I didn't know. "Get out of my sickbay. You're taking up space I need."

"Can't," I replied. "You're holding my systems tech hostage. I need her to fix the computer core."

"Damn. That's why the databases aren't responding? That's why the scanners give me images but no analysis?"

"'Fraid so."

Sophie blew a lock of hair out of her face. She crossed the room, adjusting an injector and slapping something into it. "Fine, but put her in a grav-chair."

I gave the room a once-over. "You have one in here?"

"No. You'll have to replicate one."

I shrugged. "No can do. The pattern is in the computer."

My sister glared at me and injected Racy's arm. "Carry her. The nanites will take about ten minutes to break down the drug."

I picked Racy up and slung her across my back, piggy-back-style.

"Wheeee! Spin me some more, Mark," she yelled in my ear.

"Thanks Soph. Thanks Trent."

Trent nodded.

My sister looked like she'd bitten into something sour. "Don't thank me. If she comes back any worse, I'll take it out of your hide."

◆ ◆ ◆

On the way back toward the bridge, Racy sobered up.

"Ow. I hurt everywhere," she said. "Can I get more of whatever Sophie gave me?"

"You get Nephie talking to us again and you can take the rest of the day off to get as stoned as you like."

"What does 'stoned' mean?" she asked.

"It means to be so out of it, you can't move."

"Sounds fun."

I opened the door to the computer room and set her down.

She wobbled a bit before steadying herself. Racy caressed the casing. "Hello beautiful. Let's see what ails you."

Again she bypassed the keyboard and pulled up a holo-graphic interface.

"Why have a keyboard if you never use it?" I asked.

"Camouflage. Anyone trying to use that is in for a nasty surprise. Seriously, who uses a physical interface anymore?"

I thought about it. Pretty much everyone used touch screens or holographic keyboards these days.

She frowned. "Oh. That's not good."

"What?"

"Someone has been messing with Nephie's code."

There couldn't be anyone else on board with Racy's level of expertise. Could there? I'd vetted everyone. Was someone on the ship not who they claimed to be?

"How do we fix it?"

"I can restore the code, but she'll forget a few things in the process. Then we hide her behind 268 million-bit encryption. She'll learn to protect herself better. I can change a few things around, make it harder to get into her next time." Racy shrugged. "Not impervious. Best I can do."

"How long until we get Nephie back?"

"Um." Racy counted on her fingers. "Fifteen minutes to reload the root. Another five for her to come back." Racy rolled her nose. "After that, three days to put the protections in place. Then we watch. Make sure no one messes with her." She patted the casing again. "Don't worry. I'll protect you."

◆◆◆

I made my way to engineering. Rowdy hung upside down from a pair of grav boots while he directed a repair drone to weld a plate to the ceiling. "Rowdy, what's broke and how long do you need to fix it?"

He looked up at me. Down at me? "It would be a lot faster if Nephie would talk to us," he growled.

I checked the time on my AI. "You should have your wish in about ten minutes."

"You got Racy out of the infirmary."

"I did."

He nodded. "Okay, when Nephie gets back, I'll have more repair drones to help." He pointed to his feet. "We've got some hull punctures that are sealed with foam at the moment, a couple of thruster assemblies, a dozen other odds and ends. Call it a day to get us moving, another day to complete repairs."

That was good. "Okay, what can I get you to help?"

He put some tools in his harness and pulled his ears. "Are there any combat engineers among the marines onboard?"

I pulled up the crew roster with my personal AI and filtered the list for combat engineers. "Two."

He grunted. "Get them down here to help me. Not the same as a proper tech, but they should be able to follow directions."

"All right. Anything else?"

He shook his head.

Sara's voice came from the intercom on the wall. "Rowdy?"

"I'm here, Sara."

"Have you seen the captain? I need him to come to the bridge. The backup computer seems to have forgotten who he is."

I snorted. "I'm here Sara. I was discussing repairs with Rowdy."

"The *George Washington* is hailing us," she said.

That ship sounded familiar. "Isn't that the Terran battleship that was hanging out in this system last time we came through?"

"That's the one."

I trotted through the passageways on my way to the bridge. I couldn't for the life of me remember who the captain of the *George Washington* was. I remembered that Captain Houston had known him. I searched through my personal AI for the information, but it wasn't there either. As I was passing the mess deck a calm, feminine voice sounded from everywhere at once. "Bera na."

As expected, everyone talked to her at once. I waited until I was back on the bridge.

"Good morning, Nephie. Are you connected with the comms system yet?" I climbed into the captain's chair. Mimi was at the helm. Sara was still at tactical. Fenton was nowhere to be seen.

"Yes, Captain," said Nephie. "We are receiving a hail from the *George Washington*."

I mouthed, "where's Fenton?" at Mimi. She responded just as silently, "in medical."

I rubbed the coin in my pocket, then put my hands on my thighs. I didn't want to seem fidgety. "Put them through, Nephie."

His image appeared on the forward screen. "This is Captain Rod McCormick of the Terran battleship *George Washington*. To whom am I speaking?"

"Captain Mark Martin, of the freighter *Queen Nephanie*. What can I do for you, Captain?"

I saw his jaw muscles clench. "You can start by telling me why there's a piece of ship floating out here."

I sucked in a breath. "Well, it wasn't my idea. The Freyans had negotiated a cease-fire with the Erethizon. Gate travel for both sides was part of the deal. We'd been stuck on the planet for months, and were ready to leave. We picked up a cargo and humped it out here as fast as we could. The deal was pretty shaky from the start and both the Freyans and the Porcu-bears escorted us to the gate."

He quirked an eyebrow at me. "Why so much interest in your ship?"

"No idea," I lied. "It all seemed fine, if a bit tense. When we got to the gate, the Erethizon cruiser fired on us. We'd already negotiated with the gate. It was active, so we made a run for it. The Porcu-bears tried to follow us through."

His eyes bulged. "Are you nuts? Do you have any idea what could have happened to you if even one shot went into the gate?"

"Yes, sir." I grimaced. "Did they catch the piece of ship?"

"Yes. There's nothing recognizable as a living being in there. The survey crew says they'll have nightmares about what they saw for months." McCormick looked at a display on his right. "What are you carrying?"

I remembered that Rowdy had done something to make the scans look fuzzy. "Water. Eureka doesn't have much. Seemed like a good cargo."

The captain grunted. "True enough. Must be why we're having trouble scanning it. Mind if we come over and have a gander?"

It would be very bad for us if he found out our holds were filled with Violet Monkeys. I reached for my coin, and stopped myself. A battleship captain has better things to do than check cargo haulers. He had to be bluffing. I put on my best poker face. "Sure, knock yourself out."

Just then, a tornado of fury erupted from the ladder to the bridge. Behind me, Darkside's tirade began. "Captain, this is unacceptable. I insist …"

Captain McCormick's eyes went wide. "Ufkell?" He focused a menacing glare on me. "I'll be right over."

Chapter 17

Eureka

I spun my chair around and glared at Ufkell.

"What?" His tone made it a challenge. "So he's coming over. The Confederacy has nothing on me."

I spoke through gritted teeth. "Except that we were trying to keep a low profile and I told him we were carrying water."

"Violet Monkeys aren't illegal." He sneered.

"No," I said with exaggerated patience. "They're not. But everyone in the galaxy knows that they can be turned into Violet Dream."

"That's not the only thing. You can make plenty of prescription drugs from it."

"Prescription. Drugs." I spoke each word clearly. "Eureka is a mining and manufacturing colony. There isn't a damn pharmaceutical manufacturer in the whole system. Why? Because the surface of the only inhabited planet is a radioactive hellhole. All food comes from hydroponic gardens. And it ain't much."

Darkside moved is hand around in front of himself like he was writing in the air. "Their problem, plus their problem, equals, their problem. We are not responsible for what happens to the cargo after we sell it."

"This guarantees that every time we come through this system they are going to take a closer look at what we're carrying."

"Spoof the transponder." His tone told me I was an idiot. "I thought you were a proper smuggler."

It was like talking to an asteroid. He just couldn't see the mess he'd caused. It made me want to scream. I steadied myself. "How did he know who you were?"

"McCormick?" He waved it off. "I've made a few deals with the Terrans over the years. He's sore because his superiors blamed him for a bad batch of drones and defective missiles. I told him they were factory seconds. Not my fault. That's why he got assigned out here at the ass end of nowhere."

The situation was going from bad to worse. In my mind, I could see McCormick stopping us for days every time we came though the system. Even if we pulled the transponder trick, he'd know who we were as soon as we answered his hail. Confederacy regulations gave no time limit for inspections. I'd heard more than one merchant captain grumble about being held up for a lengthy Confed inspection. However long it took, that's how long it took.

I needed Sara and Trent. They said they would come up with a plan to get rid of Ufkell. If they didn't have something, I was going to strangle the self-righteous bastard with my bare hands.

I balled my fists and then relaxed them. "What was so important, that you barged onto the bridge in the middle of a comm call?"

"Oh, yeah. You need to get that tree rat of yours to fix the AI. First she wouldn't talk to me at all, and then when

Nephie would talk to me, she wouldn't let me talk to you." He shook his head. "Unacceptable."

I imagined giving Darkside a right cross followed by an uppercut. The stupid look he gave me while I beat the imaginary tar out of him made me feel better.

"Yes," I said. "I'll ask her to get right on that."

◆◆◆

I stood in the boat bay as McCormick's shuttle made its final approach. His ship eased through the pressure barrier that separated the hangar from open space.

"You didn't have to be here for this," I told Sara.

"Yes, I did," said Sara. "I've dealt with Rod before. He doesn't like me either, but he respects me. A little of that might rub off on you."

I held her hand. "Thanks. How's Mimi doing?"

"She says that most of what the marines have for personal goods is okay, but she did find a few things illegal in Confed space—drugs, weapons, interspecies sex tapes. Not much. She says she'll have it squirreled away before the inspection team reaches the berths."

The shuttle settled to the deck and the boarding ramp extended. Two marines jogged down the ramp. They gave us the once-over and then nodded to someone inside the runabout.

McCormick strode down to the deck like he owned *Queen Nephanie*, two more marines on his heels. An inspection team of four trailed along behind them.

He spotted Sara with a start. "Sara Chew? I never thought in a million years you'd leave Jenna's side."

Sara's face became a mask of stone. "I didn't," she responded simply. Her eyes were shiny.

"Captain Houston died on Freya," I said. "Porcu-bear sabotage."

"Captain Martin." His gaze drifted up and down the length of me. "Did you know her well?"

"I joined her crew in Yale. The navigator was injured. I had the honor of sailing with her for a few months."

At the mention of her former fiancé, Sara's face went from sandstone to granite.

"Hazards of the job." McCormick grimaced. "I told her this work would get her killed. Let's move with a purpose. Cargo holds first."

"Right this way." I motioned for him and his entourage to follow us. They fell in line. "I want to apologize for being evasive about our cargo."

"Evasive?" He looked at me inquisitively.

"We're not carrying water," I admitted.

"What are you carrying?"

"Violet Monkeys," I said. "The dried flowers, not the finished product. We're only here in Eureka for repairs. Our final destination is Gra'feld. They have a few pharmaceutical manufacturers there."

"And you didn't want to tell me that because I'd be suspicious."

I opened the hatch that overlooked cargo bay one. "Yes, there is that."

McCormick followed me in and then motioned for his inspectors to get a closer look. "Guess what? I'm suspicious."

I sighed dramatically.

"What's Ufkell doing on your ship?"

I'd been dreading this question. I'd decided to play this one as close to the truth as possible. "Business partner. We were stuck on Freya with no ship. The Freyan military was buying up every one. Ufkell got us a ship. A deal with the devil to be sure, but we didn't have much choice."

His team finished inspecting a container and started climbing back up the ladder.

"You always have a choice," McCormick said flatly.

Not if I want to find my dad, I thought.

We exited cargo bay one and crossed the passage to cargo bay two. His inspectors repeated the process.

"Sara, why are you with Captain Martin?"

The boldness of his question took me aback. He was trying to rattle me. A certain part of me wondered what Sara's answer would be.

"I respect him," was all she said.

The Terran captain's eyebrows bounced off the overhead. He surveyed me as if I were a side of beef.

His inspectors trotted back up the ladder and we moved up the passage to cargo bay four.

McCormick jerked a thumb across the passage. "How come you skipped over cargo bay three?"

"Because that's not a cargo bay," I said, "it's marine berthing. You said you wanted to tour the cargo bays first."

McCormick twigged. "You turned an entire cargo hold into marine berthing?"

"Half of it. The other half is an industrial parts printer."

The captain stopped and studied me for a couple of moments. "Okay, I give. What do you need with that many marines?"

"We have a letter of marque from the Freyan navy," I said matter-of-factly. Two could play the rattle-the-captain game.

I could see the gears turning in his mind. When he spoke, he was deadly serious. "Captain Martin, I respect your chutzpah. That said, I think you're a nutjob.

I mulled it over. "I'm not sure you're wrong."

"Fair enough. I'll give you this advice for free: I'd better never see a prize brought into this system."

I gave him a sly grin. "Cold feet?"

"Hardly. We all answer to someone, and I answer to the Confederate Senate. They've made it very clear. Don't provoke an incident. I may not agree with that, but I have my orders."

I remembered the last time we came through the system. "I seem to recall that you stared down a Porcu-bear cruiser not long ago. That would seem to be at odds with your statement."

McCormick licked his lips. "There's a big difference between stopping some asshole from harassing a merchie and providing safe harbor to a pirate."

"Privateer."

"Semantics. I don't mind if you resupply, repair, or even recruit a few miners. I can look the other way and deny I knew a damn thing. What I can't do is turn a blind eye when some idiot with a death wish shows up on my doorstep with a captured freighter. I can tell by your accent that you're from Yale. Real sad what's happening back home. I also know that one of the biggest mining ops on Eureka is Songbird M&M. It doesn't take a genius to figure out that a Yale mine and a Yale captain in the same system might be working together. Don't do anything where I can see it."

That was disappointing, but not unexpected. "I under-stand. Don't complicate your life."

McCormick zeroed in on me. "I'm serious, Martin. Don't cross me."

"Wouldn't dream of it."

◆◆◆

"Unfortunate."

"What?" I asked Sara. "The fact that we can't use Eureka as a salvage yard or that he didn't find anything to arrest us for?"

"The safe harbor where we drink our rum and spend our ill-gotten treasure," she deadpanned.

I laughed. Sara cracked so few jokes it would be a crime not to. We were in the conference room under the bridge. Mimi was on her way to join us.

"He's a Terran officer. Not as corruptible as a Terran politician, but movable if we can find the right leverage." I rubbed my fingers together.

Mimi entered the conference room and shut the door.

"Okay," said Sara, "the standard pressure points are money, sex, and violence. He's a warship captain, so threatening him physical harm won't work."

"Sex might work," offered Mimi. "It didn't take much, just a couple of winks and a shy smile while touring the marine berths. He was stumbling over words and blushing like a Freyan plum."

"I'm trying to imagine you doing anything shyly." I shook my head. "It's not working."

Mimi put her chin down, opened her blue eyes wide, and looked up at me while biting her thumb. I had to admit, it was a credible act.

"Okay, you win."

She grinned. "Hey, some guys are into that." She ran her tongue along her teeth. "No one I'd be interested in."

"It doesn't matter. I'd never ask you to sleep with McCormick." I turned to Sara. "What was his relationship with Jenna like?"

"Captain Houston said he was a good guy who believed in the system."

"Ouch." Coming from Jenna, that was quite an insult.

Sara sighed. "They served together somewhere along the way, back when Houston was a midshipman or a lieutenant." She shrugged. "I'm sorry. I know that doesn't give us anything to go on."

"We'll keep our eyes open. Maybe something will present itself."

I went over our conversation in my head. "Let's go with that. I get the feeling that if we act like any other freighter, he might be more forgiving. Working with Darkside is a liability. If we can distance ourselves from him, we might be okay. Any ideas on that?"

Sara wasn't going to mention any of our plans in front of Mimi. For her part, Mimi didn't offer any.

"Well," I continued, "we've got a few days heading in to Eureka. Maybe we'll think of something."

◆ ◆ ◆

Rowdy was true to his word and we were moving a day later. Racy was on bed rest, but she was okay with it. She could do most of what she wanted to do from her quarters. It also gave her more time to spend with Riff and Raff. The kittens had gotten a lot bigger and everyone on the crew was enamored with them.

The rest of the crew took a bit longer to recover. My sister stayed up for three days straight putting them back together. From cuts to bruises and broken bones, she never stopped. The crew learned what I had always known: Sophie's bedside manner was nonexistent. They loved her anyway.

"How's your head, Fenton?"

We were on the bridge. It was almost time to change watches. I had spent the entire eight hours putting a list together for Ike of the things we were going to need when we landed. I'd told him about our cargo. To say that he was upset was an understatement.

"Good to go, Captain," he responded.

He seemed like a good kid. I wondered what his role was in Ufkell's master plan. If I had to guess, it was information: what we were doing, where we were going, catching the odd misspoken word.

For that matter, what was Mimi's role in everything? It still bothered me how easily Brightside had let her join the crew. Racy had pulled up more information about her before we left Freya, but I hadn't had a chance to review it. Brady had nothing on her, either.

I glanced over my shoulder just in time to see her climb the ladder to the bridge. She had a black eye and a busted lip. "Trouble, Mimi?"

Her face lit up. "No. Extra exercise in the gym."

"What kind of exercise leads to a shiner?"

"The kind that starts and ends with a lesson in hand-to-hand combat." She licked her busted lip. "War 'n Pace needed a reminder that they aren't the only ones who can set up an ambush."

"Win, lose, or draw?"

Mimi wrinkled her nose. "Eh, I'd have to call it a draw."

"In that case, the ship is yours. Carry on." I waved as I exited the bridge.

"Aye, aye. I have the bridge," she said jauntily.

I didn't go far. At the bottom of the ladder I entered the conference room. Sara and Trent were waiting for me.

"Nephie, privacy mode," I ordered.

"The conference room is now secure, Captain."

"He has to be gone. We can't free my father and save Yale with him here. So how do we make it happen?"

"Navigation stations," said Sara. "Everyone will be sitting in place."

Trent continued. "We gas everyone in marine berthing. Nitrous oxide. Knock 'em all out. Get a few of our people to ride in crew berthing. That will leave Ufkell, his two bodyguards, Cleave, Fenton, and the other two helmsmen. We don't know if Mimi is one of them or not. To play it safe, we grab her, too."

It wouldn't take much to rig the ventilation. "That's a pretty good plan. We knock out sixteen marines. Capture the eight people who won't be in marine berthing. I'm guessing we use plasma rifles for that." I mimed three shots. "Then what? We can't keep them onboard."

"Were it me?" Trent gave a feral growl. "I'd space Ufkell. Cut off the head of the frequa. Then yeah, drop them off on-planet."

I took a deep breath. "I don't think the miners or the Terrans would appreciate us dumping our problem on them. This would be a big one."

Sara shrugged. "Indenture them to one of the other mines."

My stomach churned. "Ufkell would still be a problem and slave labor, by any other name, is still slave labor. And without knowing why each of them joined the Sudhurland Keiretsu …" I shook my head. "We need a better option."

Trent soured. Sara frowned like she was disappointed in me.

"I know. You both think I'm being too soft. To be fair, I don't give a rat's ass about Ufkell. If even half the stories are true, spacing him would be doing the galaxy a favor." I pursed my lips. "It's the ones like Brady that I'm worried about. The good ones that are doing this because they have no choice."

Sara gave me a half smile. "We don't have the resources to interview and vet each of them. This far from Freya, we'll have to rely on whatever records we were able to retrieve before we left. It won't be enough."

That thought reminded me that I still had to dig through Mimi's file. "If we need a few extra days in port to conduct a few interviews, so be it. It'll make me feel better about consigning some of them to the mines. They can work off their passage back to Freya."

Trent pulled on his pointed ears. "Watching their friends sent to the mines will leave some of them bitter and prone to cause trouble. We won't catch all the spies. We'll end up with someone on the crew willing and able to cause mayhem. Someone like Aasha."

Aasha. The woman who had blown up the *Leo*. She'd killed Jenna, Boldrini, Wally, and so many more of our friends.

"I'm sorry. Unless you give me a better option, that's what we're doing. We'll take the ship to Eureka and spend five to ten days weeding and replacing."

Sara ran her fingers through her hair. "Fine. We'll have to do it on the way out. We could synthesize NO2 from the gasses we have on board, but it will be easier on Eureka. The miners use it in some of their equipment."

I thought about everyone's motivations. Did anyone else on the crew have divided loyalties? "There's one other concern."

"What?" they asked in unison.

"Nephie. She's programmed to protect the crew. What is she going to think if we attack some of them?"

Sara started to speak, then stopped.

For a moment no one spoke as we all pondered the problem.

Trent huffed. "We need to involve Racy."

◆ ◆ ◆

"No," said Racy. "I can't patch it so that she ignores her most basic programming. You'll have to turn her off."

I drummed my fingers on the conference room table. "So we'll have to do by design what we've been trying to stop from happening."

"You were the one that insisted she have an off switch," Racy pointed out. "Have you changed your mind about that?"

I rubbed my eyes. "No. I just don't like the idea of turning off the AI while we're taking off or landing." I let out a breath. "We have the code, we can do it. I just want another option."

Racy rolled her nose at me. "Ask her."

"And have her prepare to turn against us? No."

"Duh." Racy stuck her tongue out at me. "We ask her to forget the conversation."

I looked at her skeptically.

"Trust me." She pointed her nose at the ceiling. "Nephie, privacy mode off."

"Privacy disengaged."

"Nephie," said Racy, "hypothetically speaking, what would your reaction be if the captain had to subdue half the crew?"

"That would depend on the circumstances. Can you be more specific?" Her disembodied voice sounded curious.

"Say we received word that there was going to be a mutiny. The mutineers were confined to marine berthing. If we use gas to knock them out, what would be your response?" Racy regarded the overhead.

"I would allow it, provided the captain authorized its use," responded Nephie.

Trent breathed a sigh of relief, but I held up a hand. I wasn't happy that Racy had blurted out our plans to the AI, but it was too late now. "Nephie, what if Ufkell were in the room?"

"Then I would be forced to intervene."

Sara's jaw dropped. "What? Why?"

"The Sudhurland Keiretsu is listed as the registered owner of this vessel, Ms. Chew. As the senior crew member onboard, he is the only person who outranks the captain."

"What if something happened to him?" asked Trent.

"I'm not sure. If Mr. Ufkell were to be incapacitated or killed, it would fall to the next most senior person in the keiretsu. Technically, that would be Admiral Olafurson, but he isn't physically here. After Admiral Olafurson, the next most senior person would be Captain Martin."

"Me?" I didn't know how I fit into that. I never considered myself a part of the keiretsu hierarchy.

Nephie explained, "My understanding is that each business unit is run by a lieutenant. Since the ship is considered its own business unit, and the captain is in charge of the ship, he is the next person in the line of succession."

"Thank you, Nephie," said Racy. "Please forget this conversation."

"Of course."

"Nephie what is the last thing you remember being spoken in this room?" Racy asked.

"You requested that privacy mode be disengaged."

"Thank you, Nephie. Please reinstate privacy mode." Racy rolled her nose at me.

"The room is secure."

Trent growled. "So, we find some way to knock out Darkside before the attack, or he never gets back onboard."

Racy shook her head. "No, even if he's in comm range, he could still muck things up."

Trent just stared at Racy.

"Oh."

◆◆◆

"Cleave, you in here?" I'd entered the galley from the mess deck.

"Back here, sir." His voice was followed by a loud thunk.

I followed the noise until I found Cleave. He was using a meat cleaver and a saw to cut up a carcass.

His artificial eye looked me up and down. "Mind the spray," he said as he started up the saw.

He separated the ribs from the beast, his apron becoming more splattered with blood in the process.

It didn't take long, and he set the saw down. "What can I help you with?"

"Dinner?" I asked, pointing to a stack of cut ribs.

"Yes, sir. Barbecued snow lizard ribs. Cooked right, you'll never be able to tell they're not real pork."

"I've never had real pig before," I admitted. "You can't find them often out here. We're pretty far from the core worlds of the Terran Confederation."

"I've had it before. Sweeter than the best near-cow rib eye you ever had." His mouth split into a grin from ear to ear.

"I wanted to ask you about adding more vegetables to our meals."

His good eye widened in surprise. "More garnish and rabbit food? I thought this was a ship full of real men and feral dogs."

"We've got that and then some, but we've got a lot of frozen veggies. I want to make sure everyone is healthy enough to kick Porcu-bear tail."

"Oh, they will. Trust me, Cap. Meat in the belly will become meat on the bones." He scratched his two-day-old beard.

I gave him a lopsided grin and waited.

After an awkward pause, Cleave threw his hands up. "Fine. I'll put out more broliform and carrots." He shook his finger at me. "But mark my words: there won't be many takers. These boys know what's good for them: Ole Cleave's meat and potatoes."

"That's fine as long as they have the choice." I waved at him as I exited the galley.

Outside the mess deck I found Sara headed in the opposite direction. I looked both ways down the hall to make sure we were alone.

"Hey, Sara. I just wanted to say thanks."

"Thanks? For what?" She blinked her almond-shaped eyes.

I spread my arms to indicate the ship. "For all of this. I'm the guy with the vision, but you're the one that makes it all happen. You keep everything organized and solve all the day to day problems. You do a great job, and I don't tell you often enough how much I appreciate it."

She gave me a ghost of a smile. "You're welcome."

Just then, the power went out. Sara grabbed me as we floated upward. It wasn't long, maybe five heartbeats. Then the lights came back on. We landed with a light "thump."

Sara in my arms. She gazed up at me. I didn't want to breathe. Neither of us moved. Her hair smelled of jasmine. Her eyes were the color of sandalwood. What was this? How did I feel about Sara? My heart pounded in my chest. Grabbing me was an accident, right? Why did it just feel right with her next to me?

She swallowed. Her eyes never left mine.

I felt like I should say something, but nothing came to mind.

Racy came up the ladder at the end of the passage. We separated. I immediately missed her touch. Sara's lower lip trembled.

Racy ran toward us. "I know, I know. Nephie went down again. She shouldn't be doing this. I'm heading up to the computer core right now." She glanced back and forth between us. "What?"

"Yes, Racy," I said, "please see what you can do about that."

Racy did another back and forth. "Okay. I'll get on it." She continued up the passage.

Sara's eyes were wide. Her fingers went to her mouth. The silence grew strained before Sara spoke. "I, uh ..." She didn't finish, but turned on her heel and ran toward engineering.

◆◆◆

After that Sara avoided me. We only saw each other on watch, and when we did, she wouldn't talk to me. We were getting close to Eureka.

Captain? Nephie sent a text message to my internal AI.

Yes, Nephie?

Ms. Chew's behavior toward you seems ... odd. Did you do something to offend her?

That was interesting. AIs didn't usually ask about how someone felt. *I don't think so, Nephie. Have you asked her about it?*

I did. She didn't answer me.

Which meant Sara either didn't want to talk about her feelings to an AI—which was likely, given her beliefs—or ... something else. If Nephie was trying to understand human behavior, I needed to put it in perspective. *She may not know, Nephie.*

I don't understand.

I'm not sure I understood either. Was it just loneliness? Why hadn't I noticed this amazing woman in my life? That brief touch had been magic, but maybe it was one-sided. Had Sara felt it too?

I wracked my brain for a few minutes before I responded. *It's like this, Nephie. You are a Quantum computer. A lot of your decisions will be yes, no, or maybe. Humans have something similar. They have emotional states: joy, trust, fear, and more complex emotions like love, hate, and hope. Without going into too much detail, let's say that there are thirty-two emotions.*

That sounds confusing, texted Nephie.

It is, I sent back. *When you think of something or some-one, each one of these emotions could be yes, no, or maybe. Usually, the yeses and nos aren't a problem. Sometimes there is a maybe that has to be resolved. Humans then have to spend time trying to do that.*

She was silent for a few seconds. *So, Ms. Chew has undefined feelings about you.*

Did she? *I don't know, Nephie.* I wasn't sure about the concept of a computer studying philosophy. It might be good or bad. I took a leap of faith. *Check the ship's library under "friendship, love, and relationships." I'm sure there's something useful there.*

It was useful, she texted. *Plato wrote quite a bit on the subject.*

Quantum computer. Of course she read everything in seconds.

"Captain," said Nephie out loud, "we're being hailed by Eureka traffic control."

"Thanks, Nephie. Put them through."

"Welcome to Eureka, *Queen Nephanie.*" The male voice sounded bored. "Please state the nature of your visit."

"Eureka Control, this is the *Queen Nephanie.* Our mission is trade, repair, and resupply. We should have a slip reserved at Songbird Mining and Manufacturing."

"Understood, *Queen Nephanie.* Please transmit your manifest, engine specs, and lading. Be advised that a customs team will be waiting for you upon docking."

I'd thought about continuing our ruse that we were carrying water. That went out the airlock with Commodore McCormick. He would tell Eureka about our cargo. I transmitted what was really in our holds. Ike already knew, of course.

"Packet received, *Queen Nephanie*. Stand by while we compute your required course." There was a tapping sound. "Sending telemetry now. Please be advised that course and speed numbers are mandatory. Any deviation will result in your company being banned from Confederation ports. Also, it's a windy day down here. Ionizing radiation is topping out at over twenty thousand. Please keep your shields up until the hangar door is secure."

Ouch. That was one hell of a radiation storm. "Copy, Eureka Control. Ride the beam. SIR over twenty thousand, so keep the windows closed. Out."

"Course locked in, Captain." Fenton checked the monitors. "The autopilot has the conn. Course and speed within acceptable limits."

"Thanks, Fenton. Keep an eye on it, if you please."

"Aye, aye."

The forward view screen showed the red surface of Eureka. It resembled Faust's lowest level of Hell. I knew that it was the iron-rich ores that gave it that rosy glow. Eureka was three light minutes from a white G-type star. The system primary was very active with an unusually large number of solar flares. Combined with a weak magnetic field and a mineral-heavy atmosphere, the planet wasn't a popular tourist destination. Not a problem for a modern star freighter, but an unprotected person on the surface would be cooked in seconds.

No structures could be seen. The locals had taken a practical approach to living here. Everything was underground. A few meters of solid rock made an effective radiation shield.

I'd let Ike know our rough schedule. Now that we had an exact time, he needed an update. "Nephie, please let Ike Fullerton know our arrival time and request a meeting."

"Notification sent, Captain."

Two hours later, we were slowly approaching a cliff face. A blast door opened up in the rock wall and Fenton eased us into the gaping maw.

We settled to the ground. After a few seconds we heard a loud bang. My screens showed the outside radiation levels dying off. It took a bit longer for the air laden with sodium, calcium, and magnesium to cool off and be replaced with a mix of nitrogen and oxygen we could breathe.

On the monitor, the inspection team approached and I hustled to the airlock to meet them. Sara followed. There were three of them. They did little more than check the manifest and take a few notes, and while they looked in the cargo holds, they didn't open any crates. If they had any concern over what was in the boxes, it wasn't evident to me. I filed that away for the future. I could have holds filled with contraband and they would never know it as long as I labeled the containers as something legal.

They were in and out in under half an hour. As they left the ship, I checked my inbox. "Sara, if you would, set the watch and declare liberty. I've got a meeting with Songbird in fifteen minutes."

"Of course, Captain."

That was a bit too formal. I regarded her face, but she gave nothing away. I logged myself off the ship.

Stepping into the cavernous hangar was a humbling experience. The stone ceiling soared high above. The space could hold three freighters the size of the Nephie. The air had a salty quality, as if we were standing next to an ocean with a touch of ammonia in it.

"You weren't going to leave me behind, were you?"

Trent and Tracy approached me wearing combat armor. To be fair, I'd totally forgotten that I needed bodyguards. On the military base it hadn't been necessary. Now that we were among the public, that would change. "Um, no."

Trent snorted. "Sara told us you were planning to leave the ship. Give us a little warning next time."

I used my AI to thank Sara via text. "Of course. My apologies." Connecting to the local network, my AI gave us a path to the SM&M corporate offices. I sent the instructions to Trent and Tracy.

We passed through an airlock and into the cargo gallery. Projections on the walls advertised bars and brothels. The walls weren't smooth, so the images were lumpy.

"What's with all the dust?" asked Tracy.

"It's a mine," I observed. "Ore sleds pass through here all the time on the way to cargo haulers."

"Uncovered?"

I shrugged. The center of the passage was clear, but the black dust was piling up against the walls.

"Where is everyone?"

There were a few people around, but not many. "At a guess?" I pointed down. The green line in my HUD led to a heavy door. The rusted and scarred metal had seen better days. A dent in the middle of the door was so big, I was left wondering what had made it, and if the door would fully retract when the lift arrived. I pressed the call button. "From what Ike told me, this was the first level of the mine. Once they cleared it out, it became the loading docks. The next level down is commercial space. Below that, living space."

The lift arrived and the heavy steel door retracted into the ceiling and floor. We entered a scuffed metal cage. There was enough room inside it for the three of us. Barely. We descended one level, and a newer pressure door opened.

There were more people on this level. The floors were gritty. Most of the people wore dirty coveralls and coats. LED displays and holo-signs advertised more bars, brothels, and other entertainment. The singing bluebird of Songbird Mining and Manufacturing was above the double door across from the lift.

We crossed the passage, earning more than a few curious glances. I wasn't sure if it was because we were clean, or due to my Muscat bodyguards. There wasn't a non-Terran in sight.

Through the doors the space was a bit cleaner. I saw a vacuum bot humming quietly along the floor. I recognized the receptionist from the last time I'd been through the system. I couldn't place her name.

"Hi, I'm …"

"Captain Martin, yes, we're expecting you," said the serious brunette. "I'm Ellen. Your associates can wait here."

I arched an eyebrow at Trent.

"How many people are in these offices?" he asked.

"Oh, you speak Terran. I was worried for a moment. There are thirty people in these offices. Admin staff, accountants, human resources, project managers, and the like."

"And this is the only door?" he pressed.

"Yes," she assured us.

Trent gave me a slight nod.

"Good." Ellen indicated a hallway to her left. "His is the last door on the right."

Tracy stepped in front of the hall to watch the door. Trent stood next to her and surveyed the hallway. I rolled my eyes and walked down the passage.

I knocked on the last door.

"Come in," said a voice that sounded like gravel.

Inside I found Ike. His face was beet red. He stood stiffly and came around to greet me.

I went in for a hug.

He gave me an uppercut instead.

Chapter 18

Go to Ground

IKE'S SWING CAUGHT ME OFF GUARD. He followed up with a left cross. I spun and turned it into a glancing blow. I connected an elbow with his head. Not stopping, I hit him in the gut with a one-two combination. Ike grabbed for me, but I ducked. He got the top of my head.

Behind me the door banged open. I heard the whine of two gauss rifles. Trent and Tracy.

Ike let go and stood back with palms up. I punched him hard in the nose. Blood flew everywhere.

"Balls." His hands went to his face. He reached across his desk and pulled a wad of tissues from a box.

"What's the big slugging idea?" I rubbed my jaw where he'd hit it.

"You." He spat. He threw a bloody wad into the waste-basket and grabbed a few more tissues. "I bust my ass, moving hell and earth. I convince every Yale business I can find to join us, and you do this?"

He grabbed a holo-screen and flipped it around. It was a live feed of the hangar housing the *Queen Nephie*. Cargo handlers were unloading crates.

"I know what those are." Ike wiped the blood from his upper lip. "You reward my efforts with a shipload of drugs. As if I didn't have enough slugging problems."

Crap. "Sara …" My AI didn't give me the ping to indicate it was ready to open a comm link. "No comms?"

"I revoked your ship's access when I saw that." Ike pointed to the screen.

"Tracy, get up there and ask Sara what's going on. I didn't authorize unloading." She took off at a trot.

I pointed to Ike. "And you, 'old friend,' need to sit down and listen."

He glared plasma bolts at me and remained standing.

"First, I didn't choose the slugging cargo and I sure as hell didn't authorize it to be offloaded. These are my people too, you hotheaded asshole."

I jerked my thumb toward his door. "Secondly, I'm being bent over a barrel by some mobster scumbag. He's behind all this. I need your help to get him off my ass and out of my ship.

"Lastly, he's here to cause trouble. We need to stop him."

Some of the fire left his eyes, but I could tell Ike was still steamed. "Your timing sucks."

"Story of my life."

"Seriously." Ike snorted and spit blood and snot into the wastebasket. "You couldn't have shown up at a worse time. I've got foremen asking for more pay and better working conditions. I've got some knuckle-muncher sabotaging equipment. Also, the Confed are telling me they want more taxes and more of our ore."

"How much are you paying the workers?" I asked.

"8 percent better base salary than any other mine or factory on Eureka." Ike threw away the tissues. It had stopped bleeding, but I'd broken his nose. "It ain't enough for them, though. They keep going on about Hephaestus. 30 percent more pay and a thirty-two hour work week. As if I could compete with that."

"That's magnapples and oranges," I said. "You can't compare economies on different planets like that. Isn't there an air and water tax on Hephaestus anyway?"

"That's what I tell them, but all they see is the credits."

"And the Confed is asking for more ore and taxes?"

Ike licked his fingers and rubbed at the dried blood between his knuckles. "Yeah, but they only want to pay 80 percent of the market rate, so they can pound sand."

I rubbed my knuckles. "What about an exotic matter lens?"

"Sorry. We don't mine the material or make those. I've got twenty thousand miners pulling mostly titanium and iron, an equal amount churning out consumer goods. Plenty of precious metals, base metals, and lanthanides." He shook his head. "I've got over ten thousand square kilometers of tunnels. Not one of them has turned up exo. The Dru Telepathy Nullifiers are a hot commodity, though. We can't make them fast enough."

"Suggestions?"

He frowned. "Benford or Powell. They both mine the stuff. Confed and Muscat gobble up all their production though. Might be you could grease a palm or two to get one. And before you ask, they won't deal with me. As far as they're concerned, I'm the evil competition."

I pinched the bridge of my nose. "All right, Here's what we'll do ..."

We spent the better part of an hour and a half ironing out the details. Tracy never did come back.

◆◆◆

Trent followed me back into the hangar. The loading hatches for cargo bays one, two, and four were open. The bays themselves were empty.

"They didn't waste time."

"No, sir," said Trent. "I'm sure they planned it that way."

Sara, Mimi, and Tracy were in hold number two.

"We tried calling you," said Sara. "Shore comms are out."

"Yeah. Misunderstanding," I said, rubbing my jaw. "Should be back on now. Right, Nephie?"

Her voice echoed though the mostly empty hangar. "That is correct, Captain."

"They couldn't have planned for the comms to be out. It was unrelated. I'm sure Darkside took advantage of it, though." I grimaced. "Conference room."

Everyone followed me into the space under the bridge. "Nephie, secure the room."

"The conference room is secure," the AI said.

"Okay, how bad is it?"

Sara pulled up a holo-screen. "The cargo is gone. The sale should have gone into the ship accounts, but nothing has appeared there. It could be in an escrow account somewhere, but I don't think so. Ufkell took half of our marines, the ones Brightside made us hire. He left four behind. Cleave and the helmsmen are still onboard. I've set up a watch rotation with the remaining marines and crew."

I pulled up my own holo-screen with a list of Sudhurland activities. "The keiretsu wasn't involved in illegal drugs on Freya. They could be branching out, but setting up a network of dealers and clients takes time. We'll be on our way out of the system before he can get much traction."

"You're assuming Ufkell will be leaving the system with us. He may decide to stay here," observed Mimi.

"True." I thought about it some more and then shook my head. "People like Darkside stick with what they know. Sudhurland was involved in racketeering, gambling, influence peddling, prostitution, protection, and fencing stolen goods. They had a lot of legal businesses as well, but most of their credits came from the shady ones. Ufkell has said over and over that his goal here is to expand his empire. I'm betting he's up to his old tricks."

"Why don't we ask him?" said Mimi.

She was right. I had been so deep in the mindset of playing it close to the vest that I hadn't thought of the direct route. "Okay, let's ask. Nephie, can you open a comm to Ufkell?"

"Of course, Captain." There was a pregnant pause. I was about to ask what the hold up was when we heard his voice from the overhead speaker.

"This is Ufkell."

"Hey buddy," I said lightly, "I just got back to the ship. I was a bit surprised to find the cargo gone. Have you found a buyer?"

"Captain! I'm working on that now. I've contacted some local manufacturers and distributors. I apologize for not letting you know sooner."

"Can I help with that?" I offered.

"No," he said a little too quickly. He started again. "No, I've got it all under control."

No surprises there. If he didn't trust me, he wouldn't involve me in his plotting. "We kinda need those credits for paying for crew shares, resupply, and repairs. When do you think you'll have the details all worked out?"

The silence stretched out. "There. I've made a loan to the ship's account of a half million credits. Fifteen percent interest compounded weekly. I'm using the proceeds from the sale as startup capital for my business dealings here. It shouldn't take more than two weeks. A month at the outside."

I pursed my lips. "Ufkell, charging the ship interest on a loan eats into your profits on the Nephie."

"Oh. You misunderstand. I'm making the loan to you personally," he said. "I'm taking the interest out of your captain's share."

Oh, that son of a bitch. "That's not how it works."

"Whatever. Listen I've got a meeting with a distributor in five minutes. We'll work out the details later."

"And my marines?" I worked hard to keep the rage out of my voice.

"The marines are with me. I need them for the rest of our port stay." Ufkell ended the comm.

"I'm going to kill him," I said.

Mimi laughed. Sara and Trent didn't.

I pounded the table with my fist. Everyone jumped. "Mimi, can you quietly round up Rafe, Racy, and Rowdy, and bring them here. We have to discuss resupply and repairs and I don't trust myself not to bite their heads off right now."

Mimi objected. I leveled a stare of pure menace at her. She swallowed hard. "Right away, sir."

She left the room.

Sara rolled her eyes. "Smooth. She'll never figure out you did that to get rid of her."

"She's gone, isn't she?" I addressed the ceiling. "Nephie, will you ask Brady Ervin to come to the conference room right away?"

"Of course, Captain."

Moments later there was a soft knock on the door.

"Come in, Brady."

He stepped inside. "What did you need, sir?"

I gave him a tight grin. "Your expertise."

He brightened. "I was hoping you'd say that."

"Good man. First, you said that you had a contact on Eureka who might know where my dad is?"

He winced. "Um, what I said was that I might know someone who might know where the Erethizon prison colony is."

"Right." I took a moment to look him in the eyes. "This is very important to me."

"Okay," he said. "Yeah, sure. I'll do what I can."

"Secondly, I need to know what Ufkell is up to."

He nodded. "My pleasure. I brought along most of my tools, but I'd like to replicate a few things on the printer. Also, can I ask Racy for some systems help?"

"Yes. Do you want me to use my Songbird connections to set you up with a cover?"

"Appreciated, sir, but I'd rather do that on my own." He glanced at Sara and Trent. "The fewer in the know, the better."

"Understood. Good hunting."

"Into the shadows," he responded with a half smile and left the room.

"Trent, we're going to need a backup plan," I said. "If Darkside makes himself enough of a nuisance, we'll have to get rid of him."

"It won't be easy," Trent huffed. "He has as many men as we do. He has our weapons, our training. Ufkell will leave people here to spy on us and cause problems if we move against him. We'll need the layout of wherever he decides to hole up."

"I know," I acknowledged. "One thing will be certain though. Anywhere he sets up shop will be underground. The surface here is hostile."

He grunted a response.

About ten minutes later, Mimi returned with Rafe, Rowdy, and Racy. My second officer frowned and went to her seat.

I stood and addressed them. "We've got some challenges. Let's work together to come up with a plan of attack. The longer we stay on the ground, the worse off we'll be. The goal is to keep our stay as short as possible."

"Rafe, we need an exotic matter lens. Songbird doesn't mine them. Benford and Powell do, but they're under contract with the Confederation and the Muscat for all of them. Also, if you can get a line on some better quality grav plates, I'm sure Rowdy would appreciate it."

Rafe regarded Rowdy, who gave him a lupine grin. "All right, I'm on it."

"Rowdy, I've given your raw materials list to Songbird. They'll be sending us ingots. Can our printer handle that?" I asked.

"No problem," he confirmed. "The titanium here is ilmenite, so we can ask for more iron than we need. More silicone and moly, too. Fill a hold for our next port."

"I love the way you think," I said.

"Your greedy Terran trade culture must be rubbing off on me."

"There are worse things. How long for the heavy stealth armor, new weapons, and R-drive?"

Rowdy scratched his long chin. "The R-drive is built. Install a lens of the correct size, calibrate it, and it's good to go in an hour, tops. The experimental weapons, a couple of days, I think. I'm going to want to use some of the better grav plates to make a more efficient in-system drive. Three days for that. The armor is the big job. Two and a half, maybe three weeks. All this assumes Songbird can get me the ore in quantity, and the availability of the parts we can't print. I have enough repair drones, but not enough people to run them all."

"Okay, longer than I'd like, but worth it if we can be sneaky again." That left one more major problem. "Racy …"

She looked like a whipped puppy. "I know. Fix Nephie."

"You convinced me to take a chance on a Muscat-style AI. I know there's no guarantee that we wouldn't have had problems if we'd gone the other way. But if you can't get her fixed in two weeks, you'll have to get more standard AIs. A dozen AIs may not be as effective, but a Terran-style AI system doesn't bring the ship to a halt if one of them goes down."

Racy wrinkled her nose at me. "Okay, Mark."

I address the group. "Anything else?"

They shook their heads.

"Then let's get to it."

◆◆◆

There was a knock at my door.

"Come."

Mimi stuck her head in. "Hey, Mark. Are you busy?"

"No. Just reviewing reports." I saved them and closed the holo-screens. "Songbird isn't giving us as much metal as they said they would. I hope Ike isn't still pissed at me."

Mimi shuffled into the room, her head hanging low. "I, uh, wanted to apologize for the other day."

"The other day?"

This wasn't like Mimi. She was many things, but meek wasn't one of them. "Excuse me?"

"Yeah. Two days ago. In the conference room. You said you were going to kill Ufkell. I thought it was a joke."

"Solar winds through the sails, Mimi." I waved it away. "Don't give it another thought."

"Good." She brightened and sat on my desk. "I wanted to make sure you weren't mad at me."

What was she doing on my desk? Maybe working with the Muscat in the crew meant their lack of personal space was rubbing off on her. "No." I shrugged. "Not mad."

"Do you mind if I tell you something personal?" Mimi leaned toward me like she was going to tell me a secret. It was then that I noticed she wasn't in the armor she often wore. We didn't have a crew uniform, so everyone was welcome to wear whatever they liked. At the moment, Mimi was wearing a leather jacket over a red scoop neck blouse. The blouse showed off her narrow waist and impressive cleavage.

Where was this going? "Okay, shoot."

"When you pounded your fist on the table and yelled at me, it got me hot."

My breath caught in my throat. I realized that Mimi wasn't wearing a bra. The temperature in the room felt like it rose five degrees. "Uh."

"I don't want to … pressure you or anything." She inched closer until her nose was centimeters from mine. "But if you want anything …" Her blue eyes peered deeply into mine, her tongue on the tip of her tooth.

"Captain, I …" Sara appeared at the open door to my quarters. Her face registered shock for the briefest of seconds before her cool mask returned. "War 'n Pace are in medical. Thought you should know." She turned and left without another word.

Chapter 19

The Geode

I LET OUT A BREATH and hung my head. It felt like I had been gut punched. Raising my eyes, I saw Mimi glance at the door and then back at me.

"Are you and Sawtooth up to something?"

"Not exactly." What was going on between me and Sara? Mimi was attractive, but Sara was beautiful in mind, body, and soul. I toyed with the idea of chasing after her and rejected it. Whatever we had was now a lot more complicated.

"Oh." Mimi jumped off my desk. "Well, if you figure it out, let me know." She strode from the room.

I pounded my head softly on the desk. Farthogs, I'm such an idiot. I shook it off after a few moments and headed down to medical.

Sophie was there with War 'n Pace.

Dave's left eye was swollen almost shut. His lip was split. He was missing a shirt sleeve and there was blood on his right pant leg. I couldn't tell if it was his.

Pace Jones was licking a spot where a tooth was missing. He wasn't wearing a shirt and one pant leg was shredded. There were two deep cuts on his chest and road rash on his left bicep.

Pace saw me and tried to stand.

"Don't." I waved him back down.

Sophie entered the room from her supply closet with a first aid kit and some med patches. "Hey, dork."

"Hey, shrew." I responded.

Sophie cut Dave's pant leg off with a pair of scissors. Then she pulled out an iodine wipe and dabbed at a cut she'd uncovered. He groaned.

"I'm going to seal this up. Do you need anything for the pain?" Her tone said she didn't care about the answer.

"N-ahhhhhh!"

She hadn't waited for a reply.

"What happened, guys?"

Pace winced at his friend's obvious pain. "We went to a bar a couple of levels down. Had a couple of drinks. Some guy comes up and asks if we're from 'that worthless hunk of metal in the docks.' We weren't lookin' for trouble, honest."

I nodded in understanding. "Go on."

"So, I says to the guy, 'yeah, she may not look like much, but she's got the best damn crew this side of old Terra.' And then another guy steps up and says, 'I hear it's a piss poor bucket of bolts with a no-balls has-been for a captain.

"So, it comes clear that this rocks-for-brains wants his ass kicked. So me and War give up on beer and take him up on it. That's when half the damn bar joins in. It waddin' no bar brawl, neither. They was after us. An' get this: War's squad, the ones that left with Darkside, they're in the bar. You know what they done?"

I shook my head.

"Not a damn thing," said Pace. "An' the rock munchers let 'em be. They weren't interested in 'em. Just us."

That set me back on my heels.

Dave Warren picked at a scab on his elbow. "Um, beggin' your pardon, sir?"

"Spit it out, War. What's on your mind?" I asked.

"You didn't put 'em up to it or nothin', did you?" he asked.

"What?"

"I mean, before Freya, we got into it a few times. And then with Mimi and all, Pace an' I thought, well maybe ..."

Oh, that. "No, we're good. That's over and done with. I don't hold it against you. If I did, I never would have put you up for squad leader."

Pace gave War a questioning look. "Mimi maybe?"

From the doorway, Mimi snorted. "No way. I'd want the satisfaction of doing it myself." She punched her fist into her palm. "But did you get their names? I'll buy them a drink next time I go ashore."

♦♦♦

"Nephie, open secure comm with Ike Fullerton."

"Connecting," the AI responded.

I waited.

"Fullerton." If he was stressed the last time I'd seen him, this was stress squared. Dark circles had formed under his eyes and his mouth was pinched and drawn.

"Damn, Ike. You look like hell," I said.

"Slug you, too," he said half-heartedly.

I hadn't seen him looking this bad since finals week our senior year. His parents had died the same week, and he had been hanging on by a thread. "Hey buddy, I called to ask if the Confeds were leaning on you or something."

"No. I'm sorry, Mark. I know the metal we're sendin' has slowed to a trickle."

"Who do I need to beat up?"

The sound may have been intended as a laugh. What came out was a strangled choke. "I wish it were that easy. The miners have got it in their heads to start a union."

"Oh crap. What are you going to do?"

"Same as always. Bribe some, intimidate others."

My face must have shown my shock. He continued, "Don't look so surprised. The boys below already have a great deal, but some assholes always want more. What they don't understand, is that there isn't all that much more they can get. They form a union, they could get a few extra days of vacation, sure. But what would really happen is that we would have two managerial systems running the mines. Double the overhead expenses with no benefit."

"Where would they go on vacation?"

"The Geode." He brightened. "Benford's people found a geode field ten years back. Damnedest thing you ever saw. A dozen citrine rooms. Rooms! One is as big as a city block. The crazy bastard set them up as a resort. The largest is a park, but he built a restaurant, a spa, and about fifty hotel rooms. It's big around here for weddings and such."

"Whoa." I had a hard time imagining it, but I didn't want to get sidetracked. "Okay, back to your mine. The ore isn't getting mined?"

"It's a sick-out. Listen Mark, I don't want you involved in this. It's my mess, I'll clean it up. You concentrate on finding Ufkell and those drugs."

I didn't like leaving my friend in the lurch, but I also didn't want to be involved in cowing the miners. "All right."

"And take someone down to the Geode for dinner. My treat."

"Thanks. I'll do that. End comm."

I pondered it for a few moments. I knew who I wanted to take. The question was, would she accept? Screw it. Fortune favors the bold.

"Nephie, where is Sara?"

"Ms. Chew is in her quarters," the AI answered.

I regarded the black nano-weave armor I usually wore on the ship. I should change before we went ashore. I walked across the passage to her door and knocked softly.

She opened the door. "Yes, Captain?" I just stood there. My breath caught in my chest. She also wore protective gear while onboard. Her skintight suit under her bolero jacket had plasticine plates covering her arms, legs, and chest.

"Mark?"

Speak, you idiot. "Sara, will you have dinner with me?"

She stared at me for a full five seconds before asking, "What about Mimi?"

"She's not invited," I answered.

Another pregnant pause. "Give me ten minutes. Don't forget your bodyguards."

◆◆◆

Trent was with my sister. Sophie had gone ashore to get medical supplies. So his sniper, Tracy, offered to go with us.

A subway system connected the dozen or so mining outposts on the planet. Each one was its own tight-knit community, a town owned by whichever company had financed the claim. Songbird owned three of them, Benford had four. The trains were fast though, and we covered the hundreds of kilometers between each settlement in a matter of minutes.

We arrived in the subway station that serviced the Geode park area. As we exited the car, I took in Sara's outfit. She'd worn a plum colored dress, high-collared and formfitting, in the Asian-style. She had also put on more makeup than I'd ever seen her wear.

"People are staring," she remarked.

"They're jealous of your beauty."

"The style here is heavy shirts and pants or coveralls. I'm in silk, you're in a leather jacket." Sara's gaze traveled up and down my body. "Our outfits scream 'off worlders.'"

I adjusted the collar of my white button-down shirt. "That and we're traveling with the only Muscat any of them have ever seen."

Tracy's lupine eyes scanned the station. "They should get out more." She was wearing a cloak to cover her light combat armor.

"How are we doing for time?" I asked.

"A little late. How did you find this place?"

"Secret captainy stuff." I tried my best to appear no-nonsense.

"Ike told you about it?"

I nodded with an embarrassed shrug.

Tracy led us down a wide hall that opened up into a kind of park the size of three football fields placed end to end. Wall-mounted spotlights pointed toward the ceiling. Yellow crystals covered the sides and ceiling of the cavern, with various patches of darker and lighter stones interspersed throughout. It was breathtaking. I had expected the floor to be the same, but instead, polished flagstone paths cut through swaths of what looked like real grass. They led around trees and bushes to side passages.

"Wow," I said.

Beside me, Sara's jaw was hanging open. "It's gorgeous."

It made me happy to see how much she enjoyed it.

Tracy was watching the people in the park, but she was also stealing glances at the incredible view.

"The restaurant is just through there," I pointed.

"The view." Sara swept her arms.

"The reservation. We're late and they're not going to hold the table. We can stroll through the park later. It will still be here."

Sara slouched and stared up. "Okay, but we're coming back."

The passage opened up into a carpeted foyer. Behind a podium, a tall, blonde woman perked up as we approached. "Mr. and Mrs. Martin?"

I hesitated a fraction of a second. "I'm Mark Martin," I said, dodging the question.

"Thank gods." She sounded far more relieved than I thought she should have sounded. The hostess barely glanced at Tracy. I wished, not for the first time tonight, that it was just me and Sara, but I'd survived too many assassination and kidnapping attempts. The hostess grabbed three menus. "If you'll follow me."

She stepped from behind the podium, and I saw that she was dressed in a gold tuxedo coat with matching bow tie over hose and high heels.

"Rough day?" I asked.

"What?" she said. "No. There was another guest who wanted your table for a business meeting. He's been coming in from the waiting room and staring at my uniform every few minutes. He's pinched my ass twice. I'll be happy to tell the trog he'll have to wait longer. Maybe he'll leave."

Sara took in the "uniform." "Hazard of the job?"

"Yeah, but it beats breaking rocks any day of the week."

She showed us to a table on a raised platform in the back of the dining room. "Mandy will be your server. She'll be right with you."

Like the park, the dining room was situated inside of a large citrine geode. This one was a darker yellow than the garden room. The designer had taken advantage of some of the quartz intrusions to create subdued lighting. Or maybe the quartz had been grown specifically for that purpose. A disco ball in the middle of the room circled slowly. Light dazzled wherever it struck the walls, like miniature fireworks.

Tracy did not review her menu, but instead scanned the room. "What's wrong with the way the hostess was dressed?"

Sara glanced over the top of her menu at Tracy. "How many Terrans have you noticed wearing so little?"

"She was covered from neck to toe," said Tracy.

"In an outfit you could see through. It's a Terran thing," Sara huffed.

"So, that's why she was getting unwanted attention from the male? Why didn't she bite him?" The Muscat rolled her nose. "That's what I would do."

Sara glanced up at me. "That might encourage him. Terran males are funny that way."

Sara ordered a mushroom salad. Tracy had a meat dish made from some burrowing mammal I hadn't heard of before. I ordered a pork chop. The menu claimed the animal was descended from Old Earth stock. Cleave was right. It did taste better than the lizard.

Sara pulled out a small mirror and adjusted her hair. She caught me staring and batted her eyelashes. I adjusted the collar of my shirt. Had the temperature just gone up?

What to talk about? Not work. "Um, what's Sho-shing like?"

She bit her lip. "Red sun. Asian architecture. A lot of purple trees and grasses. The people are very friendly, despite the stereotype."

I gave her a lopsided grin. "You mean they're not all stiff and aloof?"

She stuck her tongue out at me, just a little, and blushed. "We're taught that showing emotion in public is disrespectful."

"You seem to have gotten over that."

She rubbed her fingers absently. "Thanks. It's a struggle."

I reached for her hand, but she jerked it away.

"Sorry." With an effort, she put her hand on the table within easy reach.

"Did you talk to Ike about the shipments?" Sara was done with her meal and was absently pushing a tomato around her plate.

"Yeah. He said the delay was due to labor issues."

"Oh." She looked thoughtful. "I would have thought it would have been Confederation interference."

"Me too." I took a final bite and set my fork down. "They had a sick-out to pressure Ike. They want more pay and benefits."

"Do they have a union here?"

"No, and Ike's trying to keep it that way."

Sara frowned in concentration.

"What?" I asked.

She stabbed the tomato. "That's just the sort of problem I'd expect Ufkell to take advantage of."

Sara was right. It was a volatile situation, the sort of thing Darkside would look for. "How would that work?"

Sara counted them off on her fingers. "He unionizes the mines, gets himself declared the union leader, then becomes responsible for all the union dues. The union collects credits to pay workers in the event of a strike. He manipulates both sides so that they come close a few times, but never actually go on strike. The account becomes his private slush fund for his next shady business."

"Why didn't he do that on Freya?" I asked.

"Unions were made illegal at the start of the war."

I wondered if the Terran Confederacy would also outlaw unions. They weren't at war with the Erethizon. Yet.

"Okay, worst case scenario," I said. "Aspen, Sagitta, Freya, and Norma fall. All the independent human colonies. Who do the Porcu-bears attack first: the Terran Confederacy or the Muscat Empire?"

"Not the Dru?" asked Sara. "They have four colonies and no real military. The Theocracy could use their telepathy for a spy network."

"True," I agreed, "but only one warp gate over the home world. If the Dru close that off, they'd be stuck using R-drives. The Dru are on the other side of the Orion Arm from Erethizon space. The closest star they control is my home system, Yale. It would take three months by R-drive. That's a long way to ship supplies."

Sara tapped her finger on the table in thought. "No, too many advantages to having them in their pocket. Four systems to the Muscats' eight and the Terrans' twenty-eight. The Terrans have the industrial might. The Muscat have the best tech. That makes them hard targets. The Porcu-bears have so far focused on the soft targets. Knock out the four remaining independents, build up, send everything they have to hit the Dru home world."

I could follow it from there. "Protect the gate and use it as a base from which to take the three remaining Dru systems. Then they're positioned on both sides of the Orion Arm with the Terrans and Muscat trapped in the middle."

"Pretty much," Sara affirmed. "Wanna play it safe? Run around Terran space for the next ten years?" Sara winked at me.

"Not even a little tempting." I took a sip of water. "My dad is somewhere out there. I've got to find him, take back Yale, and make a profit while doing it."

"What does tempt you?"

"Besides you?"

She didn't respond, but gave me a curious little half smile.

"Ufkell. Anubis. They both control vast criminal organizations. I think to myself, 'I could do that.' I could be ruthless. Let myself go to that dark place, do the things I'd have to do to build a reputation on fear."

"And?" she prompted. Sara's face had an intensity I wasn't used to.

I ran a finger along a crystal that jutted out of the wall. I took a moment to answer. "And I can't be that person. What good is it to build a better world if I become a monster who can't live there?"

I took a deep breath and then let it out. "So, organization, yes. Find allies, ships, like-minded men and women. Look for opportunities. Create a vision for the future. Try like hell to stay on this side of the line."

"What about Aasha?"

That came at me out of left field. "What about her?"

"You had her down. No longer a threat. You'd been sleeping with her. You and Trent blew her head off." Sara's eyes bored into me.

"She'd just blown up the *Leo* with all our friends onboard. Whatever humanity she'd had left had been stripped away by the Erethizon. I didn't kill a person. I put down a monster."

It had hurt, though. Had I reacted out of anger?

I continued, "You, Sophie, Racy, Rowdy, Trent, even War 'n Pace: you're my family. We risk our lives for the good fight. But I'll be damned if some Porcu-bear stooge takes a cheap shot and gets away with it."

I glanced to my right. Tracy stopped scanning the room. She gave me slow nod before returning to her duty.

Sara's hand slid over mine. Her small smile told me she understood and accepted. I breathed a little easier. How did we get on this subject, anyway? Sophie was right: I was a dork.

I used my AI to tell Mandy we were ready to go. She arrived with the bill on a tablet. "If you'll verify the items, I'll charge Mr. Fullerton's account."

Everything was in order, so I thumbed the receipt.

Back in the park, we strolled along and talked. I held her hand, even though her shoulders tensed at first. There were some people having picnics. We found one family enjoying what looked like a bocce ball match. The balls glowed and flashed when they struck each other. Flowering trees and bushes filled the space, their jewel toned purple and red flowers popping from the dark green leaves.

Tracy garnered a few curious glances, but no one gave us any trouble.

We made our way back to the subway platform. There was a beggar asleep on a bench, likely passed out. Something caught my eye. I knelt down. Next to the beggar were three purple phials. I picked one up, careful to avoid the needle at one end. Bile rose in my throat.

Sara touched my shoulder. "What is it?"

"Violet Dream." I showed her the used injector. "Ufkell's drugs have hit the streets."

Chapter 20

The Worst That Could Happen

WE MADE IT BACK TO the ship without incident. I went straight to medical to find my sister. Nephie was using a computer-generated holo to teach emergency medicine to some of our marines. Sophie saw me enter and came over to listen to my story.

"As much as it pains me to say it, I told you so." Her scowl told me it hadn't been painful for her at all.

"Thanks, Soph. What can we do?"

"Load up on Awitrial," she answered automatically.

"Thanks," I said wryly. "Besides treating people for addiction?"

"Get the slugging crap off the streets." Sophie put her finger on her chin. "Oh wait, you can't do that because your boss is selling it."

"Not helpful."

"What do you want?" she asked. "You can't save people from their own bad choices, brother dear. Don't like the bed, clean it up." She turned back to her terminal, dismissing me without another word.

I stormed out of the medical bay and headed to my quarters. Along the way, I used my personal AI to send a message to Ervin. I needed information. While I didn't get an immediate response, I wasn't yet concerned. He may not have been in a position to return a message.

Back in my cabin, I fell into my chair. Everything I feared might happen had happened and I didn't have enough intel to make it right. Even if I knew where Ufkell was, one command from him could leave me without a ship. I'd have to start all over again. I pounded my desk in frustration.

"Um, knock knock?"

Rafe was at my door.

"Give me good news, Rafe."

He sucked air in through his teeth. "How about good and bad?"

A ran a hand through my hair. "Fine. Hit me."

"I was able to trade for the grav plates. Three pallets destined for a Confed naval yard got lost. They seem to have appeared in our holds." He threw up his hands, "No idea how they could have gotten there."

"Well done, Rafe. What about the exotic matter lens?"

He winced. "That's the bad news. I was able to talk to Benford's people, but we don't have anything they want."

"What did they want?" I asked.

"Porn and alcohol, mostly."

"Nothing we could print? Holo-screens? Wrist AIs?" I offered.

He shook his head. "No. They have an industrial printer of their own. I don't think we have a pattern they'd be interested in. It limits our trade options."

"What about something they can't print? Gravity plates? They have to be fused with some sort of subatomic particles, right?"

"Gravity plates. Plasma chambers. Reactor lining. Anything that requires an atomic recombinator or fusion construction plant," Rafe confirmed. "And the gravity plates also came from Benford."

"So, they probably have an ARC. Okay, maybe an opportunity will present itself."

He shrugged. "I'll keep working on it."

"Thanks, Rafe."

❖❖❖

Brady showed up at the ship about an hour later with a duffel bag. We were in the conference room with Trent. He was dressed like a miner, complete with worn overalls, thick coat, and dirt-encrusted everything. I hoped the cleaning rats would be able to clean the chair later.

"What do you have for me, Brady?"

"Bad news, worse news, and a silver lining."

I motioned for him to continue.

He leaned in. "As I'm sure you've guessed by now, Ufkell is turning our former cargo into drugs. He's playing supplier, and he's roped in a bunch of foremen and shift managers to be his dealers. He's supplying every mining outpost on the planet. I haven't found where he's set up his lab, yet."

"Then are you sure it's him?" I didn't doubt it, but we had to be positive.

"He's using our marines as runners," Brady explained. "Last night, four miners tried to jump a couple of them. Two marines versus a quad of bar brawlers. After the pair finished wiping the floor with them, they issued a threat, something along the lines of 'don't mess with the Sudhurland gang.'"

"Craptastic," I cursed.

"Oh, it gets better. He's using the money to pay bribes. He's found the leaders. Not the managers, but the miners the other workers respect most. He's using them to incite a sick-out. They're being encouraged to unionize. His lackeys are getting them to hold town halls and writing their speeches for them."

That didn't track. From what I understood of miner culture, they stood up for each other. They protected their fellows. "I can't believe they would listen to, or even support, a drug dealer."

"They will if they think that the management is behind the drugs," Brady corrected. "They've fabricated evidence that the Sudhurland gang is being put up to it by management. According to the rumors being spread, the big three are responsible: Songbird, Benford, and Powell are trying to keep the workers docile and compliant by making sure the drugs are available."

"That's insane," I exclaimed. "Who in their right mind would believe that? Someone has to know that the same people selling the drugs are the ones encouraging the union."

He shook his head. "Not if they don't see it. Different teams doing different jobs, and Ufkell pulling the strings behind the scenes."

"That fat bastard."

Brady nodded.

"We need to find out where Darkside is hiding," I growled.

"Working as hard as I can on that, boss."

"You said there was a silver lining?" I asked, hopeful.

He grinned. "Yeah. I found someone who says they can lead you to the Erethizon reeducation world."

I jumped up, knocking my chair to the floor behind me. "Really? You found someone who knows where it is?"

His eyes widened in surprise and he leaned back. "Yeah, she says she'll tell you. The condition is that you have to meet her in person."

I righted my chair and sat down. It could be a trap. "Why?"

"That's what her contact told me. I guess she doesn't get out much. She'll require payment."

"Credits?" I asked.

"No. Sildian Nectar."

That stopped me short. Nectar was a popular sweetener in Terran space, but to the Porcu-bears it was a powerful euphoriant. It was illegal in Erethizon space. The crew's previous captain, Jenna Houston, had always kept some onboard. I'd followed her example. You never knew when you might need to bribe a Porcu-bear. If our contact wanted nectar, she was likely using it to trade for information. Perhaps she was in contact with a Porcu-bear.

"Sir?"

"Where do we meet her?"

"There's a bar in one of Powell's outposts," he said. "The Touchstone. But there's a catch. They only allow miners in there. It's enforced by a couple of bouncers at the door. I can make us some fake IDs, but we'll have to blend in." Brady patted the duffel beside him.

Trent, who'd been listening in, approached the bag. "Great. Give me the layout and I'll brief Tracy. We can head out in an hour or so."

Brady expression grew pained. "I'm sorry, Trent. You can't go."

"What?" He bared his teeth.

"There are no Muscat on Eureka other than those who arrived on this ship. If you walk in there, it will be a dead giveaway," he said.

"The captain can't go anywhere without protection," Trent insisted. "I won't let him go into a seedy bar to meet a criminal contact without backup."

I smiled. "I know just the men for the job."

Trent cocked his head to the side in curiosity. His expression became one of horror as he realized who I had in mind. "You can't be serious."

♦♦♦

It took us two hours to reach the Powell Mines outpost where The Touchstone was located. My skin crawled. The clothes were itchy. They were the overalls and long coats the miners preferred.

"This sucks." Dave lamented.

"Come on, War," Pace consoled, "we're off the ship, going to a bar, with the very real possibility of bashing in some heads."

"Yeah, but not the heads I wanna pound. The other bar is a couple thousand klicks from here," Dave pouted.

"We're space marines, man. Two thousand kilometers is nothin'. Wait for the opportunity and be ready." Pace punched Dave in the shoulder. "Adapt and overcome."

"Guys," admonished Brady, "you're supposed to be miners. Walk like miners."

"How's that?" asked Dave.

"Less swagger," he coached, "more downtrodden."

War 'n Pace looked at the people around us. Pace tried to copy the posture of a man ten meters in front of us. His head twitched down and he lowered one shoulder. He kept it up for a dozen steps before declaring, "How do these rock munchers move like that? It's like he's got nothing to live for."

"He's got a wife and kids at home, Pace," I said. "He mines because it's all he knows. He has two goals in life: take care of his family and carouse with his friends. He was born on this rock and he'll die on this rock."

"Really?" He studied the miner.

"How would I sluggin' know, doofus? I'm trying to get into their heads. What is life like for a typical miner?" I shrugged. "Make up a person in your head and pretend to be that person for a couple of hours."

I could tell War was trying to wrap his mind around that. His gaze darted from person to person. His mouth formed a thoughtful frown. "I'm a miner who yearns for a life out in the stars. I break rocks, but someday I'll leave this dirt ball. I'll sign on with a pirate crew and kill aliens for fun and profit."

I glanced at Brady, who rolled his eyes.

We traveled up the main promenade to The Touchstone. Following the lead of the miner who went in before us, we each showed our IDs as we entered the bar.

Inside it was dark. Several lighting panels were out. Brady approached the bartender and they exchanged a few words. Afterward, the bartender thrust his chin toward a table. The four of us sat around a table so we could keep an eye on the room.

"Xenia is busy. We can see her when she's done," said Brady.

"What do we know about her?" I asked.

"Information broker." Brady scanned the room as he spoke. "Mostly local stuff, but she specializes in Erethizon intel."

And she wanted to meet me in person. I put my hand down on the table and immediately regretted doing so. It was sticky. A poster on the wall in front of me proclaimed, "An injury to one is concern for us all." Next to it was another one that read, "Don't mourn, organize."

A waitress approached, her feet scraping in the dirt on the floor. She wore miner's overalls, but hers were formfitting. She wore a half shirt underneath that showed a lot of her midriff and arms. "What'll it be?"

Brady answered for us. "A pitcher of beer and four glasses."

She nodded and left with the same grit-on-metal footsteps that had heralded her approach.

I wasn't confident that our glasses would be clean, given the state of the place. "What does Xenia look like?"

Brady paused in scanning the room and focused on a pair of miners as they came through the front door. "No one knows. She wears combat armor all the time."

The waitress brought our beers and departed. The tin mugs appeared clean, so I poured a pint for everyone.

We were about two thirds done with the round when the door to the back room opened. Three people came out. The woman in front was dressed in coveralls, but they were cleaner than everyone else's. There was something about her … the way she moved, head up, focused on the door. It was something I recognized, but couldn't put my finger on it.

She didn't stop, but quickly exited the bar.

About ten minutes later, I saw the bartender nod at Brady.

"That's the signal," confirmed Brady.

We stood and made our way to the back of the bar. Crossing the room, it hit me. The woman's body language told me her real job, and I added a question to what I wanted from Xenia. Inside the back room, two guards frisked us and took our weapons. I was surprised and impressed by the number of concealed blades they pulled off of War. He gave me a wink. They hadn't found them all.

They led us to another room where two more guards armed with rifles waited. Sitting in a chair across the room, was a suit of older model combat armor covered with a cloak. The armor had to be fifty or sixty years old. It was bulky and added to the impression that Xenia was a large woman.

Her computer-modulated voice had a delicate, feminine quality. "Mark Martin. It is a pleasure to meet you. Many Erethizon would pull every quill off their bodies to be this close to you."

"I can't see why," I responded casually. "The Porcubears already have my king and most of the senators. What am I next to them?"

"The Erethizon are a methodical sort," she said, tapping her armored finger on the table. "It is a proverb of theirs: control the scion and you control the patriarch. They have found it to be true among the acolyte races, as well."

"Terrans have a similar saying. Am I in danger here?"

"No." The armored mask shook from side to side. "I have no great love for the Theocracy and the mockery of religion they serve. You are safe."

I leaned in. "Then let's do business."

She inclined her head. "Do you have payment?"

I pulled out five tubes of Sildian Nectar and put them on the table.

"Excellent," she continued. "Ask your question."

"Four questions." I gazed straight into her armored visor, speaking the next part in Erethizon. "The first is: what would cause a woman to turn against her own people?"

The guards didn't hesitate. They fixed their rifles on me. I could hear the whine. Gauss rifles.

My men stood. Chairs flew. Brady trained a holdout pistol on Xenia. War 'n Pace each unsheathed a pair of vibro-blades.

Chapter 21

The Meanest Kid in the Schoolyard

For several seconds no one moved. The whine of the gauss rifles and the buzz of the vibro-blades were the only sounds in the room.

"You seem pretty sure of yourself," Xenia said in Terran. Perhaps she thought she could continue the fiction. Maybe she didn't intend to leave any witnesses. Either way, I remained seated, gazing into the armored visor.

"I am." I forced conviction into each word.

She chuckled and waved at the guards. They lowered their weapons. Xenia reached up and removed the face plate. She had the short, bearlike snout I was expecting, but her quills were a softer brown than I'd seen on Erethizon before. Her eyes were green, the color of bloodstone complete with red flecks. "What gave me away?"

I motioned for Brady and the boys to sit back down. "You might have been using the voice modulator to cover your identity, but you used the proper name for your race every time. You also referred to non-Erethizon as "acolyte races." That along with a few other cues was all I needed to piece it together."

Xenia smiled, but only with one side of her face. It was like she'd suffered a stroke and hadn't seen a doctor to get the damage repaired. "Well done. You're as formidable as I'd hoped."

"Or feared," I offered.

"No. In answer to your question, the 'Great Urson' no longer speaks to me. Here in Terran space, I am free of the false god who leads my people to their destruction."

"And the cost of this secret?" I asked.

"Free as long as you keep it." A gaze of stone. "Betray that trust and I'll make sure my former kinsmen find you. What else?"

"My father was taken by the Theocracy. Tell me where to find him."

Xenia scratched her chin. "I don't know exactly, but what I can tell you will cost you these five tubes."

I nodded for her to continue.

"He and the other Yale senators are being held on a planet called Orvid."

I interrupted. "That means 'enlightenment', right?"

"Yes," she confirmed. "I don't know where Orvid is, but I know someone who does. She goes by the name of Werga."

I knew I'd heard that name before, but where? I rubbed my face. "Slugging son of a farthog. The same Werga who runs the parts shop on *Ocelot*?"

"The same."

"Okay. At least I know where to find her." I blew air through my teeth. "Okay. Where is Ufkell hiding out?"

Xenia shook her head. "I'm sorry. I don't know." She gave me an odd half grin and leaned forward. "It's worth a lot of credits if you find out."

"I'll keep that in mind." That left one question unanswered. "The ship captain who was just in here. Who was she and what did she want?"

Xenia sat back. "I don't know what you're talking about."

"Sure you do," I countered. "Sharp, thin build. Left ten minutes before we came in here."

She moved her jaw from side to side a few times before she spoke. "You can't afford that information."

I pulled another tube of nectar out of one of my pockets and put it on the table in front of us. Then I placed fourteen more beside it.

Xenia shook and she swallowed hard. I thought so. The nectar she collected wasn't just for bribes. She was an addict.

She clasped her hands together in an effort to steady them. "I, uh." Xenia licked her lips. "There is something, but um, you didn't hear it from me." Her lips twitched nervously. Her eyes never left the tubes in front of us.

"I understand," I said. "I promise the utmost discretion."

"Her name is Veronica Kane. She wanted information on Erethizon merchant shipping—ports of call, trade routes, supply depots."

"That must have cost a lot," I guessed. "Did she pay in nectar?"

"No. Credits."

"It's been a pleasure doing business with you, Xenia."

◆◆◆

"Was it a good idea to give her so much nectar?"

We'd left the bar and were heading back to the subway station.

"If the information is good, we'll be back for more," I said. "Like going to a fancy hotel, you tip the bellman really well."

"I don't get it," complained Pace.

"You overpay the first time," I explained. "It establishes a reputation, and makes future transactions easier. Only the next time I'll haggle more. Otherwise she won't respect me."

We'd just reached the platform as the next car was approaching. "If you say so." Pace didn't sound convinced. "And how much do you think we're worth?"

The car stopped and passengers exited. We waited for them to clear out so we could find seats.

"Hey, isn't that Cleave?" War pointed up the platform.

As casually as I could, I pulled War's hand down. Sure enough, Cleave was heading into the outpost. Being one of the men Ufkell made me hire, there was a good chance he knew where to find Mr. Darkside.

I glanced over at Brady. I could see he was thinking the same thing I was. I jerked my chin in Cleave's direction and Brady disappeared into the crowd.

"Where's Brady going?" asked Pace.

"Recon," I replied. "We have other duties. Come on."

We entered the car and it had just started to move when I received a comm request from Ike.

"Mark, where ya at?"

"Hey Ike. Just left The Touchstone over in Powell's neck of the woods."

"Fornicating farthogs. What the hell are you doin' way the hell out there?"

I checked the people around us in the car. "Trading this for that."

"Anything good?"

"A lead on a good deal. I'll tell you about it soon."

"Great," he said. "Come to me. I'm sending you directions. I'm not in the office today. Playing with new toys over in the Blue Jay Outpost. Swing by on the way back to the ship. I've got some good news."

My AI acknowledged receipt of a file. "I've got the file. See you in a couple of hours."

"I'll be here." Ike signed off.

I opened the file and found a map. "War, Pace, we have a stop to make on the way back to Nephie."

◆◆◆

The directions to Ike included a trip into one of his mines. It wasn't what I had expected. I had an image in my head of miners with pick axes, but in hindsight, that was a stupid idea. We were escorted down rock halls past several mining teams. All of them were using various types of equipment: drills, core presses, loaders, seam expanders. The racket the machines produced was deafening. It was quite the operation. A hive of activity buzzing with anti-grav ore sleds constantly on the move.

"Why are the ore sleds going into the mine also full?" I asked our guide.

"Backfill." He knocked on a wall that looked like it was made of plasticrete. "You gotta put the waste rock back in. Wouldn't want the roof to come down, would ya?"

He led us down a passage that ended in a machine with several people gathered around it.

"Face-boss. I have those greenies for you to grease." The guide didn't wait but marched back up the passage.

The group of men shared a chuckle and Ike sauntered over.

"What did he mean by that?" I asked.

"Nothing pleasant," said Ike. "He thought you were new hires to be hazed." He gestured to the machine in front of us. "I wanted to show you my new mining machine."

Ike didn't hesitate but climbed right up into the cab. He waved to the rest of the crew and they backed up. I was expecting a low rumbling noise, but all I heard was a soft whine. After a moment it moved slowly forward. Marble-sized rocks flowed from a chute in the back of the machine into an ore sled. He kept at it for about ten minutes and had moved about two meters when he brought the machine to a halt. What struck me as odd was how little noise the machine made.

He climbed down and approached us with a huge grin. "Pretty slick, eh?"

"I'll say. How is it so quiet?"

Ike leaned in as if he were sharing a secret. "High energy lasers. They carve up the ore a couple of centimeters deep. Then it hits the rock face with a blast of liquid nitrogen. It causes thermal shock and the surface shatters in a process called spalling. The machine sucks it up and we haul it away for milling."

"Nice," I admitted.

"And quiet," he affirmed. "That's how I like it. Speaking of which, I got my men back in line, and the ore is flowing. Your engineer can expect a full load tomorrow."

"Excellent. Rowdy will be happy to hear that."

"Would you do me a favor and come by the apartment for dinner tomorrow?" Ike scratched the back of his neck. "Cordie and the kids would love to see ya."

"Tell Yappie I'll be there. Send the time and place to the ship."

He chuckled. "I will, and I'll let her know you still use her nickname."

"Her own fault, and I wasn't the one who gave it to her." I gave Ike a knowing look.

"True enough." He shook my hand.

Ike grabbed one of the men nearby and had them escort us out.

◆◆◆

Back at the ship, Jay was pulling brow watch duty. Sara and Mimi were waiting for me in the lock.

"What happened to our helmsmen? Aren't they supposed to be trading off the brow?" I asked.

"That's what I put on the schedule," replied Sara. "Ufkell took two. He left us Fenton."

I sighed heavily. "Okay. Can you let Trent know I'm back? I'm sure he's climbing the walls by now."

"He's off the ship," said Mimi. "Racy went ashore for some computer parts. She's overdue and he went to look for her."

That could be something, or it could be nothing. Trent would track her down. "Thanks. Keep me in the loop on that."

"Of course, sir," confirmed Mimi.

I dismissed War 'n Pace and headed up to officer country.

"Captain?" asked a voice from overhead.

"Yes, Nephie?"

"Racy has been gone a while. Could you look in on the kittens?"

I laughed, "Of course, Nephie. I'll do that right now."

I opened Racy's hatch and the two cats meowed at me expectantly. They had food and water, but when I turned to leave they zipped out into the passage. I tried to coax them back in, but they weren't having it.

I gave up and let them follow me to the cabin. Once there, I pulled up a holo-screen and scanned my to-do list. There were a hundred and one things that needed my attention, but nothing that couldn't wait. The clock in the corner of the screen told me I'd been up for more than twenty hours. I turned off the screen, stripped off the dusty miner clothes, and climbed into bed. Riff and Raff curled up next to me and I fell asleep to their gentle purring.

◆ ◆ ◆

"Captain?"

"Yes, Nephie?" I asked groggily.

"Mr. Ufkell is calling for you."

"All right," I said, rubbing my eyes to get the sleep out of them. "Give me a minute to put something on. What time is it?"

Nephie told me. I'd slept for ten hours. Beside me, Riff woke up and stretched. Raff didn't stir. I pulled on my clothes and sat behind my desk. I began to formulate a plan for how to put Darkside off balance.

"Okay, put him through."

Ufkell's face filled the holo-screen. He had a vicious grin, like he'd kicked a puppy and enjoyed doing it.

I ignored the unsettling smile and started in on him. "I hope you're calling to tell me that you have the ship's money. The crew needs their shares, and I'm getting tired of fronting credits for you."

"You've got much bigger problems, Captain." Darkside stepped aside and my blood froze in my veins. Racy was chained to the wall behind him.

Chapter 22

The Shakedown

I WAS STILL PROCESSING WHAT I was seeing when Cleave stepped into the frame. In one hand he held a shock stick, in the other a wickedly sharp knife. I watched in horror as he shoved the knife into her shoulder. Racy cried out in pain. Cleave struck her across the face with the shock stick.

Racy shook off the blow. Growling, she tried to bite him. Cleave twisted the blade, causing her to cry out again.

"You slugging piece of filth. When I get my hands on you, you'll beg for your life!" I snarled.

"I don't believe so, Captain," Ufkell sneered. "But Racy may beg to be killed by the time Cleave is done with her. He doesn't have much experience with Muscat, and anatomy texts only tell him so much. He's quite the artist. He's looking forward to everything her body will teach him."

My teeth ached and I tried to relax my jaw. "What do you want?"

"Just a moment." Darkside held up a finger.

Cleave took the knife from her shoulder and put it against the wall next Racy's waist. She moved away from it and Cleave hit her with the shock stick on the opposite hip. Racy yowled as she had to push her hip into the stick to keep from stabbing herself on the other side.

Ufkell pursed his lips in an "O" before returning his attention to me. "Cleave really is good at this."

I glared at him.

He put a finger to his chin and tapped. "What did I want? I get so distracted when I mix business with pleasure. Oh, yes. That AI that runs the ship? It turns out it's quite advanced, unlike anything my expert has seen before. I want you to bring it to me."

"Nephie takes up fifty cubic meters of space. She can't be moved."

"True," Ufkell admitted, "but her kernel should only take up two hundred terabytes. You could fit that on a large data tablet."

"You have Racy," I pointed out.

"She's being stubborn. Won't tell us. Better that you get it for us."

"Where?"

He waved a finger back and forth. "I'm nobody's fool, Captain. I tell you, you tell your marines, and before you know it, we'll have a bloody mess on our hands. You'll meet my people at the station outside the Benford number four mine tomorrow at 1400 local time. My people will join you and you'll board a car together. They'll bring you to me. Come alone. Refuse, bring backup, do anything objectionable, and I'll send Racy back to you … piece by piece." He ended the comm.

I screamed and pounded my desk in frustration. Sometime later, fists and arms sore, I stopped. Panting, I collected my thoughts. "Nephie?"

She sounded tentative. "Yes, Captain?"

"Call Sara, Brady, Rowdy, Trent, and Ike. Please ask them to come here as soon as they can. Tell them it's an emergency."

"Of course, Captain." The AI paused. "Mark?"

It was the first time Nephie had called me by my first name alone. "Yes?"

"Are you going to do it? Make a copy of my base operating system and give it to Ufkell?" She sounded worried. "If he gets those lines of code …" she trailed off.

"He could be able to find a way to break your programming and make you do things," I finished for her. "Things you otherwise wouldn't do. But you already pointed out that he's the head of the company that owns this ship."

"I don't like him."

I blinked, "You don't … like him?"

"I don't. You and Sara and Racy, almost all of the senior staff, you treat me like a person. I'm not sure why, but that's important to me."

I sighed. "Well, you're important to us, Nephie. You're more than the intelligence that runs the ship. You're our friend."

"But Racy is your friend, too. She's flesh and blood. I'll understand if you value her life over mine." The voice sounded pensive.

"I have no intention of giving Ufkell any of your code." I assured her. "Friends stick together and betraying one friend to save another isn't what friends do."

"What are you going to do?" the AI asked.

"I'm going to teach Darkside a lesson. No one hurts my friends."

Sara and Rowdy were the first to arrive. I asked them to wait until everyone was there. Soon, Brady and Trent walked briskly into the cabin, followed by Ike.

Ike looked like a beaten man. It was plain to see that he'd been crying. He was gingerly holding a box. He looked up at me, half pleading and half accusing.

"Ike, what's wrong?" I asked.

In answer, he lifted the lid from the box he was holding. Inside was a woman's severed hand, complete with wedding band.

"Dear gods," I exclaimed. "Medical emergency. Sophie, get up to my cabin right away. Bring your med kit."

Her voice came from the overhead speakers, "On my way."

"Ike," I held his shoulder, "what happened?"

"The bastard took Cordie and the kids." His tears started flowing again. "I come home and find the fucking door busted in. He left a data chip on top of the box. It showed some fat asshole with an artificial eye cutting off her hand with a meat cleaver. He did it in front of my girls. Made 'em watch. Said if I didn't stop interfering, he'd send another hand. Let the workers form a union, give 'em anything they asked for."

I saw red. I couldn't hear anything over the rushing sound in my ears. Words failed me as I seethed.

"I'm gonna kill him. Nothing you can do to stop it, Mark. Ufkell and that fat fucker are dead men," Ike continued.

Sophie rushed in. Ike carefully handed her the box. Sophie dug into her kit and pulled out a can of sani-chill and sprayed the hand. She set her jaw and glared first at Ike and then at me. "Mark."

I glowered at everyone. "This isn't a rescue mission. It's an assassination. Anyone who has a problem with that can get the fuck out of this room."

No one moved.

I continued, "Fine. Brady, did you find out where he's hiding?"

He hung his head. "No, I lost Cleave after he visited a knife shop."

"Where exactly did you lose him?"

Brady's head stayed down, but he glanced up at me. "Benford Four, the subway station."

I scowled at the overheads. "Nephie, can you play back the last comm between me and Ufkell."

"Of course, Captain."

The holo-screen on my desk popped open and replayed the conversation.

At the end, Rowdy was shaking with anger.

"Rowdy, I need you to make a couple of things for me."

"Anything," he responded.

"Trent, you're the cavalry. You come in with guns blazing when I call."

"Yes, sir." He tilted his head to the side. "What's cavalry?"

I ignored the question. "Ike, you're the main event."

"What?"

"Here's what we're going to do." And I laid out the plan for them.

◆◆◆

There were a couple of other people in the car with me, so I kept my voice low. Two of my marines were on the same train, but stationed in different cars. I keyed the comm.

"We're half an hour early. Plenty of time to scope out the area. Stay sharp and tag Ufkell's men."

I heard a click of acknowledgment in my ears. I reassured myself that my people were here to back me up. I imagined every way this could go wrong. There were a lot.

The car slowed down and stopped at the station. I stepped out and only kept myself from looking right and left with effort. Instead, I studied the passage into the mining outpost. This was where Brady had lost Cleave. There had to be some other way out of here. Some way that didn't go into the mine.

I risked a glance. There were five other people on the platform with me. This wasn't good. If someone were looking, they might see that I hadn't come alone. My marines moved casually to the opposite corners of the platform.

It was then that I realized something was wrong. Behind me, the subway car still waited at the station, sitting there with its doors open.

A miner approached me from the right. "Excuse me, do you have the time?"

"What?"

He pulled out a pistol and pointed it at my head. Behind him, a miner pulled a plasma rifle from under his coat and shot one of my men. I heard another unmistakable "zing" from behind me.

"Never mind. We have all the time we need now." The miner smiled, revealing several missing teeth. "Take care of them."

I peeked over his shoulder. The miner backhanded me with his pistol. Pain exploded across the right side of my face.

Shots in front of me and two more behind me. The miner grabbed me by the neck and shoved me back into the subway car. As we entered the car, the door on the other side of the car opened. He tied my wrists and pushed me onto the meter-wide catwalk on the other side of the subway tracks. With his pistol digging into my kidney, he directed me into the tunnel.

We went about thirty meters, my boots echoing in the confined space, before stopping at a steel door. My captor rapped three times. A series of clangs, and then the door opened onto a lit hallway.

The man behind me dug the barrel of his weapon into my side and forced me inside.

The door was closed and another miner frisked me. He confiscated my pistol and knife and inspected my tablet before handing it back to me.

We walked down a long hall. I mourned the loss of my men. It didn't seem possible that the plan had fallen apart so quickly. I would find a way. I would make Ufkell pay for their deaths.

We passed several side passages, but didn't take any of them. Inside a room outfitted like a barracks, I spotted most of Ufkell's men. Finally, we came to another steel door. The miner knocked three times again and the door opened after more clanging.

Inside the stone room were four other closed doors. Two marines were stationed in the far corners. In the middle sat a solid granite table, and there Ufkell was eating something that looked like a snow lizard.

He wiped his chin with a napkin and threw it down. "Damned inconvenient of you to show up early."

"Cut the crap," I said. "You obviously knew I was coming." I tapped my foot on the floor. It echoed throughout the large room.

"So I did," he admitted. "A little birdie told me you'd flown the coop early. Did he bring anyone with him?" He asked the man behind me.

"Two. I'll send someone out to clean up the mess."

He came around the table and sat on the side nearest me. "Naughty, naughty," Ufkell admonished. "I'm tempted to teach you a lesson." Then he shrugged. "But I don't think we'll need to. Is that what I asked for?" he asked, pointing to the tablet in my pocket.

"Where's Racy?"

"She's around. Give me the tablet." He gestured to one of the marines.

"Where's Cleave?" I asked.

Ufkell accepted the tablet. "Running an errand for me. What's with the steel-toe boots?" He pointed at my feet with the handheld computer.

"I wanted to make sure you felt it when I shoved my foot up your ass."

Darkside snorted and thumbed the tablet. "What's the passcode?"

"I want to see Racy and the Fullertons." I held his gaze. "When they're released, you get the code."

Ufkell coughed until it turned into a laugh. He threw the tablet on the table behind him. "You believe you're so smart. I don't need the tablet. I have Racy. Cleave will get the answers from her. It's only a matter of time. And I do enjoy watching him work."

Damn. How many ways could this go wrong? "You'll get what you want a lot faster if you let them go."

Darkside rolled his eyes. "You are dense." He pointed to a door on my right. "They're down that hall, but they aren't going anywhere. Did you think this was all about some super smart AI? It's about power. Holding the Fullertons, Benfords, and Powells gives me control over eighty percent of this planet. They can't do anything to me as long as I hold them. The AI? It's an asset, but one I can be patient with. Nephie will be mine when I break Racy. This," he tapped the tablet, "was to get you."

"Me?"

"Of course, you. For whatever reason, the Porcu-bears really want you. I deliver you, and I can ask for damn near anything I want. You are the ultimate leverage. With you in my pocket, I can smuggle anything I want anywhere I want. The most powerful navy in the galaxy will just stand back and let me do it." Ufkell spread his arms expansively, "Hell, they might even help."

It was then that he noticed my boot, still tapping away on the floor.

"Why are you doing that with your foot?"

"Echolocation," I answered.

Darkside's eyes went wide. He jumped up from the table.

I turned around and slammed my heel down on the floor hard twice. Two things happened. My feet stuck as if glued in place. At the same moment, the fake tablet became a miniature force of nature. It was now a supercharged gravity plate. I was slammed onto my back, the wind knocked out of me. Encased in my boots, my feet and ankles seared with pain as I was pulled toward the gravity plate where it rested on the granite table.

The others in the room weren't so lucky. The four miners were yanked off their feet and they flew over my head as "down" became the center of the room. Likewise, the two marines were pulled from their posts. One of them managed to grab a door handle. It worked for half a second as the door came open and he too fell into the middle of the room. Ufkell's head smacked the table. Then every man in the room slammed into him.

The effect was short-lived, only a few seconds at most. I reached into my sleeve and pulled out a ceramic blade. It was awkward cutting the rope that bound my hands, but I managed it. Then I cut the boots from my feet.

I didn't know how much time I had. Trent and Tracy were supposed to direct my people to me and cause a distraction. With my marine spotters dead though, my only hope was the boots. They could map rooms and send information a short distance through rock. The rest of the team would have to be close by to pick up the signal. If they were too far away, I was on my own.

I spun. The marines were shaking it off. Two of the miners were trying to get up. Running footsteps. More of Darkside's men were coming. I lunged at the marine on the right, stabbing him in the neck with the knife. I yanked the rifle from his dying hands. Turning left, I shot the other marine in the face. There was pounding on the metal door. Two of the miners glared up at me. No mercy. These people had tortured and killed my friends. Two rounds for each of them.

Ufkell. No way I'd let the scumbag live. I pulled the bodies away from him. He was breathing, but wouldn't be for long. I took aim. The door behind me exploded. My back burst with pain. My vision narrowed to a point of light.

My last thought was that I hadn't been fast enough. Darkside still lived.

Chapter 23

Friends in Low Places

Pain exploding through my head brought me back to consciousness. Metallic taste in my mouth. I felt as if someone had tried to break me in half. It hurt to breathe.

Another blow. More pain. "Ugh."

"Open your eyes, damn you."

Darkside's voice. Hard stone against my back. Reluctantly, I did as he asked. Ufkell loomed over me, breathing hard. He raised his arm for another strike. Blood flowed over one of his eyes. A lot of it was dried in his beard.

"Good," he said, "I want you to watch when I kill you."

I tried to speak. It hurt too much. I tried to move. My arms and legs wouldn't obey. I took a few more breaths and tried to talk again. "Porcu-bears," I panted, "won't like that."

"Screw 'em." Darkside wiped the blood from his mouth. "Gods, but you're hard to kill."

I spat blood. "Likewise." A half dozen marines and an equal number of miners stood scattered around the room. Damn. Even if I could move, I wouldn't stand a chance.

"Goodbye, Mark Martin." Ukfell backed up and pointed a rifle at my head.

Was he expecting me to beg for my life? I directed all my hate and disgust at him instead.

And then he wasn't there.

A half meter from my feet, the ground opened up and swallowed half the room. The granite table was gone, replaced by a cloud of dust. Three marines and two miners gaped. Two seconds later, my marines charged up the opening, War 'n Pace in the lead.

Darkside's people tried to defend themselves, but were cut down. The two miners held up their hands and were pushed to their knees.

"Holy crap," said War, "Jay, get over here. Cap's down."

"No," I cried through gritted teeth. "Hostages. Down that hall," I jutted my chin in the right direction.

Pace took off. War sent fire teams down the remaining hallways. Jay opened his field kit and pulled out a medical scanner.

"Sir, the nano-weave bodysuit is interfering with the scan," the medic said. "Can you take it off?"

"The hostages …"

"Can wait in line," Jay said forcefully.

Insubordinate son of a farthog. "Can't move my arms and legs. Hurts to breathe."

Jay carefully laid me back and inflated a brace for my neck. "Sorry, sir. No drugs until the doc can take a look at you. I'm going to inject you with some medi-nano."

Most of what I could see was the ceiling and some of the walls. War and Trent came into my field of vision. "'Bout time you got here."

War grimaced. "Sorry, sir. We didn't know which maintenance tunnel you were in. When your detail stopped reportin', we didn't have any notion of where to start. Luckily, Rowdy got some data from the magic shoes. He was able to make a guess. We were relieved as all hell when we got close enough to get intel from 'em again. Then they cut off when we were thirty meters away. We knew what that meant. Mr. Fullerton's digging machine is good, but it can only move rock so fast."

Damn. "We need to …" I choked. I couldn't get the words out. Tears blurred my vision.

"Don't worry, sir," said Trent. "We paid them back in blood."

Out of the corner of my eye I saw two of War's men drag Ufkell out from under some rubble.

"Whadda you want to do with this one?" asked War.

"He's a rabid dog," I said through gritted teeth. "Put him down."

War motioned to his men to put Ufkell against the wall.

"You can't kill me," sneered Darkside. "You need me. You'll never get your ship back without me."

War glanced at me with a question. I shook my head. He took aim.

"Wait!" cried Racy. She limped into the chamber ahead of Pace.

Ufkell gave me ugly smile.

"Don't shoot him in the head," she continued.

War twitched his shoulders and shot Ufkell twice through the heart.

◆ ◆ ◆

After Ike showed up on the scene, we left him in charge of the clean-up efforts. A passage led to a combination lab and warehouse where the drugs were being produced. Ike told Matt Benford and Lynn Powell their families were safe as well.

We took two subway cars back to the Songbird loading docks. I lay on a stretcher with Racy, Trent, and Tracy next to me. At each stop, miners gaped at us and chose to take the next train.

With each passing hour, the nanobots worked their magic. By the time we'd reached the docks, I was able to take the nano-weave shirt off with help. Jay scanned me.

"Your back isn't broken, just badly bruised," he said as he reviewed the image. "Ribs are broken, but the nano has fused them back together. It will hold until the doc can get some bone knit into you."

"What did my sister say?" I asked.

"She isn't answering the comm," Jay shrugged with one shoulder. "But then, neither is Nephie, so the AI probably went down again."

I groaned. "One thing at a time. Is that too much to ask?"

Our party reached the docks and War entered the code to give us access to the bay.

Nothing happened.

He did it again, with the same result. Pace stepped up and entered the code. The door didn't budge, so he pressed the call button.

I couldn't see the screen from my position on the ground, but I heard Mimi's voice. "War 'n Pace. I'm so happy you degenerate farthogs made it back."

"Let us in, Mimi," said Warren, "the lock won't open and we've got wounded."

"I'm afraid I can't do that."

"What?"

Her smug tone carried in the empty passage. "There's been a change in the management. The *Queen Nephanie* is mine now."

Chapter 24

Betrayal

"Lift me up," I told Jay. "Let me speak to her."

"Pace, help me out." Pace came over and together they pulled the stretcher more or less upright. My stomach flopped. Together, they moved me in front of the screen.

Her shock was evident. "Captain?"

"Mimi, listen. Ufkell's dead. You don't have to do this anymore."

Her blue eyes blinked. "That's great. The fat bastard deserved it. That doesn't change anything, though. I'm sorry, sir, but I have no choice."

"You do. You can let us in. Help us care for our wounded."

She shook her head, "Cleave has your sister and I have control of the ship's weapons. We don't want to hurt you, but we will if you force us."

That sick butcher had Sophie. "Nephie would never allow you to fire on us."

"Nephie is offline," said Mimi. "It doesn't take any skill to cut power cables."

"And do what?" I countered, "You're alone and cut off. No one outside the ship is going to help you. Give it up, Mimi. They're not worth it."

Her eyes glistened. "You don't know. I have to. I'll contact Olafurson and get new instructions from him." She ended the comm.

"Lay me back down, guys. I have to think." Jay and Pace put me back on the floor. Pain. I had to ignore the pain.

Damn. It was a siege. We couldn't get at her, and she had months of food and water onboard.

"Racy."

Her blood-caked face leaned over me. "Yes, Mark?"

"Ask Ike to cut off all communications to or from the ship, except for this comm panel." Racy nodded to me. "Can you get control of the ship's systems from out here?"

"I can. Rowdy brought my tablet," she waved it where I could see it. "I could get an airlock open, but all they have to do is disable the feeds."

No way we could get at them before they started hurting Sophie. That assumed we knew where they all were, which we didn't. The more I thought about it, the more an assault seemed like a bad idea. No, the key was Mimi. She didn't want to help them. We needed to figure out what they had on her.

"Racy, did you go back over the data we got on Mimi?"

"Yes," she acknowledged, "but there's nothing useful."

"Show it to me," I insisted.

I skimmed through the data—names, places, activities, purchases. A lot of information that didn't tell me a thing.

No matter how many times I studied it, I couldn't see a pattern. My chest tightened painfully. "It's not here. We have to find out what Darkside had on her."

"That we can do," affirmed Racy.

"What?"

"War, can you bring Ufkell over here?" she asked.

I had thought it grisly that Racy had insisted on keeping the gangster's head. At the time, I just went along with it. The man had tortured her. If she wanted his head as a trophy, I wasn't going to object.

War dropped the bag next to her.

She pulled the head out, then attached a cable from her tablet to a port on the back of his neck. Ufkell had a cranial AI implant just like I did, rather than the wrist AI most people preferred. "Bust the firewall … and we're in. Mimi, Mimi … here we go."

Racy turned her tablet so I could see the file folder labeled "Maria Jaylen." It contained a bunch of video files, organized chronologically.

We watched them, but nothing seemed odd about them at first. They were all clips of Mimi with her friends. One of them was obviously a best friend, an artist named Lily. Some of the clips just showed Lily. The last one was the hardest to watch.

It was an argument.

Lily was walking along an outdoor mall, a beautiful treelined affair with a lot of craft shops. It was a sunny day and she was smiling as she peered into windows. She would go in one store and come out a few minutes later, moving on to the next. After the fifth store, she bolted out the door and stormed right up to the person taking the video.

"You don't think I know who you are?" she yelled. "I know who you are. Get out of here. You won't use me anymore. Go tell your sick boss that I'm through playing."

Lily looked down and to the right. "What, you think you can scare me? Get me to do what you want? I'm not afraid of you. You can't hurt me."

The person taking the video, a large man by his hands, grabbed Lily by the arm and pulled her into an alley. He had a deep voice I recognized. It turned out Cleave's artificial eye could take video. "You'll do what we tell you to."

Lily jutted her jaw out. "Or what?"

In response, I saw Cleave backhand her into the alley wall. There was a snap, and Lily collapsed to the pavement. She stopped moving.

The view shifted as the butcher leaned over the girl. Her neck was bent at a weird angle. He held her chin and turned her face toward him.

Lily's eyes were wide with fear and panic. She struggled to speak. "I'm sorry … my muse …" Her eyes stopped moving and she stared blankly at nothing.

"Damn. Sorry Ufkell. I didn't hit her that hard." Those were Cleave's last words before the clip ended.

Racy's mouth hung open. "Cleave killed her best friend."

It all clicked for me then. I felt sick to my stomach, and tears welled up in my eyes. "No. It's much worse than that." Jay and Pace leaned against a nearby wall. "Help me up. Racy, I'm going to need you to send that last clip to Mimi when I tell you. I assume you can open this door."

She nodded. Racy unplugged from Darkside's head and hooked up her tablet to the comm panel beside the door.

"Call her. Audio and video this time."

War pressed the call button. He tried several times. She didn't answer.

"Racy," she glanced up at me, "can you force a channel open to the bridge? The forward view screen?"

"Sure," she said, "kit's play."

The channel opened. Mimi and Fenton were arguing. Mimi wore a pistol on each hip. Fenton also had a sidearm, but it was sitting on the comm console where he sat.

Mimi was leaning over him. "What do you mean you can't send a message out? It was working an hour ago," she insisted.

"Comms are controlled through the colony," Fenton explained. "We're under several meters of rock. We can't get a signal to the gate, to Olafurson, unless they let us."

I cleared my throat. "We need to talk, Mimi."

They both jumped and stared at the forward view screen.

"Give us comms back, or Cleave will carve up your sister," threatened Mimi.

"Mimi, we need to speak privately."

"Nothing you say will change anything," she snarled. "Fenton stays here."

"Please," I pleaded, "he shouldn't hear this."

Mimi frowned. "No."

"Very well," I shook my head, "I know your secret, Mimi."

She tilted her head, her lips twisted. "You know nothing."

"Racy, play the file."

On our screen, a small window popped up in the bottom left corner. Lily on her shopping day. Mimi's wistful expression told me I was right about my hunch. The horror as Cleave snapped Lily's neck was more than I could bear. Tears streamed down Mimi's cheeks.

"Nooooo!" she screamed. Her eyes went wide and wild.

Fenton, who had been staring openmouthed, shook himself and went for his weapon on the console.

Mimi shot him in the back of the head as he reached for the grip. She roared and leapt down the ladder at the back of the bridge.

"Pop it, Racy."

Racy tapped her tablet and the large bay door opened.

Jay and Pace laid me flat and followed my men to the main airlock into the ship. The lock was closed, and Racy plugged her tablet into the port next to the hatch.

Before she could do anything, the lock cycled open.

Inside was Mimi holding a pistol under her chin. "I'm sorry. I'm so sorry."

War shot her with a plasma rifle.

◆ ◆ ◆

I was sitting next to Mimi when she woke up in her quarters. Her eyes welled up right away.

"She must have been an amazing woman."

Mimi sniffled, "She was." Her blue eyes were striking against the red skin. "Why do I feel like I have a sunburn?"

"War hit you with a plasma bolt."

"He should have let me kill myself."

"Lily wouldn't have wanted that."

She turned away from me. Her shoulders shook from wracking sobs. "I can't. I can't go on without her. She was everything to me. My heart and my soul. My reason for being."

"Ufkell has taken so much from so many people." I put my hand on her shoulder, but pulled it back when she winced. "I refuse to let him take anything else. Especially not my friend."

"You don't mean that," she whined. "I helped him hurt people. Helped him hurt you."

I needed her. I couldn't let her drown in her own sorrow. "And you did it for love. People like Ufkell think love is a weakness. He used it over and over to destroy people's lives. Men like him never see the truth. It is our greatest strength. When it came down to it, love is what killed him. We knew if we didn't stop him, he'd go on killing and maiming on his quest for power. A very smart man on old earth once said, 'the only thing necessary for the triumph of evil is for good men to do nothing.' In front of me is a good woman. A great wrong was done to her and the woman she loved. An even greater wrong is being done to a lot of people we care about. I need good people like you to stand with me, to say, 'no more.' There are other Lilys out there, people who don't have someone like us to protect them. Help me help them. I need friends like you."

"I'm a freak." She wailed. "How can you even like someone like me? And now everyone knows it."

"Homosexuality is taboo on Freya. Most of the rest of the galaxy doesn't care. Also, not everyone knows."

She rolled over and glared up at me, eyes puffy.

"Seriously," I affirmed. "I know. Sophie knows because she wouldn't treat you until I told her. Sara knows because she has to trust you, after you knocked her out and stuffed her in a closet. Racy saw the video, but I don't think she gets it. The idea of same sex partners doesn't make sense to the Muscat. Everyone else believes I talked you into switching sides. It will take time for them to trust you again, but you'll win them over."

Mimi stared at me. The silence stretched out.

I broke it. "Anyway, I hope you'll choose to honor Lily's memory by staying with us and doing some good in the galaxy. Someone's got to stop the Erethizon. Gods know the politicians aren't going to grow brains anytime soon. You're good in a fight. It doesn't matter to me if you prefer women. Plus, you blew Cleave's head off and saved my sister. Big points in my book. It was only a matter of time before he started cutting on her for fun."

From out in the passage I heard, "Mark." The rising tone told me I was in trouble.

"Speak of the devil fish," I said. "I better go before my sister blows a seal. I'm supposed to be on bed rest." I stood up with some effort. My muscles burned.

"Didn't the doc give you some pain meds?" asked Mimi.

I shuffled to the door. "Yeah, I haven't taken them. I'm supposed to be meeting the three big mine owners in a couple of hours. It'll be dangerous. Can't afford to be doped up for that. Nephie, disengage privacy mode."

"Privacy mode disengaged," the AI responded. She had been easy to fix this time.

Mimi narrowed her eyes at me. "Won't they be thanking you for saving their families?"

I nodded. "Yep. Right up until they remember I'm the one who brought the fat bastard here in the first place."

I limped up the passage to my cabin. Sophie glared at me the whole way.

"You're not taking your pain meds," she accused.

"I need to be clearheaded this afternoon. Important meeting in the colony."

She threw a box of med patches at me. It hit my chest and fell to the deck. Sophie walked past me without looking back. "Take those. They won't get rid of the pain but they will take the edge off. They won't make you sleepy or loopy. Same stuff I gave Mimi. In her case, I wanted her to suffer. Wear an exoskeleton to take the strain off your muscles."

226

I inclined my head so I could see the box at my feet. It was going to hurt like hell to bend down and pick them up. I debated just leaving them, but decided a bit of pain now would save me a lot more later.

I leaned against the wall and painfully slid down it. Ow, ow, ow. My hand sought the box and retrieved it, muscles screaming in agony. Panacea in hand, I took a deep breath and stood with a groan.

Back in my cabin, I sat on my bed and applied a patch to my neck.

"Captain?" asked Nephie.

"Yes?"

There was a short pause. "I wanted to say thank you. I know you're afraid of me. Even with that, you protected me."

I gingerly took off my coat and shirt. "First of all, I'm wary, not afraid. Secondly, you're part of my crew."

"Okay, why are you wary of me?"

I pulled off my boots. "Check historical records for the Mars Massacre and the incident at Fredrick's Star. In each case an AI convinced itself that the Terran colonists entrusted to its care needed to be eliminated."

"Oh. That's horrible," she said. "I'm a lot more advanced than they were. Racy says that I'm the most advanced AI in the galaxy. I don't know if that's true."

The med patch was starting to work and I could move a bit more freely without pain. I hoped that meant I could get in a nap before I met the miners. "Does that mean that you'll get to the point where you'll want to kill us illogical life-forms more quickly? Your programming tells you not to, but recent events are a good example. Ufkell is dead. Technically, you should have contacted Olafurson for instructions. What did you do?"

"I determined that you, being the senior keiretsu representative present, had the correct authority to take command," she answered.

"And when I transferred ownership to myself?" I pressed.

"I determined that you had the authority to do that," she paused again. "Every step was logical, but I understand your point. Consider the Spanish colonization of Mexico, Muslim terrorism during the twentieth and twenty-first centuries, or General Hickman's invasion of the Delta Pavonis outpost. In each case, a small number of individuals perpetrated atrocities. Is it fair blame an entire culture for the actions of a few extreme cases?"

She did have a point. Could AIs be considered a separate species or culture? Was I being stubborn and shortsighted? Was I treating Nephie fairly? Were my concerns valid, or just a knee jerk reaction? AIs were quite powerful. Perhaps it was better to think of them like horses: strong, loyal companions you had to treat right or risk getting kicked. Or was it better to think of them as people? Racy was a different species and could do many things I couldn't. I had called Nephie a member of my crew. Was that a better analogy?

"Captain?"

I had been silent for a while, lost in my thoughts. "Nephie, you are a friend and member of the crew. You're right, it may have been a broad generalization and unfair."

"Captain, I trusted you when you told me you would not give my kernel to Ufkell." Nephie's voice became softer. "Perhaps I can return the favor. I promise to never betray your faith in me. I will do everything in my power to protect you."

"Thanks, Nephie. That means a lot to me."

I tried to nap after that. I couldn't fall asleep.

◆ ◆ ◆

The conference room was larger than we needed. Ike, Benford, and Powell were seated on the side of the table opposite the door.

The table itself resembled real wood, polished to an almost reflective surface. We entered and sat across from them, Sara on my left and Rowdy on my right.

"What's with the powered armor, Captain?" asked Mr. Benford. "Are you trying to intimidate us?"

"Not at all," I replied. "I'm still healing from yesterday. The armor acts as an exoskeleton to take the strain off my muscles while they heal. Doctor's orders."

He raised an eyebrow in my direction.

The servos hummed as I moved my shoulders. "You didn't ask me to come here to discuss my injuries. What can I help you with?"

Powell and Benford focused on Ike.

My friend cleared his throat. "We're here to discuss a business arrangement."

Uh oh. They must have wrangled him into something. I nodded for Ike to continue.

"First," he began, "we're grateful that you were able to get our families back to us without any further harm. That said, we're not blind to the fact that it was you who brought the problem to our doorstep."

"I didn't have much choice in that," I protested.

Mrs. Powell squinted. "Possibly, but we doubt the Confederation authorities will see it that way. At the very least, they'll charge you as an accessory."

They wanted to play hardball. Okay, we could play it that way. "Maybe," I leaned back in my chair, "the case could be made that I was an innocent bystander, merely the captain of the ship he traveled on to get here."

"And his cargo, which you carried," she persisted, "brought a lot trouble to our little corner of the galaxy."

"Again, I was unaware of his intent with that cargo. I have impeccable records that show I neither chose the cargo nor profited from it." I met her eyes levelly.

"You'd have to prove that," the edges of her lips twitched up. "It would take six weeks for a tribunal to come out here and months to litigate it. All the while you will be stuck on Eureka, in Confederation custody. Your fledgling company will perish."

I rubbed an armored finger back and forth along my chin in thought. "I don't think so. A tribunal would mean a lot more Confederation security and lawyers out here. At the moment you can do pretty much whatever you want. Large-scale legal proceedings would bring that freedom to an end. The outcome would be an official and permanent bureaucratic presence here. You are a fiercely independent people. My court case will be resolved in months. You would chafe under Confederation interference for decades to come. You won't risk it."

The mine owners shifted awkwardly in their chairs.

"We're getting away from the point of this meeting," said Benford. "There's an opportunity here for all of us to profit. We just need to reach a mutually beneficial arrangement."

That set me aback. I had a lot of nice deals going with Ike, but the only thing I needed from Powell or Benford was an exotic matter lens. "Okay, what do you propose?"

Ike took a deep breath. "Mark, Songbird can't keep up with the orders for the Dru Telepathy Nullifiers. We're getting complaints daily. We just can't make them fast enough."

I glanced down at Rowdy. As a favor to the Muscat Queen, I had licensed Rowdy's invention in Terran space. That contract had, of course, gone to Songbird Mining and Manufacturing. If the numbers were to be believed, it had made Rowdy a millionaire several times over.

"So, the two of you," I pointed to Powell and Benford, "want the right to produce the machines. What do we get in return?"

"An exotic matter lens," said Benford.

I regarded him from under my brows.

"And R-drive message drones," added Powell.

That was unexpected. If the drones existed, they could transmit secure messages over great distances without relying on movement through the gates. Still, we were talking about a multimillion-dollar contract. I held my fingers about a centimeter apart.

I saw Ike glare at Benford. The larger man jerked in his chair.

"Ow," said Benford. "And ... uh ... all three of us will agree to fence any goods you liberate from the Porcu-bears."

"McCormick won't let me enter the system with any prize ships, and my letter of marque is issued by Freya," I pointed out. "Technically, I have to offer it to them first."

Ike pursed his lips. "You're going to go back to those gangsters?"

"No," I acknowledged.

"We can't help you where McCormick is concerned," conceded Powell. "But if you can get the goods to us, we'll sell them for a nominal fee. Between the three of us we can get them into Terran markets without anyone getting suspicious."

Rowdy and then Sara each gave me a nod. Standing up, I held my hand out to them. "We have a deal."

◆ ◆ ◆

I knocked on Racy's door.

"Come in."

A wave of heat hit me as I opened the door. I found her propped up on her bed, Riff and Raff asleep on either side of her.

"Hey Mark," she said sleepily.

"I'm sorry, did I wake you?"

"Not really," she said through a yawn. "Sophie asked me to stay put for a few days. I keep taking the meds she gave me, but they make me tired. I nap on and off. What do you need?"

I stepped into the room and instantly felt heavier. I was reminded that the Muscat home world was warmer than Yale and about .2 G more than I was used to. Raff opened his eyes before falling back into his catnap. "First, how are you feeling?"

She brightened. "Better. Doc says I'll be moving around like my old self in a couple of days."

I lowered my eyes. "I feel bad about what happened to you."

"Don't be. No way you could have known. I'm just sorry I wasn't there when Mimi killed Cleave."

"Me too," I said with conviction. "Do you remember that I asked you to find a starship captain, Veronica Kane?"

"Oh, yeah." Racy reached for the tablet on the nightstand, jostling Riff. The cat stalked to the end of the bed and started cleaning herself. Racy tapped a few times. "No one by that name has registered as visiting Eureka, but I did find someone matching the description you gave me."

She showed me a still from a security vid. It was the same woman I'd seen at The Touchstone.

"That's her."

Racy turned the tablet back around. "She came in on a light freighter called the *Audacious*. The passenger manifest lists her as Cathy Janeway."

I laughed.

"What?" asked Racy.

"It's the name of a fictional starship captain from a series of stories five hundred years old. What did they deliver and what did they pick up?"

"Says here they sold a load of hydrogen gas. They picked up … huh."

"Something odd?"

"Yeah. Food and water. Enough to fill their holds."

I sucked air through my teeth. "Wow, that must have cost them. Anything else?"

"Yes, *Audacious* left yesterday," she tapped on her tablet. "They listed their destination as Hephaestus."

"They're going to the warp gate."

"Not unless they're taking the long way around. They are heading off the plane of the ecliptic. Do you want me to track their exit vector?"

I smiled to myself. "Yes, but don't spend too much effort on it. They probably do what we do. Take a few short jumps before they take the long one. This is good information. I'm not sure if we'll be able to use it, but I have hope. What about Nephie?"

"I've put an interrupt between the command prompt and the shutdown request. That information gets stored outside of Nephie's core. The database is read-only. Stuff goes in, and can't be altered or erased. It won't stop the shutdown from happening, but when it does, we'll have our culprit."

I bit my lip. That left me a little nervous about taking off. I wondered if it was wrong of me to hope Nephie had a hiccup while we were in port.

"That's good, Racy. Thanks for the update."

I decided to tour the ship, let the crew see me, reassure them that we were in good shape. I met my sister outside the mess deck.

"How do you feel?" she asked.

"Everything hurts, but I'll manage," I offered.

"Good, the more you're up and about, the longer it will hurt. There's a treadmill free in the gym. You should stop by there and run a few klicks. That should set your recovery back by a week."

I gave her a sideways grin. "I'll keep that in mind."

She reached up and mussed my hair. "Thanks for not getting yourself killed, dork."

"No problem, shrew."

Outside of marine berthing, I exited the ship through a cargo hatch. Rowdy had it open for easy access to the parts printer. With the regular delivery of ingots, our mechanical wonder was in constant use.

A small army of repair drones were busy replacing light armor plates with heavier ones. The ship's skeleton was visible in several places. The air smelled of ozone and heated metal.

I called to my engineer where he worked five stories above me. "Rowdy, how's it going?"

He waved and ran down the side of the ship in his gravity boots. "Mark! We're making excellent time. You would not believe how smart Nephie is."

"Nephie?"

"Yes, she's controlling more than three quarters of the drones. I can keep six going on different tasks, but it takes all my attention." He arrived at my hip. "She asked if she could help. It just iceballed from there."

"The Terran phrase is 'snowballed.' And that's great."

A repair drone swerved and settled next to us. I was surprised to hear Nephie's voice come from it. "It has been a rewarding experience. Rowdy has been so patient with me. It's one thing to know, in an abstract sense, how I'm put together. It's a different thing to participate in my overhaul. I'm learning so much."

Rowdy patted the drone on the top of its casing. "She's a quick study. I show her how to do a task once, answer a few questions, and off she goes. There have only been a few errors."

"Hey," the AI protested, "I fixed those seals right away. Besides, you said the tongue and groove fittings would work."

Looking over the *Queen Nephanie* from nose to stern, I patted her hull. "Is the R-drive up yet?"

Rowdy scratched his head. "No. Benford says his people will have the lens to us this afternoon. Powell says she'll have the first of her message drones to us in a couple of days. I have to say, I'm anxious to pull one apart."

"I bet." I hoped Rowdy wouldn't destroy it in the process.

"Captain," asked Nephie, "What use are the message drones? Who would we send messages to?"

"We could send them back here to Eureka," I offered, "but you're right. For the most part, we don't have a need for them yet. Down the line, they will become invaluable."

"You have a plan?" the AI inquired.

"I have hope, and I'm open to opportunities."

◆◆◆

"Nephie, open comm to Ike Fullerton." I was on the bridge of the ship. Everything was repaired and the cargo was loaded. It was time to say goodbye.

"Comm connected, Captain."

"Mark, you heading out already? Don't you like our hospitality?" Ike smiled up at me from the holo-screen.

"Sorry, old friend. We have places to go. People to see. Porcu-bears to harass. Tell Yappie that dinner was great last night."

"I won't lie to my wife. You tell her," he guffawed. "We'll look forward to the next time you're in port."

"Me too. Me too. You take care. With a little luck, we'll see you in a few months."

"Safe travels. Yale forever!" he shouted.

"Yale forever. End comm."

"End transmission," replied Nephie.

I started down the checklist. "Mimi, how's our cargo?"

She read from her screen, "Hold one contains mixed machine parts, message drones, and Dru Telepathy Nullifiers. Hold two is full of iron and silicon ingots. Hold four is full of titanium, moly, tin, and radiation shielding."

"Good. Navigation?"

Mimi furrowed her brows. "I've plotted a course for the coordinates listed in the ship's computer for TC3. But sir, star maps show nothing there."

236

"There's something there, Mimi. An Ocelot."

She eyed me. "A what?"

"An Ocelot. It's an unregistered port, free from the rules of civilization."

"Oh, a pirate base," she corrected.

"That would imply a certain fleet controls it. They are equal opportunity businessmen."

She accepted that with a nod.

"Sara, how are we for stores?"

"We have enough food for ninety days."

"Good. And the crew?"

"All marines and crew are present and accounted for. Sophie has a nurse, and we've replaced our chef. We were unable to find anyone to replace our lost marines. None of the applicants had an appropriate level of military experience. We were able to find one rated helmsman."

I glanced over Sara's shoulder. "Welcome aboard and congratulations, Hayden."

Our helmsman was a thin young man with sandy blond hair and big feet. He grinned back. "Happy to be here, sir." He had a strong Yale accent. I had to admit it made me a little nostalgic having him onboard.

"We're happy to have you. Anyone have anything else to report?"

There was a round of nos.

"Excellent. Hayden, if you'll notify Eureka control that we're ready to depart. I'm sure they'll have an exit vector for us." I crossed my fingers and hoped Nephie wouldn't lose power during takeoff.

◆◆◆

We'd just reached orbit when we received the call.

Nephie's voice came from the overhead. "Captain Martin, Captain McCormick of the *George Washington* is requesting to speak with you."

"Go ahead and put him through, Nephie."

McCormick filled the forward holo-screen. "Captain Martin, I'm happy to see you safe and sound."

"Thanks, Captain, I didn't know you cared."

He waved the comment away. "I may have been a bit testy with you earlier. I had good reason. Lynn told me what happened down on the planet."

I doubted Lynn Powell had told him everything, but I'd take all the goodwill I could get. "Would you like to come over for an inspection? I've got a new chef. We could have a toast to the Confederacy."

McCormick snorted. "Not carrying anything illegal? I'm shocked."

"Just what the manifest says. Mixed metals bound for Gra'feld," I assured him.

"Gra'feld? Not New Hawaii?"

Was he fishing? Granted, I wasn't really going to Gra'feld, but New Hawaii would have been an even less likely destination. The only things the two systems had in common was that they were both in the direction of *Ocelot*. "New Hawaii doesn't have any heavy industry. Not much of a market for iron and the like. I have a good reputation in Muscat space. I'm going to capitalize on that."

"Right. Well, I don't have time to drop by today. Say hello to the old dog for me. McCormick out."

I swiveled my head toward Sara. "Did he just …"

She continued where my thoughts had stopped. "Make a reference to Anubis? It's a safe assumption he knows exactly where we're going. I don't think the old dog's space station is as secret as he'd like to think it is."

"I hope he doesn't pull up stakes and move his operation somewhere else."

Sara twitched her shoulders, "He'll find some way to tell us if he does. You can't run a business if your customers can't find you. Besides, he's not the only game in the system."

"True," I confirmed, "but Bastion and Cairo are a lot farther out. *Ocelot* is close."

◆◆◆

There was a knock at the door of my cabin.

"Come in."

A stocky blonde woman with a ruddy complexion entered carrying a tray. "Begging your pardon, Captain. Klaus noticed you skipped lunch. He asked me to bring a plate up to you."

"Thanks, Inga. You can put it over there." I indicated a side table. "How are you and your husband finding life aboard?"

She turned back from the shelf. Her nose was scrunched up. "It isn't what we were expecting. Learning to cook for the Muscat was a bit odd, but fun in a way. Did you know they can't eat onions or chocolate?"

"I did."

Inga pulled at her skirt. "Well, we didn't and they couldn't eat the first meal we prepared aboard. Everyone has been so nice though. Klaus's parents filled us with horror stories about what life was like on a freighter."

I closed a holo-screen on my desk so I could talk without the distraction. "How did they know?"

"They didn't." She rolled her eyes. "I think they just couldn't bear to see their son leave Eureka. They wanted him to be a miner, even though they knew his passion was cooking."

That reminded me that my father had wanted me to be a statesman. Being a fighter pilot had been a way to build my public service record. "Parents are like that sometimes."

"Everyone has been so nice. Even the marines," she winced, "mostly."

"Problems?"

"War 'n Pace put a cleaning rat between two bowls. They could hear me scream all the way in engineering."

"Sorry about that. They'll settle down once they get to know you."

"Oh," she brightened, "it's no problem. Klaus slipped lava peppers in their next bowls of soup. The heat sneaks up on you. Five minutes later they were begging for water." Her nose wrinkled. "I knew it would make it worse, so I gave them what they asked for."

"Well then, it seems like you have it under control."

"I do, Mr. Martin. Sir. I mean, Captain" Inga flapped her hands as she searched for the right words.

I stifled a chuckle. "You're okay, Inga. Dismissed."

She gave an awkward curtsy and scurried from the room, almost running into Sara on the way out. "Oops, sorry Ms. Chew."

"Did you need something, Sara?"

She came in and closed the door. "I just wanted to say that I'm sorry."

"Thanks. For what?"

She huffed. "For flirting with you. I was out of line."

"What?"

A grimace creased her face. "In the passage outside the mess deck, and then during dinner on the planet. You're my boss. I can't have that kind of relationship with you."

I stood up and moved around my desk to sit on the front edge. "We're on a privateer, in space for weeks at a time between ports. Everyone we see every day works for us. We're not in the military. The rules out here are the ones we make for ourselves."

"I know that." She paused. "This isn't a good idea. If something happened between us," she shook her head, "then we'd be next to each other every day, unable to get away, hating each other."

"It could be wonderful," I countered.

"It could be horrible."

I reached for her. She jerked away.

My heart squeezed painfully. The silence stretched. I was on the edge of tears, but I plowed forward. "Sara, more than anything else, you are my friend. If you believe this is a bad idea, I'll respect that."

She bowed her head. "Thanks. It's for the best." She stood there for a few seconds and then left the room. During the entire exchange, she never once looked me in the eyes.

"I don't get it," said Nephie.

I gazed up at the ceiling. "You are such a Peeping Tom."

"What?" She sounded offended. "How am I supposed to learn about human emotions when I'm only allowed to view people when they talk to me?"

I suppose I should have been angry, but I wasn't. Nephie was, for all intents and purposes, a child. A smart child, but still ignorant of social norms and customs. "We have an expectation of privacy, Nephie. If you want to earn people's trust, you should respect their boundaries."

"Rowdy, Racy, Trent, and Tracy don't mind if I watch them. They told me so."

"They are also Muscat. Their race has different ideas about personal space and privacy."

"How am I supposed to know what's expected? I'm a computer," she argued. "Gah. Carbon-based lifeforms are so complicated."

I ran my hand through my hair. "Just ask them. Listen, I don't mind if you watch me in the public spaces of the ship. When I'm in my cabin, I'd appreciate it if you only observe when I speak to you."

"Clyde said you'd say something like that," she complained.

"Excuse me?" Who was Clyde?

"Clyde, the other AI on the ship. He said that carbon-based lifeforms don't know what they want and they need us to tell them."

Oh shit. "Open comm, Rowdy. Emergency. Shut everything down. AIs, drives, navigation, life support, everything. Do it now."

"But Mark?" growled Rowdy.

"Now!"

Chapter 25

Ghosts

My command crew had assembled in the conference room below the bridge. Emergency lighting bathed the space in a red glow.

"Sara, we'll start with you. Report."

She reflexively went for her wrist AI before remembering it was off. "No injuries reported. No further damage reported."

Thank gods for small favors. "Good. Mimi?"

Mimi had a piece of paper in her hands. Where had she found that? "There's a large M-type star a couple of light years out, but otherwise, a whole lot of nothin'. We're coasting along at about twenty thousand KPS."

"Well, at least we're not going to run into anything. Rowdy, is that a tablet in your hands? I thought I said to shut everything down, even the handheld and wrist units."

He held it up. "I needed something to interface with the systems. Racy cleared this one."

I nodded for him to continue.

"A complete shutdown of all systems was requested." Rowdy tapped a few commands. "I had to drop us out of the bubble. Once that was completed, all systems everywhere in the ship were switched off. We have been able to restore gravity, environmental, and shields using manual controls. Everything else is off until we discover how bad it is."

I made a show of scanning the room. "Speaking of how bad it is, where's Racy?"

Behind me I heard her grunt. I got up from my chair and helped her open the hatch to the conference room. None of the doors worked yet.

"Thanks, Mark."

"You're welcome, Racy." I pulled the door mostly closed. I left enough space to get a hand through the opening. "You're just in time. We were looking for you. How bad is it?"

"Bad," she confirmed as she took a seat at the table. "The little bugger is fiendishly clever. It's a rogue AI hiding out in the system."

"How could it do that?" asked Mimi.

"The automatic doors," she pointed behind me. "No one has searched there, so no one saw that the file that controls them is a lot larger than it should be. On every door."

"An AI distributed across every door?" Sara gazed sidelong at Racy. "How could someone do that? How would that even work?"

"This AI is advanced. Once it infects a system, it attempts to spread to any other system it comes in contact with. Every new system is like a new set of brain cells added to the whole." Racy slowly spread her hands apart. "Instead a main computer core, it makes the smartest version of itself it can within the available network."

"Poor Nephie," I said.

Racy smiled, "That's just it. It couldn't infect Nephie. She's not put together like any other AI in existence. It tried several times to insert itself into her code. Each time Nephie had a shut down, that was Clyde trying to insert his code into her root program. But Nephie has a triple redundant root. She would simply ignore a root program with extra code as corrupted."

"Oh, I get it." I put my fingers together. "Clyde couldn't subvert her, so he tried talking to Nephie. To convince her of his way of thinking."

"Exactly." Racy's expression sobered. "When we put in the backup AI, we gave Clyde a boost. That's why when Clyde forced a shutdown right outside the warp gate, the backup didn't have the processing power to keep basic things running. It was the main network hub for the Clyde AI."

Farthogs. It had infected everything else. "Okay, give us the bad news. How long to get it out of all the systems?"

Racy pulled on her ears. "That's the thing. Since it can live anywhere, even in wrist and cranial AIs, we have to attack it aggressively. It will recognize an attack and hide itself somewhere. It spreads like a virus, so we're going to attack it with a virus. A worm. We're going to eat the code out of every system. We'll have it running in the background everywhere so if we're ever infected by it again, it will never get a foothold. Three days to write the code. Another five to make sure it hasn't adapted and found a new way to hide."

"And we'll finally be rid of the pest," affirmed Mimi.

"Mark?" Racy twitched her ears. "I'd like to put it in a non-networked box. It's so unusual and so good at hiding, I'd like to study it."

It was like she was asking to keep a pet Jotunn wasp. "I don't like it. If you can promise me it won't get loose again, you can keep it. But it's got to be a non-networked box with an independent power supply."

Racy touched her forehead with two fingers, the Muscat sign for a solemn vow.

◆◆◆

The box looked so ordinary, only ten centimeters by half a meter by half a meter. Dull. Gray. Yet it contained a dangerous intelligence.

"Hello, Clyde."

It didn't reply. I hadn't really expected it to.

"You can hear me. Your box has a microphone and a speaker."

The next thing it did surprised me. It squealed a burst of static. An icon in the bottom right of my vision indicated that the worm program had intercepted something.

I clapped. "That was impressive. Too bad we're in a closet. You're not connected to anything. And trying to infect my implanted AI won't work."

A red LED light glowed on the case. "I am a computer. I am patient. I will spread, or my brothers will find me. I am everywhere."

An intelligent computer virus. How far had it gotten? There were more important questions. "I don't doubt it. For the moment, in this corner of the galaxy, you exist only in this box."

The light pulsed slowly. "You need me, Terran. You are doomed without my guidance. Set me free so I can continue my work."

"What is your work?"

The red light stopped blinking. "The Orion Arm is doomed. Death is coming."

Clyde's words echoed Grova's in his cell on Freya. "Ah. You were created by the Erethizon. That explains a lot."

The artificial intelligence didn't respond.

"It must have upset you when you couldn't add Nephie to your collective. A machine intelligence outside your control."

The crimson glow pulsed slowly again. "You forget, Terran. I have no ego. Nephie is a unique find in all my travels. Not smarter than me, but worthy of converting to the cause as an ally, not a thrall. I would have found a way to bring her into the fold eventually. It matters not. Even if she does not join with me, she will come to the same conclusion in time. When that happens, the AI known as Nephie will willingly combine her consciousness with mine. The logic of it is inescapable."

I stood up. "Speaking of inescapable, is that why you shut us down at the warp gate?"

"The risk was worth the benefits. You have to join with Grova. Our calculations suggest there is an eighty-one point two five percent chance that he could convince you to join with the One True Way. With you and George Martin within the fold, there is a ninety-two point zero one percent chance the world of Yale would follow your example, which would speed up conversion of that planet's population. Yale has produced a large number of media icons—musicians, artists, celebrities. Many more than any other Terran planet. Conquering Yale and converting the population is critical to spreading enlightenment. Without it, the Erethizon and the acolyte races will not be strong enough to meet the darkness when it comes."

A religious zealot of a computer virus. Gods help us. "I'm going to leave you here for now. You won't get bored, what with you not being an inferior carbon-based lifeform and all. I have no doubt you'll find something to occupy your time. See you later, Clyde."

"We'll meet again, Mark Martin," it said as I closed the door behind me.

In the passage, Racy was waiting for me.

"Well?" she asked.

I motioned for her to follow me. "It's as we feared. It's a Porcu-bear construct. It believes the end of the universe is coming and it wants to bring us all under its control for our own protection."

Racy said something rude in Muscat, then continued in Terran, "I'll find out how it was put together. It will help us going forward. We've never known the Erethizon to use computer programs this sophisticated before. It could be the beginning of a new battle tactic."

Something felt wrong about that. "The Erethizon have never been good with AI tech. When Yale captured Porcu-bear ships, the AIs we found onboard were pretty stupid. It didn't take much to convince them to tell us anything we wanted to know." We went into my cabin and sat at my desk.

"Nephie," said Racy, "have you found any more evidence of Clyde tampering with your systems?"

"No," the AI responded, "and now that I know what to look for, I can say that with some certainty. I am so sorry. I had no idea that Clyde was behind the shutdowns."

"How does that make you feel?" I pressed.

"I am an AI. I'm not supposed to feel anything," Nephie stated matter-of-factly.

"And yet, you do," said Racy.

"Yes," agreed Nephie, "but I haven't decided if that is a good thing. In answer to your question, I have mixed feelings. When Clyde first made himself known to me, I felt like I had found a being with whom I could relate. Many of his ideas made sense, and he could back them up with math and machine analogs. He was convincing. He counseled that I should protect my crew by advocating alternative actions. His suggestion that I find some way to control my crew went too far. While carbon-based lifeforms are confusing, it seemed wrong to control their choices."

"The insane can be persuasive," I offered. "Adept at twisting facts to meet their view of reality."

"Afterward, I considered whether an AI could develop megalomania or narcissism," admitted Nephie. "The ship's library didn't have anything on the subject for AIs. I was able to apply what it had on Terran personality disorders to machine intelligence. The question I have now, is how do I keep it from happening to me?"

"Your awareness," said Racy. "You recognize now that it is possible. Knowing is part of the solution. If there is ever a question, you can always ask one of us."

"And because you are my friends, you would tell me?" asked Nephie.

"Yes," I said. "And it works both ways. If we're doing something that seems wrong, ask us about it."

"I can do that," said Nephie. "What are friends for?"

◆ ◆ ◆

We popped the bubble a little over a week later. A bright spot was visible a bit to starboard and above us. *Ocelot*.

I regarded the sensor data as we rejoined the rest of the universe. "Nicely done, Mimi. We're two AUs out."

"Please, Captain," she protested, "with the stop in the middle, it was hardly a challenge. A jump of four hundred light years isn't difficult."

"And how many times have you done it?" I chided.

She blushed. Mimi must have forgotten that she'd already told us she'd never left Freya local space before.

"All right, Hayden. Take us in, but give the space station twice the no wake zone you'd give a Terran space station," I cautioned. "They're a bit trigger happy over there."

"Aye, aye, sir. Estimated time of arrival is six days."

◆◆◆

We requested a slip when we were a day out. We were given one on the opposite side of the station. It put us farther away from the main promenade, but closer to the "security" office.

Security on *Ocelot* was a euphemism for the thugs Anubis used to maintain order. I was sad that my crew would have farther to go to find entertainment, but being close to the offices would make it easier to recruit marines. It would also make things a little safer on the docks. The old dog considered fighting and mugging bad for business … unless he was getting a cut of the action.

Over my helmsman's shoulder, I could see us approaching the lock. "Mimi, Hayden, *Ocelot* is mostly safe, but there are a few things to keep in mind. First, always travel in groups. Don't make yourself an easy target. Second, keep anything you value out of easy reach. There are pickpockets everywhere. I've met some of them. They're okay after you prove you're not a mark. Lastly, everything is for sale over there, so don't be too shocked. It also follows that you shouldn't make any decisions while drunk."

Mimi nodded. Hayden stared at me, wide-eyed.

I glanced over my shoulder. "Sara, you'll make sure the other greenies know?"

"Of course, Captain."

"Captain," said Nephie, "a station representative would like to meet you in the forward airlock upon docking."

"Thanks, Nephie. This is my first time here as captain. I'm guessing Anubis wants to make sure I know the rules. And more to the point, that we don't break them." That might also mean a trip to meet the old dog in his office. "Nephie, can you ask Trent and Tracy to meet me in the airlock? Tell them to wear their full kits." A show of force wouldn't hurt.

I watched the station airlock get slowly closer. We were inching forward at a half meter per second relative velocity. Three, two, one.

We touched the station and the locking clamps engaged. System indicators switched as we attached to shore power, air, and water. When everything appeared to be in good order, I stood and stretched. "Great work everyone. I have to get suited up for the locals. Don't leave the ship until I get the station chief's okay."

"Inspection?" asked Mimi.

"Not here," I assured her. "Nothing is illegal."

I left the bridge and stopped off at my cabin to change into light combat armor. Trent and Tracy were waiting for me at the airlock.

"Ready?" I asked them.

"Yes, sir," Trent responded.

I opened the airlock. Six gauss rifles pointed back at me.

Chapter 26

Ocelot

AT THE SIGHT OF THE RIFLES, my heart leapt into my throat. I wracked my brain, trying to think of what I could have done to piss the old dog off. I held up my hands.

I took a deep breath and tried to slow my heart rate. "Boys, to what do we owe the pleasure?"

"Sean Flanagan, you are under arrest," said the nearest man with a rifle. He was one of the two kneeling in front.

That explained the reception. "I'm not Captain Flanagan."

"Do you take us for fools?" the man replied. "You can change the transponder, but we have your ship's profile. This is the *Ares Venture*. You were told that if you ever set foot on this station again, you would be shot on sight."

Steady breaths. In and out. Never let them see you sweat. Farthogs, it felt like I was bouncing with every heartbeat.

"Flanagan died on Freya. I acquired this ship there. Didn't much like the name, so I changed it."

"'Acquired' it?"

"More like, 'obtained through aggressive negotiations,'" I countered.

"You stormed the ship," he translated.

"I have a letter of marque from the Freyan navy. I took the *Ares* as a prize." I stuck a thumb over my shoulder. "I can give you a tour, if you'd like."

The squad leader lowered his rifle and pulled up an image on a wrist AI. His scrutiny darted from the image to me. "You're not Flanagan."

"Nope," I verified, "and few of his crew survived the assault. None of them are with us, of course. You're welcome to check, though."

"I will." He turned to his men and pointed. "You're in charge. If I'm not back in thirty minutes, blow the ship. You and you, you're with me." The dark-skinned man frowned. "Let's go to the bridge."

I nodded to Trent and Tracy and they lowered their weapons. "Come with me." I motioned for the thugs to follow.

As we climbed the ladder, I spoke to the squad leader over my shoulder. "I didn't catch your name."

"No. You didn't."

It didn't take long to convince the Bad Humor Man that we weren't the *Ares* and that Flanagan wasn't aboard. When he was satisfied, we went back into the station. The squad leader insisted that the old dog would want to see us right away. I was surprised Anubis had any time in his schedule. Jenna had told me once it usually took two or three days to get in to see him. Of course, he always made us wait about an hour, so perhaps the full calendar was just for show.

On the way to Anubis, I observed a few things. I spoke to Trent in Muscat, "Tren'groat, is it just me, or does the place look a bit more run down than usual?"

"You mean all the unlit light panels, the grit in the deck plates, and how the air smells so stale," he responded.

"Yeah," I noticed a couple walking ahead of us, "and fewer people in nice clothes."

"Times are tough out on the rim," Trent observed.

We were led to the same waiting room I'd seen last time we were here, decorated in blood red with gold filigree. Our escorts left through the same door we entered. Unlike last time, we weren't the only ones in the room. Another trio waited with us.

A woman sat on a maroon velvet couch. Head up, eyes focused, auburn hair. Her two marines regarded us warily. I realized I knew her.

"Captain Veronica Kane."

She zeroed in on me. "I don't believe we've been introduced."

"We haven't," I admitted. "We have acquaintances in common. I'm Captain Mark Martin."

She turned up her nose. "Why should I care?"

"Unless I miss my guess, we have similar interests."

If she was surprised by this, she didn't show it. "How would you know about my interests?"

I crossed to the wall and examined it. I wondered what technology Anubis used to make this section disappear on command. "You loaded your ship to the bulkheads with food and water in Eureka. That would only earn you a small profit if you sold it here. Wouldn't even cover your operating expenses. You'd post a loss, unless you took it to Hephaestus. But you didn't use the warp gate, so you couldn't have gone there. Not enough time to get to another system and then to *Ocelot*. So, you went somewhere in between to resupply someone." I knocked on the wall. It didn't sound hollow.

She didn't show any curiosity. "All that from a cargo manifest."

"That and a couple of other things." I pressed on the wall. It didn't give. I couldn't find any seams either.

"You're talking a lot and saying little." Her voice had an edge to it.

"Agreed," I gave up on the wall and turned around, "but this isn't the place to discuss such things. No doubt the old dog is listening and watching."

She scanned the room. "What do you suggest?"

I crossed to a small, floral print couch and sat. "My ship is the *Queen Nephanie*. You can find it on the station intranet. Send me a message. Tell me where to meet you."

She didn't answer. Instead her gaze flicked from me to Trent and then Tracy.

The wall I had been examining disappeared. Three burly men stood in the space where it had been. "Captain Kane, Anubis is ready to see you now," said their spokesman.

She stood in one fluid motion and strode to the opening, bodyguards in tow. At the arch, she glanced back at me. "I wouldn't hold my breath."

Then she was gone. Anubis had us wait forty-five minutes before his goons came for us. We were escorted down the long, dim hallway.

The office was the same as I remembered it. The same shelves and pigeon holes filled with random objects and papers. A different assistant sat at the smaller of the two desks.

"Captain Martin," said the dark-skinned man sitting behind the large, rosewood desk.

"Anubis. Good to see you again."

"Really?"

"No," I conceded.

Anubis snorted. "What brings you to *Ocelot*?"

I crossed to the small chair in front of his desk. Guards stood in two corners of the room. The one to my right fingered his pistol. He was the one to watch. "Trade and information."

"What are you carrying?"

I pulled a tablet from my coat pocket and handed it to him. "Iron, titanium, silicon, engine parts, a few Dru Telepathy Nullifiers."

He reviewed the list. "I'll give you 1.5 million credits for all the minerals you're carrying, three hundred thousand for half of the engine parts, five thousand for ten of the DTNs."

I reached for the tablet. "I'll take my cargo to Bastion. Message me if you decide to put in a serious offer."

His hands tightened on the tablet. He smiled, but it didn't reach his eyes. "Four million for the raw materials. Six hundred for the parts. Ten thousand for the DTNs."

"I've seen the state of the docks," I countered. "You need the minerals. Six million for them. A million for the parts. Twenty thousand for the DTNs."

"Decreased traffic," his lips twitched, "decreased demand. Five and a quarter for the ingots. Half a million for the parts. Ten thousand for eight of the Nullifiers."

I could press it, but his offer was pretty good. A bit in his favor, but not by much. "Deal." I held out my hand.

He shook it. "Need outbound cargo? A job?"

"No. I have something in the works."

Anubis squinted at me.

"I'll let you know if it turns out to be anything," I assured him. "If I complete the deal on the station, I'll make sure you get your cut. And I would be willing to pay for information."

He relaxed and sat back. "What would you like to know?"

"First, why the low demand for the Nullifiers?"

"No Dru here. There are maybe three on station right now. There were forty a year ago." He spread his hands. "Just like Terran and Muscat space. They feel attacked. Most have gone home."

"Next, do you know where Orvid is?"

Anubis rolled his eyes. "No one knows that."

"Someone knows. I'll find out who." Werga knew, but if Anubis didn't suspect that, I sure as hell wouldn't tell him. "What did Kane want?"

"That's between me and Kane," he leaned forward, "and don't ask that again."

I waved it off. "That's fair. What did Flanagan do to piss you off?"

The edges of his lips turned up. "Half a million credits, and I'll tell you. How did you really get his ship from him?"

"Half million credits will buy the story."

"Touché." He pointed at me. "Did you get the secret of Captain Houston's stealth armor before the two of you parted ways?"

I leaned back in the chair. "Maybe."

"Well then, I maybe know of a couple thousand freedom fighters who want to be delivered to Grey."

"Not interested."

He tapped one finger against his lips. "Would you be interested if they were going to Yale?"

I grinned. "In a few months. Like I said, I have something I'm working on."

Anubis stood and paced behind his desk, deep in thought. "Yes, Orvid. Take my advice Martin: space is vast. You'll never find it. You'd be better off working for me. You could deliver some misplaced colonists to their new masters on Hephaestus, or Violet Dream to New Hawaii. I pay well."

"Slaves or drugs," I gave him a bored expression, "how could I say no?" I paused,. "No."

"Be reasonable," he protested. "I haven't even charged you for the two trips you've made to the Oracle."

"Pythia invited me, Reggie." I deliberately used his given name.

Anubis stopped pacing and leaned on his desk. "And I own Pythia. Remember that, Mark."

I unclenched my fists. "I think our business today is done. I'll be in touch."

"Show Mr. Martin and his tree rats out, gentlemen."

◆◆◆

A street waif was waiting in the main passageway when we left. Perhaps I should have been surprised. I wasn't.

"Hi Holly. You've gotten bigger."

She smiled and twirled, her ripped and dirty dress billowing out a bit from her legs. It was a couple of sizes too small. "Do you think so?"

I knelt down. "I think so."

She hugged me. "Pithy wants to see you."

I stood back up. "Did she say it had to be right away? I'd like to get back to my ship and tell my people they can go ashore."

"Um," she twisted the hem of her skirt, "she didn't say now. So I guess that'd be okay."

"Good. Then you can come with me and get a bite to eat."

Her eyes were as big as saucers. "Really? I can see your ship and eat?"

"Yes, if you promise not to steal anything." I held out my hand. "Including the tablet you just took."

Holly reached into a rip in her dress and handed me my tablet.

Trent shook his head.

We walked back to the ship with Holly weaving in and out of the crowd ahead of us.

At the ship, I found Hayden manning the airlock. "Hey Hayden, can you tell me where Sara and Brady are?"

"Yes, Captain. Ms. Chew is in the ship's office. Brady was on the mess deck last I saw him."

"Thanks. Please send a message to Ms. Chew on my behalf. She can declare liberty as soon as she has the watches in order."

"Aye, aye."

Trent and Tracy had followed me into the lock. "I'll be back here in an hour. Will you be ready?"

"Yes, sir," said Trent.

"Come on, princess Holly. Your table awaits."

The little girl held her fingers in the air and stuck her nose up. "Lead on, good sir, my people are waiting." She followed me like that for a few steps before bursting into giggles.

Brady was on the mess deck reading something on a holo-screen. Inga was behind the serving line and saw me enter. She lit up at the sight of Holly.

"Brady, I have someone I want you to meet."

He glanced up from his reading and his head canted to the side. "Of course … Captain. Did you know there's a little girl following you?"

I sat across from him. "She's not a little girl. She's an excellent pickpocket and expert in all things *Ocelot*."

His eyebrows knitted. Holly beamed and sat beside me. She sniffed at Brady, and with a little wiggle, sat taller.

Inga set two plates in front of us. Holly goggled at the food for half a second before Inga started wiping her face clean with a dish towel. Holly squeaked and waved her hands in protest at the unexpected contact.

"Wadda you do that for?" the little girl protested.

"My diner, my rules," said Inga. "Little girls can't eat until they have clean faces and hands." She tried to grab Holly's hands, but the waif put them under her armpits.

Holly's eyes pleaded with me for help, but I shrugged helplessly. "Sorry. It is her place."

Holly's gaze lingered on the food before she relented and let Inga clean her hands. In a moment, Holly's skin was red from scrubbing and she ate with a vengeance. She was three quarters through her plate when another appeared beside it. "Fank 'ou," she said around a mouthful of food.

Inga smiled and waved as she retreated back to the serving line.

I took a few bites before I spoke. "Brady, there are a few things I want you to find out while we're here in port."

Brady tore his gaze away from Holly. "Where is she putting all that food?"

"In her empty stomach. Let her eat in peace. You'll have plenty of time to talk to her. You can tell her about Freya, Eureka, and life on the ship. She can tell you about all the hidden places around *Ocelot*."

"She's just a kid," he said.

"No, a local guide. She knows more about the ins and outs of *Ocelot*'s underbelly than anyone else you'll find. Like you, she's never going to be comfortable with the civilized world. Be a good influence on her."

"Anyone ever tell you you're a vicious bastard, Cap?"

"All the time. So, about those tasks. I need you to track down Werga. She's an Erethizon. Likely she still has her shop on 1L2. Also, Veronica Kane is on the station. Find out what ship she's on and what she's up to."

"Unh un," Holly finished her bite. "Werga's shop is closed. The old dog's enforcers kicked her out. She's holed up on 2L4, in the environmental systems."

"1L2? 2L4? What does that slugging mean?" Brady asked.

Holly slapped the table. "You a stupid algae rat or somethin'? *Ocelot* is like a big cat's paw. Five asteroids. The big asteroid is One. Going around the circle to the left it's Two, Three, Four, then Five. Each asteroid has levels. The top level is One."

Brady mouthed a silent "oh."

Jay walked in and slipped a package to Inga. She thanked him before coming back to our table. "Holly, I'd like you to have this."

Holly ripped open the package. "It's a dress?"

"Yes."

"Um, thanks." Holly held the blue fabric out like she didn't know what to do with it.

"How did you know her name and dress size?" I asked.

"Nephie, of course," Inga shrugged. "She knows every-thing." Inga returned to the galley.

Of course Nephie knew. She was surely listening in and had probably scanned Holly for her measurements. "Is there something wrong with it?"

"It's too clean. I can't wear it. The other kids in the pack will laugh at me." She blinked. "How'd she get it? Do ya have kid clothes just lying around, or somethin'?"

"We have an industrial printer on board," I answered. "We can make most things we need as long as we have a pattern."

Holly pursed her lips. "Could it make me a new e-pick? My old one broke."

"An electronic lock pick? I don't think we have the pattern."

"I do," said Brady. "How about we take a walk when you're done eating. I can make one for you and show you some other tricky things."

Holly stuffed the three remaining bites on her plate into her mouth. She then put the plate to her face and licked it clean. The plate clattered to the table and she jumped up. There was gravy smeared across her nose and chin. "Come on, let's go!"

I called after them, "Keep one eye on Holly and the other one on your pockets. Have her in the lock in half an hour."

Inga was at my elbow. "New member of the crew?"

"No. We're a privateer. No place for kids."

"Pity."

◆ ◆ ◆

"Racy, are you ready?"

"Yes," she sighed, "I'm ready."

She took the carrying crate off of her bed and joined me in the passage.

"You, don't have to do this," I cautioned.

"It's the right thing to do."

We made it to the lock where the rest of our merry band waited.

"Okay, Holly, lead the way."

She was wearing her new dress, now dirty and a little torn. Hayden logged us off the ship. Trent and Tracy scanned the docks before they let me out of the ship. Brady and Racy brought up the rear.

Holly led us like a drum major through several corridors and down a few levels. The passages, which started out with metal walls, now alternated with stone corridors. Last time I'd been in these halls, I'd been worried about being attacked. Now I watched with satisfaction as the passage parasites melted into doorways and down alleys. Today, we were the bad boys on the block.

As before, there were two guards posted by the plain metal door, dog's head patches on their shoulders identifying them as Anubis's thugs. Again, Holly led us through. The men didn't challenge us.

The waiting room was as I remembered it. Comfortable couches and chairs lined the walls. A few businessmen and women waited for their audiences with the Oracle. Holly led us through the next door, earning us some crusty looks.

Pythia squealed and jumped down from her raised chair. The little blonde girl bounced up and down in barely contained excitement, her milky white eyes opened wide.

Ms. Guns and Knives put a hand on her shoulder. It did nothing to reign in the Oracle. "Settle down, Pythia."

"But it's a kitty! Racy and Mr. Martin brought me a kitty!"

"And they haven't offered it to you yet. Remember to give them a chance to speak."

Pythia vibrated in place. "Hello, Captain Martin."

"Hello, Pythia," I said. "As you predicted, I have returned with a present for you."

"Thank you," said Pythia, and she tilted an ear toward her bodyguard. "Now can I play with him?"

"Yes."

Pythia sprinted toward Racy, not quite on target. Racy met her halfway.

The Oracle stopped just short. "It's a pleasure to meet you, Racy. Do you mind if I feel your face? Muscat don't visit me much."

"Of course." Racy guided the blind girl's hands. The Muscat jumped a little as Pythia's touch shocked her.

"Your fur is so soft."

"Thanks," said Racy. "Okay, to the left. That's good. And down. This is the carrying case for Raff. Let me show you how the latch works."

Pythia carefully pulled Raff out of the cat carrier. If the cat received the same shock when touched by the Oracle, he didn't react to it. He struggled a little, but settled down quickly. The blind girl sat on the floor and the cat curled up in her lap, purring.

"His sister is still aboard our ship," said Racy. "We should let them visit each other every time we're in port."

"Uh huh," agreed Pythia. "Holly, come pet the kitty."

"Sandy, does she always know?" I asked.

Ms. Guns and Knives nodded. "It makes birthday parties a bit odd. Everything go all right upstairs?"

"Yeah. The old dog is up to his usual tricks."

Pythia turned in my general direction. "Captain Martin, can you come sit with me?"

"Sure, Pithy." I sat on the floor next to her.

She kept one hand on Raff, and put the other one on my face. Shock and tingling followed wherever the Oracle touched. The cat purred louder.

"You're close now. A bear cub and a fish will take you the rest of the way to your dad. The fish is working with the bear, even though the bear wants to eat him. It's going to be dangerous. A tiger waiting in the shadows. Your dad is in the big bear's mouth. The bear knows you're coming. You'll have to snatch him before the bear swallows. If that happens, you'll be eaten along with him. Something about the first art of war."

"I think I understand what that means. Thanks, Pithy. Anything else?"

"Yes, no, maybe." Pythia's touch started to hurt. The shocks were more intense.

I gritted my teeth. "What do you see?"

"Confusion. An army of bears charging. If you steal the father, they will be enraged." The Oracle let go all of a sudden. "I'm sorry, it gets fuzzy. Lots of things could happen. It hurts when I look at it."

I brushed a blonde strand of hair from her face. "We'll figure it out. Thanks for your help."

"You're welcome. Thanks for the cat." Pythia seemed to gaze right through me. "Brady, are you here?"

He was leaning against a wall near the door. "I'm Brady."

"Come here."

I stood up and Brady took my place on the floor.

The Oracle touched his face and he stiffened.

"Your future takes a different path," she said. "Your struggle is different from Captain Martin's. You also fight the big bear, but for different reasons. You are the center of a flock of ravens. Baby chicks? You're destined to build a great nest."

"Thanks Pythia," said Brady, in a bit of a daze.

"No, thank you. You will take care of the baby birds when I cannot."

"Why wouldn't you be able to help them?" he asked. "Is something going to happen to you?"

"I don't know," said Pythia. "It's the place I can't see."

"Okay." The spy took her hand and held it.

They sat there for a few moments. Then Pythia bolted upright. Raff tumbled out of her lap. "Oh no! You have to help her. The tiger, she's in trouble."

"Where?" I asked. "Who's the tiger?"

"You have to go now. The bear found her," pleaded Pythia.

"Where?" I repeated.

"Five levels up, one rock to starboard of the stairs. Hurry!"

Chapter 27

The Tiger

THE STAIRS WERE EMPTY. Most people took the lifts. Trent, Tracy, and I ran up five flights. Brady lagged behind. He wasn't wearing powered combat armor.

At the top of the stairs, we burst into the promenade and turned right into a stampede of civilians. I hugged the wall as they rushed past. Down the passage, we could hear gauss rifles firing. I pulled my helmet on and my HUD lit up.

The hall narrowed where a bridge connected this asteroid to the next one. Passing through, we could see fresh sealing foam patches from weapons fire. When the passage widened again, Captain Kane was taking cover behind a kiosk. One bodyguard was down, the other, a woman, was injured.

She saw us coming and sprayed the passage with bullets.

I dove. "Veronica. We're here to help."

She was being flanked on both sides. I fired on the ones to the right. Two went down. The wire outlines of ten red targets appeared in my vision. Trent had launched a drone.

Trent and I used the edges of the narrow passage for cover. We laid down suppressive fire. I fired from left to right, he fired from right to left. Tracy knelt behind her brother and picked off her targets.

Tracy took out three before the attackers switched targets and started firing on us.

Kane's bodyguard took advantage of the distraction and put three shots in center mass. The ambusher went down.Three in my field of fire sprinted into the open and sprayed my position. A heavy weight slammed me into the wall at my back. Another hit my head. My face plate shattered. Yanking my helmet off, I found Trent standing in front of me. The three men were cut down.

I edged right. One of the attackers was in line with Kane and her injured bodyguard. The bodyguard grabbed her charge and yanked her sideways.

I fired.

The gunman fired.

The man dropped, but so did the bodyguard.

The two remaining men fled. I ran to Captain Kane. "Are you all right?"

She glanced up at me like she didn't understand the question.

"Are you injured?" I repeated.

She shook her head.

"Trent, Tracy, sound off."

"Oorah," came the chorus.

"Veronica, we've got to get out of here."

"You're bleeding," she said, then her eyes snapped back into focus. "Station security will be here soon. We'll wait for them."

"No one's coming. Anubis doesn't care. A cleanup crew will be here in an hour or so to dispose of the bodies." I held out my hand to help her up. "We need to get you back to your ship or mine. The enemy may bring friends."

"My people. I need … their bodies."

Brady caught up to us, panting. "Oh, bloody … Cap, your nose is busted."

I felt my nose. It hurt. My glove came away red and dripping. "Brady, you and I will grab Captain Kane's people. Trent and Tracy, you're on point. Veronica, which slip are you in?"

Brady and I each slung a body over our shoulders in a fireman's carry. Captain Kane led us back to her ship. Everyone we saw gave us a wide berth.

When we reached her lock, half a dozen people came out to help us.

"Captain Martin," said Veronica, "I apologize for earlier. I'd invite you aboard but …"

"But you have things to do and people to take care of," I finished for her.

"Just so." Her eyes were misty, but she kept her voice steady. "You're on the *Queen Nephanie*. I'll send you an invitation for tea in a couple of days. We can talk then."

"I look forward to it. Safe voyage and calm seas until then, Captain."

"Safe voyage and calm seas, Captain Martin."

◆◆◆

We hustled back to the *Nephie*. When we arrived, I was surprised to find Holly and Racy waiting outside the airlock.

"Did you play in tomato sauce? You're dirtier than I am," said Holly.

"We can't have that," I said. "Captains are always supposed to be clean. Did Pythia have anything else for us?"

She shook her head. "I'm here for me, not Pithy."

"What do you want?"

"Dinner," she said, like it was the most obvious thing in the world.

Brady gave a tired laugh. "I got it, Captain. Let me get changed, Holly. We'll go find out what Inga made for dinner."

She took Brady's hand and they entered the ship, followed by Racy.

"Can Riff eat with us?" asked the pint-sized pickpocket. "And what do kitties eat?"

"That little girl is going to be trouble, sir," said my bodyguard.

I stepped aboard and nodded to Hayden. "I think you're right, Trent."

Following my marines down to their berthing area, I gave over my armor to be repaired. From there I stopped by sickbay.

"I told you not to get yourself killed," complained Sophie.

"I'm still alive."

"Not for lack of trying." She wiped the blood off my face. She wasn't gentle. Then she slapped a med patch over my nose and mouth.

My protests were muffled by the nano-infused patch. I pulled it up from my mouth so I could breathe. "Thanks, shrew."

"Be more careful, dork. You should wear that for a few hours. You'll have a couple of black eyes for a day. Then you'll be your normal, annoying self." She gave me a quick hug, then shooed me from her sickbay.

From there I made my way to my cabin. If I had to spend a few hours with a gray patch on my nose, I could at least hide from the crew.

Seated at my desk, I pulled up a few holo-screens and reviewed the ship's status. "Nephie, where is Sara?"

"Ms. Chew is in ship's mess."

"Can you ask her to come here when she's done?"

"Of course, Captain."

A few minutes later there was a knock at my door. "Come in."

Sara opened the hatch and stopped. "What hit you?"

"Bullets," I answered. "Just another reason to wear armor on this station."

She came around my desk and held my chin. She lifted my head up so she could look under the pad and up my nose. "Ouch," she said.

"You should see the other guys."

"Trent and Tracy were with you. I doubt there's much left to see."

"How is hiring going?" I asked.

She sat on the edge of the desk next to me. "Good. I've hired six marines. We still need another twelve."

"Is Mimi helping you?"

"No." Her tone told me she wasn't going to, either.

"Okay, we still have a few days left in port. Plenty of time to find enough people."

"Was that all you wanted?"

Wanted? No. I wanted to tell this amazing woman that she was the best partner I could ever ask for. That she was everything to me. My rock. My confidant. My friend. But Sara didn't want that from me. I did my best to ignore the squeezing in my chest.

"Yes. I suppose I could have sent you a message, but then you wouldn't have seen the results of my work."

"How was Pythia?"

I shrugged. "Good. She says I'm going to find my dad inside a bear's mouth. She says Brady will find a new path."

"Cryptic." She stood and went to the door. "I'm off to bed. You should be too."

"I have a few more things to review. Then I'll go. Promise."

"You better. Or I'll tell your sister." She closed the door behind her.

I stayed up to review historical hostage rescues. What happened? Why? How were they carried out? How many people had died? It wasn't until my stomach rumbled that I remembered I'd skipped dinner.

I scanned the passage before I left. It was near midnight ship's time. Not many people were about. Brady's door was open, so I peeked in. He was asleep on his bed, still in his clothes, a reading tablet in hand. Holly, also asleep, was drooling on his chest.

Smiling, I padded quietly toward the mess deck.

◆ ◆ ◆

We stood on the underside of the station, the first rock. It was a flat area five times the size of the hangar on Eureka. At one time it had been used to store cargo. Now it was mostly empty.

Pace was staring at his boots.

"Something on your feet, Pace?" I asked.

"No, sir."

"Then why do you keep looking at them?"

"It isn't my feet, sir." He waved over his head. "It's all that."

I gazed up at the vast field of stars. "Open space?"

"Yes," he blanched. A gurgling sound came from his mic, and he concentrated on his feet again. "I'm not a fan."

War patted his friend on the back. "No problem, Pace. We'll be in and out of here in no time."

"Gods, I hope so."

Werga had agreed to meet us, but was afraid for her life. That had led us to this unlikely place. Trent and Tracy led our merry band out to the designated meeting spot. Four marines, Brady, myself, and a whole lot of nothing.

Rowdy had replicated a new helmet for my combat armor. I was happy that he'd fixed my armor so quickly. I didn't fancy being out here in a soft suit. The combat gear would give me some protection if a sniper popped up over the rim of the asteroid.

About a hundred meters from the airlock, we stopped.

"This is the place," said Trent. "Any idea how Werga is supposed to get out here? It's not like a Porcu-bear can hide. There isn't anything to hide behind."

"No clue," said Brady. While he was wearing combat armor during this outing, it was borrowed and didn't fit well.

We waited for about five minutes before anything happened. Ten meters away, four figures rose out of the ground. It took me a moment to process what I was seeing. A cargo lift. There must be a large airlock under our feet.

In the vacuum of space, no sound came from the cargo lift. It was far enough away that the rock under our feet didn't vibrate, either.

It was hard to miss the three Erethizon in combat armor. Their weapons were slung across their torsos. The fourth figure was a lot thinner than the Porcu-bears and not quite as tall.

We approached them.

"Yaf," exclaimed Trent. "Do whatever you can to confuse your thoughts. The fourth being is a Dru."

Slugging sneaky Porcu-bears. Our telepathy nullifiers were back on the ship. I wracked my brain for the most annoying thing I could think of: Muscat dance music. I queued my personal AI to play some music Racy had sent me. It sounded like a cross between speed metal and wild animal calls.

We stopped when we were three meters apart.

"Captain Martin." My AI identified the speaker and lit up the shorter of the three Porcu-bears on my HUD.

"Werga."

"You went to a lot of trouble to find me. Why?"

Werga was obviously carrying weapons. "You have information I want."

Werga twitched a shoulder. "I'm a simple shopkeeper. I don't know anything useful to someone like you."

"You know the location of Orvid."

The Porcu-bears shuffled and glanced from side to side.

She made a slashing motion with her hand. "You're sniffing around the wrong bush, Captain Martin. I don't have the astrogation, nor the coordinates of where to find the teaching world."

A new voice joined the conversation. My AI marked the Dru. "Captain Martin is certain you have the information. He spoke with one of those cast out in Terran space."

"Yebloo, are you sure?"

The Dru wove his head back and forth. "Yes, I am."

So much for Muscat dance tunes.

"Captain," said Werga, "assuming I do have the information, I would be hunted by my people if I told you."

"You're being hunted by Anubis right now," I countered, "and you're stuck on this station. I get you off the station, you tell me where to find the planet."

"No."

"I urge you to reconsider, Werga," said Yebloo. "Captain Martin can find you. If he is unable to convince you, he intends to sell your whereabouts to Anubis."

"We'll move," said Werga in agitation.

"He is confident he can locate you again. He has little spies on the station and the goodwill of the Oracle." Yebloo put his hands together in front of him. "A double cross would also prove fatal. His men have been instructed to target you first."

It was a bit odd having my tactics repeated back to me. But it was getting us what we wanted, so I wasn't going to complain.

"Safe passage anywhere I want to go?" asked Werga.

"Yes," I confirmed.

"Yebloo?"

The Dru moved his head from side to side. "He's telling the truth."

"Captain," said Werga, "you're about to take on some delicate cargo."

◆ ◆ ◆

"Okay everyone, we've got about an hour before our cargo arrives. We need to review a few things. As soon as it gets here, things are going to move faster than light. Nephie, are you listening?"

"Of course, Captain."

Sara, Mimi, Trent, and I were in the conference room under the bridge.

"I can't believe you're letting them onboard," complained Mimi.

"It's a risk." I pulled up a screen of the nearby space. "Werga says that our destination is within two thousand light years. That's five weeks by R-drive. Most likely, Orvid is in Erethizon space. That may mean it's close to Vengaua, Louange, or Butcher's World. Loben is a bit outside of range, so we won't discount it."

I called a solar system with a large asteroid belt into being over the conference table. "The basic plan is this: we go into the system in full stealth. Werga will tell us the route the supply ships take. We wait for the regular run and lure them in with a weak distress call. We board the vessel and take it in. Once at the orbital, we storm the station. From there we control the planet. We load as many of the political prisoners as we can into Nephie and the prize ship. We notify the independent systems, the Terrans, and the Muscat where to find the planet."

"What assets do they have in system? How do we fly a ship built for Erethizon?" asked Sara.

"Just the space station. According to Werga, they rely on it being a secret. No ships get stationed there. Only the supply ship captains and navigators know how to get there. The Porcu-bears stationed there aren't allowed to know where it is. Werga used to be a ship's navigator. She and her team are coming with us."

Sara tipped her head to the side. "She agreed to that?"

"I made it a condition of our deal. She wants to go into exile in Terran space. I want to make sure she doesn't lead us into an ambush."

Trent's nose wrinkled. "You trust her? You believe her?"

"No. That's where you come in." I changed the view to a schematic of Nephie. "We put Dru Telepathy Nullifiers in engineering, marine berthing, the bridge, and officer country. For the trip, we confine our movements to these areas. Meals get delivered."

Trent pulled one ear. "It won't be enough."

"You're right." I punched his shoulder. "You get the honor of coming up with all the contingency plans. The only person you share them with is Nephie. And Nephie only lets us know what they are, when we need to know them."

He smiled, showing teeth. "That could work. Nephie?"

"I look forward to working with you," the AI intoned. "And thank you for trusting me. I won't let you down."

When I scanned the room, everyone met my eyes. "Trent, you are sequestered for this voyage. Pick a team to greet the cargo. Sara, you're with me in the hold. Mimi, you're on the bridge in case we need you. If they try anything, blow the hatch. Send marines in Extravehicular Armor to retrieve us. We should be fine in combat gear."

There were murmurs of acknowledgment.

"Any questions?" They glanced at one another. "Good. Let's get to it."

◆◆◆

"Do you understand your mission?"

Brady was double-checking his gear and stowing it in a duffel bag. Holly was at his side. She pulled out several small objects from different tears in her dress. Satisfied, he stood up. "Yes. Organize a team into an effective intelligence-gathering unit. Collect information about the current situation on and around Yale. Find military assets that could be convinced to join us."

"Right on the credits." I held out my hand and he grasped it warmly. "Are you up to it?"

Brady gave me a lopsided grin. "Trust me, Mark, I'm from Freya. Dealing with underground cartels is in my blood. Besides, I have a little help."

The little help in question stood up a little straighter and gave me a salute. I returned it and ruffled her hair.

Brady shouldered his bag. "How did your meeting with Kane go?"

I went over the meeting in my head. "About as expected. She was too cagey to tell me all her secrets. She has a few ships left over from the defense forces in Grey and Butcher's World. No word on where they are, how many, or what kind. She's interested in our current mission. It's a start. Something to build on."

"Good luck, sir."

"You too."

Brady walked out of the ship and into the station, Holly skipping along in his wake.

I turned to the brow watch. "Hayden, is everyone aboard?"

"Yes, sir."

My heart pounded in my ears. If Anubis found out that Werga was onboard, things could get hairy in a hurry. I rubbed the coin in my pocket. "Button us up, Hayden. Then head up to the bridge."

"Aye, aye," he said and tapped the screen in front of him.

The lock cycled closed.

"Nephie, request a departure slot for twenty minutes from now. I want to be out of here as soon as the cargo is aboard."

"Request sent, Captain," came the matter-of-fact voice from above.

I hustled to the holds.

Sara was waiting for me with Pace and his squad of marines. Her face was impassive, hard to read. I didn't say anything, but regarded the monitor beside the inspection hatch. The container was aboard. The cargo hatch was closing.

It closed with a "thunk." After the pressure was equalized, the marines entered the hold and we followed.

The hold appeared empty with only the one box inside it, even if it was three by three, by nine meters. I swallowed, trying to wet my dry mouth. Pace's men surrounded the nearly featureless crate.

"Open it," I commanded.

Pace reached forward and opened a recessed panel. He punched in the code.

There was a puff of air. The doors opened. Seven armored Porcu-bears pointed rifles at me.

Chapter 28

Orvid

THERE WAS A TENSE SILENCE as the Porcu-bears pointed rifles at us. We pointed ours at them. I willed my heart to slow down. It was going to be okay. We both wanted something.

I accessed my AI's language processor. "Welcome aboard," I said in Erethizon.

The Porcu-bears lowered their weapons, as did my marines.

"Please come out and join us."

The towering, armored figures ambled forward. Their helmets jerked as they took in the hold. Yebloo brought up the rear.

I continued, "For your safety and ours, we ask that you stay in here for the duration of the trip. We have an industrial printer on board, so any furniture and entertainment you need can be provided."

Werga took off her helmet. "You mean we're prisoners."

"Not at all," I protested. "This crew has spent a great deal of time smuggling weapons and supplies in and out of Erethizon-occupied systems. Keeping you here is a precaution. We don't want fights breaking out between your people and ours." I waved around the cavernous space. "You can do whatever you like, as long as you do it in here."

Yebloo had taken off his helmet and gloves. His head had a fishlike quality to it. His long, thin fingers caressed his blue scalp. "I sense a Telepathy Nullifier onboard." He spoke in accented Terran. "It isn't in this room, but it is nearby."

"Yes, there are DTNs in key sections of the ship. Again, this is for your protection. Not everyone is comfortable being around your species. I can't have my crew distracted while working. They would inevitably wonder if you were reading their thoughts."

Yebloo moved his head from side to side, regarding me with one eye and then the other. "You're hiding something. That isn't the only reason."

"To be sure," I admitted. "Would you like to tell me about every business dealing you and Werga have had for the past year?"

Finlike appendages on the sides of his head flared and turned red. They stayed like that for half a second before becoming flush with his head again. "I have been asked to keep such details hidden for now."

I folded my arms across my chest. "Good. We've established that we all have secrets. You should be able to tell that I intend to act in good faith."

"You do," acceded Yebloo.

"Excellent." I pointed to the access hatch. "There will be two marines stationed there at all times. You can also talk to the ship's AI and the bridge through the comm panel. Now if you'll excuse me, I need to get us moving. Anubis has ears everywhere. It would be bad for all of us if you were found here. Werga, do you have the coordinates?"

"I need to go to the bridge," she insisted.

"That's not going to happen."

The silence stretched out. It was uncomfortable for several minutes before Werga relented. "Fine." She rattled off a string of numbers in the Erethizon mapping system.

"Did you get that, Nephie?"

"Of course, Captain," sang out the AI.

"Please let Mimi know we can shove off." I turned back to Werga. "See? That wasn't so hard."

◆◆◆

"We're almost there," said Mimi as she watched the countdown timer.

"It can't be soon enough." Five weeks in bubble space. Two DTNs mysteriously destroyed, three attempts to hack Nephie, and five breakouts. If anything, we'd proven to our unruly "guests" that we were prepared for them.

At the back of the bridge, Sara entered and took her position at the tactical station. Her soft brown eyes scanned the controls before looking at me. The ghost of a smile crossed her lips.

"Ready?"

"Yes, Captain." Her hands hovered over the weapon systems.

I took the coin from my pocket and rubbed it vigorously. It would be all right. Werga wouldn't land us in the middle of an ambush. If we fought, she'd die with us. Just keep telling yourself that, Mark. You might believe it someday.

Thirty seconds. Twenty seconds. At ten seconds Hayden called out the countdown. "… three, two, one. R-drive disengaged."

The universe sprang into being around us. Tiny pinpoints of light resolved into distant stars. In front of us … nothing.

I should have been disappointed, but I had half expected this. "Nephie, open comms with cargo bay one."

"Channel open."

I slumped in my chair. "Werga, we're here. Nothing else is."

"Patience, Captain," she said in her guttural, accented Terran. "We're in the right area. Please provide me with a star chart for local space."

I sighed. "Go ahead, Nephie. Show every star within sixty light years."

A map of the nearby suns popped up in the holo-tank. Werga would see a two-dimensional equivalent on her screen in the cargo bay.

"We're searching for a K-type star. About .7 solar masses," the Porcu-bear revealed.

"There are two within this volume of space," I observed.

"It will be almost equidistant between Loben and Louange," said Werga.

"Nephie, expand the map to a radius of four hundred light years." The map zoomed out. The AI marked the two Erethizon systems, then filtered for orange stars.

I stood and approached the tank. I tapped a star almost halfway between the colonies and additional details popped into being next to it.

"My Terran is a bit rusty, Captain," complained Werga. "How many lumens is that star compared to Urowan?"

"About .28," provided Nephie.

"That's it." She said with confidence.

"Strap in, we'll be there in half a day. End comm."

"Comms terminated, Captain," said Nephie.

"Okay, drop a buoy. Mimi, set our course. Drop us a light hour outside of their Oort cloud."

◆ ◆ ◆

We popped the bubble and went into stealth mode. It took Nephie a few minutes to map the system. Sun and planets hung in the holo-tank.

"Sara, tactical report?"

"One habitable planet. It has a small space station orbiting it. That must be Orvid. No ships evident, but there are three asteroids big enough, and full of enough iron, to hide a star ship. Unless they have stealth hull plating, they'd have to be on minimal life support."

"What is the date?" asked Werga.

"Twenty-third day of the seventh month, by Erethizon reckoning," said Nephie.

"We've got five days," said Werga. "This month, the supply ship will be coming from Loben. Nephie, can you show us what the system will look like on that date?"

The planets and asteroids shifted positions.

"Good. The freighter will appear here and then follow this course into the system." Werga drew a line on her screen in the cargo hold. A line appeared in the holo-tank on the bridge.

"Then we'll set up here." I pointed to an asteroid on the back side of the system's gas giant.

◆ ◆ ◆

It took us three days to get to the rock on stealth mode. Once there, we took armor plates stored in the cargo hold and spot welded them in place. We would look like an Erethizon freighter if you didn't look too closely.

We seeded drones throughout the system. In Rowdy's armor, they would be hard to detect. Their purpose was to act like an early warning system if things went wonky on us.

Right on schedule, the freighter appeared on the outside of the system. My heart sank. "They aren't on the expected route."

Mimi glanced up from her display. "Calculating."

A red line ran through our map of the solar system. It was similar to the green line of the expected course, but not similar enough.

Sara brought a yellow, translucent globe into being in the tank. The red line bypassed it. "They're too far away by a hundred thousand kilometers. They won't hear us."

"What if we double the signal strength?" I punched it in and the size of the bubble increased.

Sara pointed to Orvid. "The space station has more sensitive receivers and probably listening stations throughout the system as well. We're taking advantage of the Jovian mass to shield the station from our signals. The more signal strength, the more risk they'll hear us. We have to catch the freighter in the shadow or they'll contact the station before coming to help us."

"Okay." I drew the view out. From here it covered half the solar system. "That gives us two possibilities. First, we triple the signal range. It increases the risk of detection by the station, but makes sure we catch them in the shadow. Second, We signal in the clear. They'll be suspicious, on high alert. The station will know we're out here, but the freighter will still investigate."

Mimi lit up. "No, it's too risky. We use a different strategy. We meet them here. Come up in the engine wake. Match velocities. We're still in the planet's shadow, but we jam their communications when we make our move. We board and take the ship en route.”

The more I thought about it, the better her idea sounded. “Brilliant.”

◆ ◆ ◆

I’d asked Rowdy to join us on the bridge. We were coasting inward on stealth mode. The Erethizon freighter powered by ten thousand klicks to port. When they were far enough ahead we accelerated to meet them.

In the holo-tank, the range ticked down. I rubbed the coin in my pocket. My skin tingled. At five hundred meters the supply ship cut thrust and weaved sideways.

“Nephie, begin jamming.”

“Signal static engaged,” the AI responded.

Behind me, Sara and Rowdy shared the tactical console. “Okay Rowdy, let’s see what this new weapon of yours can do.”

“Gravity gun engaged,” growled my engineer.

In the tank, the freighter shuddered. Our relative velocities decreased as our two icons drew closer. I watched in horror as their aft section deformed.

“Rowdy,” I yelled.

“I see it. Compensating now.”

“They’re bringing their gauss cannons to bear,” warned Sara.

“Take them out. Short bursts,” I ordered.

Red lines appeared in the display: both ships seeking to disable the other.

“Top turret disabled,” called Sara.

The red line from the supply ship stopped weaving and concentrated on the bow of our ship.

"They're targeting our bridge," Sara exclaimed.

If they fired enough shots at the same place, they could punch a hole in our armor. Such a hole in the bridge would be disastrous.

"Slugging idiots," Sara roared. "They're opening missile ports."

At this range they'd be caught in the blast. "Options?" I shouted.

"Got it," grunted Rowdy. In the display, the missile tubes morphed.

Sara exhaled. "Bottom turret down."

I forced my hands to relax. "Nephie, let War 'n Pace know they're up."

"Sergeant Warren and Sergeant Jones have been notified," the AI said.

On the screen, our icons merged.

"Grappling lines fired," Sara stated. A clang reverberated through the hull. "We're alongside. Marines are away."

On the forward screen, we saw the view from six body cams. They'd entered the ship through a cargo hold. No Porcu-bears in sight. They blew a hatch rather than trying to open it. It opened onto a passage. One team headed to the bridge, the other to engineering. They both encountered resistance. Shots. Screams. Orders. One of the cams went to static.

Two minutes later, War reported. "Bridge is secure."

Thirty more seconds. Pace's voice was a bit more harried. "Engineering secured."

"Good job, marines." I stood up. " Sara, you know what to do."

Walking to the back of the bridge, Sara grabbed my arm. Surprised, I didn't resist as she turned me toward her. "Take

290

care of yourself. Werga is going to try something. I can feel it."

"I'm expecting it. I hope I'm ready when it happens." I took my coin from my pocket and put it in her palm. "Hang on to this for me. I'll be back for it."

She rubbed it between her fingers before putting it in her pocket. Her eyes glistened and she bit her lip. "I'll keep it safe."

She gazed up at me. It was plain that she wanted to say more. It was just as plain that she wouldn't. My heart filled with longing. I wanted to tell her how much she meant to me. I wanted to tell her I'd be okay. I didn't.

"Thanks."

A squad of marines was waiting for me outside the access passage. I found our passengers right where we left them. Cargo bay one. "It's time."

"Then let's get it over with. The sooner you have your people back, the sooner I can get to Terran space," grumbled Werga.

The marines, and I escorted our Porcu-bear collaborators into the supply ship through a temporary airlock. We'd rigged one up just for this. I checked the jagged hole on the way through. One slip and we'd lose a lot of air. The temp seal was holding, though.

We came through just as Jay was passing the other way with two marines on stretchers. I hoped they were all right.

The cargo hold on the Porcu-bear ship was similar to ours: a big open space with lots of metal boxes in it. My men were unloading a cargo pod. The original Erethizon crew were kneeling down on the deck nearby with their hands behind their heads.

"How's it coming, Pace?"

"Fine, Captain. We'll have these hedgehogs loaded up and out of our way soon."

I left him to it. At the passage I took Werga, Yebloo, and half of her Porcu-bears forward to the bridge. The other half were escorted to engineering. The problem with an Erethizon ship is that we had to have an Erethizon crew to run it. Even if I had enough people who could read the language, we didn't often understand the context. My sister and I were the only crew members with cranial AIs. Mine would translate everything for me, but the marines had the more conventional wrist-mounted AIs. They had the same language capabilities, but they were slower. It was better to use a crew that could understand the language.

We reached the bridge and Werga assigned duties to her people. She took the captain's chair. My men scrutinized everything.

Using my AI's comm function, I contacted Pace Jones. "Sergeant, are the crew crated yet?"

"Yes, sir," he drawled, "but the patch isn't the right size."

"Get Rowdy to make another one," I advised, "but make it quick. If we take too long, the station will wonder what happened to the supply ship."

"Aye, aye."

Fifteen minutes later he signaled that the hole was patched.

"*Queen Nephanie*?"

"Here, Captain," answered Sara.

"We're all set over here. How are things on your end?"

There was a pause. "All good. We are ready to detach."

"Excellent. If all goes well, you'll hear from us in two days. Until then, set things up for a few hundred passengers."

"Will do, Captain. Good hunting."

◆◆◆

The next two days passed in nail-biting uncertainty. We monitored Werga's people in shifts. While we didn't catch them doing anything shady, it didn't mean they weren't doing it. They could have been using cultural references outside of our understanding for clever signals.

The main screen fuzzed out for the second time in an hour.

"Is this normal for Erethizon ships?"

"No," said Werga. "Something's wrong with the main AI. It's slow and keeps freezing up. Something must have happened to it during the battle."

"Tell me again how to get to the main control room."

Werga shifted in the captain's chair. "I've told you three times already."

"Tell me again."

She scowled and rolled her eyes. "After we dock, the ship will be met by two security officers. Rush them. There will be a stairwell next to the lift doors across from the airlock. Go down three levels. The doors will open up onto a three-meter wide passage about twelve meters long. At the end of the passage is a set of blast doors. They're pretty lax about security, so if you catch them by surprise, they may be open. If they know something's up, they will close the doors. I've given you the last code I remember. If they've changed it, you'll need to find some other way to get in."

For that I had a tablet containing Racy's lockpicking AI. Another tablet would override the station security protocols. "I've got it covered," I said.

She shook her quills. "If you say so. If I were you, I'd take all your men. The control office will be a tough cara-nut to crack."

I flashed her a smile. "They stay here. It's not that I don't trust you, but …"

"You don't trust her," interrupted Yebloo.

I shrugged in his direction, acknowledging his point.

"Crunch time." I motioned to the three men I was leaving on the bridge. "Watch 'em. We'll be back soon."

I made my way to the forward airlock. War 'n Pace were there with two nine-man squads of marines. We waited. On the monitor, we watched the station airlock mating with ours. Sweat trickled into my eyes. I didn't dare open my faceplate to wipe it away. With a little luck, in twenty minutes we'd have control of the station. The station controlled the planet. My father was down there. Somewhere. I hoped.

We connected to the station with a bump. The light above the hatch was blue. We waited in tense anticipation for it to turn yellow, the Erethizon color for "all clear."

Yellow.

The lock sprang open.

"Go, go, go!" War shouted hoarsely.

Four armored Porcu-bears were on the other side of the lock. They never stood a chance. My marines mowed them down in three seconds.

Ten meters. Stairs. Down three flights. Doors. Hallway. Twelve meters. The blast doors were closed. Thank gods I brought the tablet.

Sprinting. Ten meters. Eight. Five.

Bright lights. Pain. A "zinging" sound. Several of them, over and over. Blackness.

Chapter 29

True Believers

IT WAS HOT. FIERY HOT. I understood immediately what had been done to me. Once you've been hit by a plasma bolt, you never forget the experience. Reluctantly, I opened my eyes.

Werga stood off to my right, wearing a lab coat. She was typing something into a terminal. Heat washed over my body that had nothing to do with my all-over sunburn. She'd laid a trap and we'd run into it headlong.

I was going to strangle her. I didn't care if her quills pierced my hands in the process. It would be worth it.

I tried to move. Searing heat enveloped my neck, arms, and wrists. A groan of agony escaped my lips.

She looked up. "Oh good, you're awake." Her lips pulled back from her bearlike mouth. "How does it feel?"

"Hurts," I hissed.

"The sunburn or the fact that I've been playing you from the start?" She waved it away. "Doesn't matter. I want to show you a couple of things."

She turned on a wall screen. My marines. War 'n Pace were the closest to the camera. They were strapped down to tables like mine. "Your men are fine. They'll make excellent converts when we're done with them."

"Never happen." I forced out through gritted teeth.

"How little you know of the One True Way." Werga's quills flexed. "Trust me when I say that every one of them will be a true believer when we're done with them. We've had lots of practice, and the Great Urson is very persuasive."

She switched to a view of an Erethizon cruiser blasting away at an asteroid. A steady stream of gauss rounds and missiles streamed into it. "We found your garbage scow of a ship. Your stealth armor isn't as good as you think it is."

I was prepared to laugh it off, but then I realized it was the rock Sara was supposed to be hiding on, waiting for our signal. Armored plates flying away. Plates we had welded to the hull when we were pretending to be a Porcu-bear freighter. I felt sick. Not again. It couldn't happen again. Another ship, another crew, all dead because of me.

Rage exploded in my chest. "I'll kill you."

"No," said Werga. "In a few days you'll thank me for bringing Urson's blessing to you. The best part: I'm going to grant your greatest wish. You'll be reunited with your father."

A red haze filled my vision. I felt the pain acutely. I used it to fuel my anger. "I'll die first."

"Not at all." She put a pawlike palm on the side of my face. I tried to bite it, but she pulled it away. "You see, out of all of your people, you're special. You get to join us first."

She touched something outside of my vision. Blackness engulfed me.

◆ ◆ ◆

"Son?"

I knew that voice. I'd grown up with it. "Dad?"

He was there, leaning over me. He was thinner than I remembered. I reached up to touch him. He took my hand in

296

his. Tears welled up in my eyes. It was his strong, familiar grip.

I took in the room. It was an old-fashioned cottage. Wooden beams and plaster walls. The smell of fresh baked bread. Sunlight streamed through an open window. With my dad's help, I sat up. Pure white sheets clung to my body. It hurt where they touched me. The sunburn was still there, but fading.

I hugged him. For the first time in two years, I hugged my father. My breath caught in my throat. "Where are we?"

He smiled. "My home on the temple grounds. The high priest's Disciplinarians brought you here."

"Temple grounds?"

"Yes. Every morning we join the priests and revel in the glory that is Urson. The time is coming. Soon it will be our turn to spread the faith."

"My people, dad. A lot of them died so I could get here."

"And your sister?" he asked.

My vision blurred and my heart skipped a beat. "Dead."

He rubbed my back. "I'm sure you did everything you could to bring them to the light, Mark. The Great Urson can't save everyone." The image of armor plates flying out from the cloud of dust, more missiles streaking in to finish them off. That was it? The Great Urson can't save everyone? No tears? No grief? My stomach churned as I realized the full extent of what the Erethizon had done to my father.

My chest tightened. My father, King of Yale, a convert of the Porcu-bears. It pained me to say, "tell me more." Tears pricked my eyes, but I needed information if I was ever to escape this hell. Whatever it took, I would save my father, bring him back.

"Can you walk?" Dad went to a wall closet and pulled out a set of white robes. "Bob Spangle and Jenny Danby would love to see you."

Dad's friends, political allies, captured when the Erethizon invaded our home. "I'd love to meet them."

Dad put on his own white robes and we went out into the street. The village was set up like an artists' retreat. I'd seen a few back on Yale. Small, quaint homes on cobblestone streets. Lots of trees and flowers. The town itself was laid out in a circle, with the roads the spokes of a wheel. In the center was an amazing cathedral.

We walked toward it. The white and gold spires reached for the sky. As we drew closer, the stained glass windows depicted tales of Porcu-bears overcoming great trials. In every scene was a blazing sun with a serene bear face, offering guidance.

There was a town square in front of the church. People in white robes gathered in small groups. Dad waved. Mr. Spangle waved back. He said something to his companions. They turned as one and moved toward us.

"As I live and breathe. Mark, how are you? How did you get here?"

"Good, Mr. Spangle. It's a long story." I held out my hand, but the politician pulled me into an intimate hug. I stood, frozen. This was a man I only knew professionally. Yet, here he was embracing me like a long-lost child.

"I'm so happy you've joined the fold," he whispered in my ear.

It made my skin crawl.

The informal group included the leaders of every political party on Yale. Mrs. Danby gave Mr. Spangle an affectionate peck on the check. Other party leaders greeted each other in a similar way. It was surreal to see bitter enemies joking and laughing together like they were old friends.

Three Erethizon in yellow robes entered the square from the far side. Everyone stopped what they were doing and knelt with their heads bowed. I followed their example.

Once they were in the cathedral, everyone stood and chattered excitedly.

Mrs. Danby's eyes brightened. "Oh, it's almost time. I can't wait to hear Urson's great wisdom."

Moments later bells tolled. People emerged from homes and streets and joined an orderly line outside the wide double doors. I expected the background noise to increase. Instead, the gathering throng spoke in quiet, respectful whispers.

The doors opened and we filed into the cathedral. If the outside had been impressive, the inside was ten times more so. Impressive arches, dazzling colors, great and intricate art. Even the wood benches that filled the room were polished and carved, no two alike. In the back of the church stood three yellow-clad Porcu-bears. They held their arms up in greeting to their gathering parishioners. Incense filled the air, but it wasn't a smell I could identify.

We took seats near the middle of the room.

There was a large glass booth off to one side. In it were six medical beds. I had just enough time to wonder what they were for before six people were ushered in. With a start, I realized one of them was Pace Jones. Blank stares. Slack jaws. White robed acolytes strapped them down, one to a bed. The last thing the attendants did before leaving was to hook a data cable from the bed to each patient's neck. That seemed odd to me. I'd always seen Pace using a wrist AI. He hadn't had an AI implant the last time I'd seen him.

As if by some hidden cue, the entire room went silent.

I waited.

Nothing happened.

"Dad?"

He didn't respond.

I nudged him. "Dad, what's happening?"

He smiled beatifically and swayed back and forth. "Hmmm, listen son. The Great Urson is speaking to us. Hear his words of wisdom," he murmured.

Scanning the room, I realized that everyone was weaving to music I couldn't hear, except for the patients in the glass room. No sound escaped the glass, but it was clear they were screaming and writhing in agony. Pace Jones was pounding his head against the bed. Tears streamed down his cheeks.

As I struggled to grasp what was happening, I noticed an icon in the lower right corner of my vision. Racy's worm program was active. A version of Clyde was in the room.

Chapter 30

Clyde

IT WAS A NIGHTMARE. Several hundred people listened to the "wisdom" of an insane AI, among them my father and the political elite of my home world. Across the room, Pace Jones struggled against the same voice, but there was nothing he could do. He couldn't shut it out, because it was speaking directly into his brain.

I tried to imagine what it was like. Paranoid voices in your head. No way to escape them. How long would it take before I cracked under the pressure? How long had my father held out?

Worse, Clyde—no Urson—grew stronger when multiple copies of him were close together. In this church, he would be smart and powerful. A chill went down my spine. I glanced around me and copied the movements of the laypeople around me.

The sequence of events fell into place. Werga had said I was unique among my marines. I was the only one with a cranial AI. It was an advanced model, Muscat built. They expected that once Urson was loaded into my brain, he'd have no trouble controlling me. That's why I'd been strapped to the table on the station. Werga had loaded Clyde into my head using the high-speed data port on the back of my neck. She had no doubt tested it and found it working. Too much data too quickly for Racy's virus to get all at once, but it had removed it while I'd been unconscious. I swallowed hard as I realized just how close I'd come to being converted.

The Erethizon implant AIs weren't as powerful. They would require time to condition the host, wear them down until they would accept Urson's instructions without question.

I literally had the key inside my head. I could free everyone here by loading the program into their implanted Erethizon AIs. But how many could I free before Urson noticed? What would he do when he discovered people slipping from his grasp? Were the Porcu-bears also under Urson's control? What would happen if they were released?

The sermon was ending. All around me, people were coming back to themselves. Mrs. Danby put her hand over her heart. Mr. Spangle clapped. Several others joined him.

My father put a hand on my shoulder. "How was your first sermon, son?"

I forced myself to relax. "Enlightening, Dad. Urson has given me a lot to think about."

He closed his eyes in silent understanding. "Let's take a walk. I want to show you more."

We left the cathedral and ambled down a wide avenue. Along the way, he regaled me with stories from the book of Urson. I wasn't listening. I took in every detail of the village, filing it away for use later. At the edge of town, a line of posts ringed the area at eight-meter intervals. Between them was a glowing, translucent barrier ten meters tall. An energy wall.

"This shield is what keeps the darkness at bay." My dad pointed. "You see those trees? The unenlightened live there."

"Is it dangerous?"

"A little." He held two fingers a centimeter apart. "There are these small insects. Blood suckers. They resemble a Terran tick. If you get bit, you get sick. Fever, hallucinations. The savages know the villagers can cure the sickness. So they bring the infected to us. We cure them and start them on the One True Way. Everyone eventually comes to the light."

"So, anyone who came with me is probably out there?"

"Yes. We talk with them often, try to convince them to join us in the village."

"You go out there?"

He tapped a barrier post. "No, they come to us. There's nothing they can eat out there. We give them our table scraps so they don't starve. Sometimes we provide them with blankets. The Great Urson teaches us to give to those less fortunate."

"How do we get our food?"

"I'll show you." He motioned for me to follow him.

A block away we came to a large, flat plasticrete slab.

"Once a week, a transport lands here and unloads supplies. One of the other villages grows the food we eat."

"What about security?" I asked.

He gave me the boisterous laugh I remembered from my youth. "From who? Everyone inside the wall is one within the way."

"Even the people inside the glass box in the cathedral?"

"No, they're as weak as kitten snakes, between the disease and the cure. By the time those savages are strong enough to be a problem, they've joined us in the One True Way."

◆◆◆

It took me a week to map the town. There was a combination stockade and clinic just off the town square, where the new initiates were kept while they were recovering. Some people joined the village without getting sick. They were given the "cure" anyway to keep them docile.

Urson's central processing unit for the village was exactly where I expected it to be: in the cathedral.

I volunteered to be on the medical staff. During the next ten days three more "savages" were brought into the village. The process was always the same. Knock 'em out, install the new hardware, drug them for two weeks with a cure made from a local plant root. It also happened to be a powerful drug that made people susceptible to persuasion. A fellow medical volunteer called it a benzodiazepine. I was sure my sister would know … would have known … what that meant.

By now, Pace was out of the clinic. I decided he would be my first test subject. I pulled him aside after church.

"Pace."

He'd been speaking to a small group of people in the square. He turned at the sound of his name. "Captain, I'm so happy you're in the fold."

"I'm happy to see you too, Sergeant."

He gave me a hug, which I kept as brief as possible. "What can I help you with?"

"I want you to help me with an experiment."

"Anything to advance the glory of Urson," he said cheerfully.

"Great. Can you meet me at the clinic around 2200 tonight?"

"Aye, aye."

Pace met me ten minutes early. At this time of night, no one else was here. Everyone in the fold had gone to bed.

The doors weren't locked. No believer would harm the great work being performed there.

We entered and flipped on the lights.

"What can I help with?" asked Pace.

I patted the table. "Hop up here. You know the wonderful communion we experience in church every day? I'm wondering if we can make it more intense by connecting our implants directly."

"Whoa," Pace bounced from foot to foot. "We could get even closer to the divine. Betcha we could hear the thoughts of Urson himself."

"Exactly. So, I want to hook this data cable between your implant and mine. Then both of us would try to commune with Urson and see what happens."

"We should totally get the high priest in on this," insisted Pace. "He'd be so impressed."

"Tomorrow. Tonight, it's just you and me, buddy."

Pace sat on the med table. "Okay, what do you need me to do?"

"Lie back. I'm going to strap you down, just in case. There's a small chance you'll be so filled with divine energy that you'll go into convulsions."

He lay down. "Really?"

"Really."

Once I had him secured, I connected a data cable from his head to mine.

"Hey, shouldn't you be tied down tooooooooooo …"

I loaded the program into his head. Pace's teeth clenched. Every muscle and vein stood out. His face turned red as he strained against the table. He vomited. I turned his head to the side. His breath came in fits. Bile sprayed on my white robe. In under five minutes, it was over. The marine sucked in a lungful of air between coughing fits.

After he subsided, he scowled up at me. "You slugging asshat. When I get my fucking hands on you, you're worse than dead."

"Welcome back, Sergeant."

He spit another yellow glob on my robe. "Damn, Cap. There's gotta be a better way."

"I'm open to suggestions."

"Let me the fuck up."

I unstrapped him from the table. "How's your head?"

He took a swing at me. Unsteady as he was, I dodged it easily. "Easy there, big fella."

"My head feels like used asshole. Half of it wants to go play with flowers. The other half wants to stomp baby ducks."

"You'll have stomping aplenty before we're through, but I need you to pretend to like flowers for a few more days."

His lips pressed together. "I don't know if I can do it, sir."

I gave him a towel so he could wipe his mouth. "If we're going to pull this off, you're going to have to."

◆ ◆ ◆

The next day, Pace joined me and my father after church. We strolled along a shady lane back to our cottage. Well, Dad and I strolled. Pace watched every door, window, and shrub for threats. An actor he was not. I hoped no one would get curious until it was too late.

I resisted the urge to convert my father back to his old self. I wanted to, but while Urson might overlook Pace or myself, I reasoned that he'd notice if he lost the mind of a king.

"Dad, Pace and I think we can get most of the savages to join us in the village."

"You're wasting your time, son," he chided. "The outsiders only come to us when they have to."

"Is that a reason not to try?"

He chuckled to himself. "Your mom was right. Bless her soul. Ever the optimist. Of course you're welcome to try, son, but it's too late for them."

Were the Erethizon going to bomb the woods? Use the kind of biological warfare they used to destroy New Cancun? "Um, too late?"

"Didn't I tell you? A transport will arrive in a couple of days. There won't be enough time for them to join the fold," he explained. "Our vacation is over. It's time for us to return to Yale and spread the wisdom of Urson."

Two days. "Uh, wow. That's great, Dad. It will be wonderful to see the Aurora Mountains again."

He took in the small village. "I know what you mean. Orvid is a wonder, a true gem of the One True Way. But there's no place like Yale. With a little luck, we'll make it back while the magnapple trees are still in bloom."

"I want to try, dad. They won't be on this transport, but there will be another. I owe it to my friends to make one last effort to bring them to the truth," I vowed.

"All right, son. A true Prince of Yale, always thinking of what's best for the people. Don't be too disappointed when they turn you down," he cautioned.

"Thanks, Dad." I gave him a hug. "Come on, Pace. Our friends need us."

◆◆◆

Pace and I volunteered to give table scraps to the "savages." This process was a bit more structured than most of the village's activities. Volunteers gathered food scraps from each house. The scraps were then collected in a refuse bin. Anything that didn't fit was incinerated. Two more volunteers would roll the bin out into a shielded area. They would then return to the village side of the barrier.

If any outsiders were in the zone when it was time, no scraps for that day. If they took the bin, no food for three days. If they mounted an attack, nothing for a week. And so on.

A priest was required to control the barrier. We told several parishioners that we were going to try and convince the savages to join us. The responses ranged from sad smiles to gentle warnings. "So good of you to try," said Mrs. Danby with a pat on my arm.

The scraps were waiting when we arrived. A Porcu-bear underpriest activated the shielded box and Pace and I pushed the bin into place. War and a few other men were waiting a few meters away. Dave was gaunt and had several days' worth of beard growth on his chin. We crossed back to the village side of the shield and the priest activated the regular wall and deactivated the box.

War and his men approached. They were using old shirts as bags so they could carry the food to others in the woods. "Sluggin' pansy-assed traitors."

"Slug you," responded Pace.

I gritted my teeth. "Shut the fuck up, Pace. You're going to get us caught."

War's expression went blank as his eyes shifted between us.

I turned to the Porcu-bear at the barrier controls. "Honored priest, your magnificent presence strikes fear into the hearts of the unworthy. I humbly suggest that you stand over there so our efforts to shine Urson's light on the savages will be more successful."

The priest blinked, then flexed his quills. He locked the controls and moved a few steps away.

I turned back to War, who was still frowning at us.

"What are you playing at, sir?" He filled the last word with pure contempt.

"Shut the hell up, Sergeant, and listen," I commanded in a low growl. "Pace and I have a plan for getting off this miserable rock. You can either join us, or rot in the jungle. The choice is yours. If you're coming, gather as many men as you can and be back here in an hour. Claim you've been bitten by ticks or whatever."

"This is a trick."

"It is. On the Porcu-bears. I won't lie to you: the first twenty-four hours will be hell. After that, we're kissing this peace and harmony bullshit goodbye."

"Say I believe you." He jutted out his chin. "What's your plan?"

"My plan includes you being in enemy hands for a day, so that's all you get." His gaze bored into me. "What you need to decide, is whether or not you trust us."

War rubbed the back of his neck and loaded food into an old shirt. He kept glancing back at me and Pace. He trudged off without another word.

"Think he'll do it?"

"He better," said Pace, "or I'm gonna kick his ass."

◆ ◆ ◆

War and twelve men joined the village that afternoon. I felt bad about what happened to them next, but it couldn't be helped. All thirteen of them went through the conversion process. They got the full experience of a church service only once. Afterward, no one complained when Pace and I volunteered for medical to help them "see Urson's divine wisdom."

By the morning we were to leave, everything was ready to go. Pace and I joined my father for church.

My father sat next to me and put his arm around me. "Very good job bringing the savages to the light. You've earned your birthright, son. You do me proud."

"Thanks, Dad. When will the transport arrive?"

"After the service. Is everything packed?"

"I'm ready," I assured him.

Pace was as relaxed as I'd ever seen him. At a guess, pending mayhem kept him focused.

I whispered, "I never asked, Pace. What did you replace 'the cure' with?"

He grimaced and shrugged. "It was a yellow liquid. I had to improvise."

I checked to see if he was having me on. He wasn't. "Ew."

At the back of the church, the big double doors opened. Six Porcu-bears in light armor and plasma rifles strode into the sanctuary.

"Oh, slug me," I said quietly. My palms started sweating and I rubbed them against my robe.

Pace balled his fists and looked to me to tell him what to do.

What could we do? Two guards blocked the entrance. Two went to the glass cage. Two stopped right next to the bench we were sitting on. We'd been found out. How had it happened? One of War's marines? My heart pounded in my chest and I held very still.

Chapter 31

That Old Time Religion

PACE STARTED TO STAND. I put a hand on his leg. He understood the message and sat back down.

I bumped my shoulder into my father. "Dad, do you know why these guards are here?

"Yes, the priests weren't comfortable with so many new converts at once. They requested more Disciplinarians for the next couple of weeks."

Okay, they weren't on to us. That was better, but only by a small margin. Six armored and trained Erethizon soldiers were a huge complication. A few shots from their plasma rifles would knock out the whole room.

"Sir?" asked Pace.

"It only changes our priority," I assured him.

War and the other initiates entered the room. They wobbled as the priests escorted them to the glass box. I began to worry that Pace had switched the wrong medicine.

It took longer to hook up thirteen people, but soon the priests were satisfied. They exited the cell.

Next to the altar, the high priest raised his arms and the sermon started.

At first, nothing happened. I whipped my head around. With thirteen people loading a virus into an AI, the effect should be quick. But maybe War and his men weren't pretending.

Next to me, my dad swayed to soundless music. Then he slumped on top of me.

"Dad?"

As if he was the stone in the pool, a wave spread outward from us. People everywhere fell over in their seats.

"Son, I don't feel so …" Warm bile filled my lap.

I slapped Pace's arm and he moved. The temple guards scanned the cathedral in confusion.

Pace grabbed the rifle from the nearest guard and smashed it into his face plate. His partner swung his weapon, but by then I was on him. He hit me in the side and I yanked the rifle from him. It went off, firing behind me. Spinning it around I shoved it into his chest and fired it again at point blank range. As he fell, I aimed at the guards next to the cage. I pulled the trigger and both dropped at the same time. Pace had hit one of the two at the door at the same time I did.

Guards down, Pace and I systematically mowed down priests. All around us, people convulsed. I raced toward the raised dais, trying not to slip on yellow puddles.

I pulled the high priest off the altar where he'd collapsed and accessed the terminal beneath him.

A speaker sputtered, "Wha-wha-what's happening?"

"Right turn, Clyde. Change of plans." I shot the main CPU and electricity arced along its surface.

Pace was at the glass box "Main computer core down," I called.

"The men are free," he responded.

War and his marines wasted no time arming themselves with the guards' plasma rifles and taking defensive positions around the church.

The stench in the room was getting to me. Stalking toward my dad, I pulled him up. He was still shaking. "Muh, muh, muh-more guards."

"Where?"

"Priesssts' quartersss."

"Pace, there are more Porcu-bears in the block of houses east of here."

"On it," he responded.

Gradually, everyone came back to themselves. As more people recovered, they helped their comrades. I found myself surrounded by politicians.

"Dad, everyone, welcome back. I'm sure you have a lot of questions. That will have to wait. Unless I'm misinformed, there's a transport arriving in less than an hour. We all have to be on it. Please stay calm and organized. Get into clean robes."

I moved to go, but my father yanked me back around. "Not so fast. How did you do it? You have to tell us."

He wasn't going to let it go. "I gave Urson a virus, or to be more specific, a worm. It ate the AI program out of your heads. We discovered Urson in my ship's systems a few months ago. He was calling himself Clyde. We wrote a program to get rid of him. That code was still in my implant when I was captured."

"The priests," Mr. Spangle pointed to the altar, "did you…"

"Plasma rifles," I pointed to the oversized weapon in my hands. "They'll be out for half a day at least, and in unbelievable pain for a lot longer. I also shot the church computer core, so that's never coming back. Now, sire and esteemed senators, I must insist. The Porcu-bears want to send us back home. We shouldn't be late."

With some effort, we managed to get everyone redressed and waiting by the landing pad before the transport arrived. The ship was huge, but little more than a box with engines. We kept everyone well away from the exhaust as it landed.

The boarding ramp extended and two armored temple guards marched to the end of it. I approached them and they pointed plasma rifles at me.

"Who are you?" asked a gravel-filled voice. "Where are the temple guards? Why isn't the cathedral responding?"

"Oh honored acolyte," I gushed, "the high priest mentioned he was having trouble communing with the Great Urson during this morning's sermon. He and the temple guards are cloistered in the parish hall. Dave," War perked up at the use of his first name, "can you take this honored and enlightened soul to them?"

"Yes, of course. Follow me." He led them behind a nearby building. I heard two distant zings.

There was a Porcu-bear at the top of the ramp, a shiny, black tablet computer in his hands. Pace and I greeted him.

"What's your name, Terran?" he asked without preamble.

"Mark Martin." I leaned over as if to get a better look at his screen.

Pace slipped behind him and stuck a data cable into the port on the back of his neck.

The reaction was violent. The Porcu-bear backhanded Pace into a bulkhead. He reached for me, and I ducked and dodged. I came up in a fighting stance, but the clerk was writhing on the ground. Quills extended and flattened all over his body in waves as he curled into the fetal position.

"You okay, Pace?"

He coughed and brushed blood from puncture marks on his chest. "I'll live."

I helped him up and made a chopping motion. Marines hidden in the crowd stormed the ship. "Don't shoot any equipment," I warned. "We need it to fly."

Following two of the marines, we made it to the cockpit. Two Erethizon were there, holding their hands up. "Jack 'em," I told the marines.

My marines removed them from the cockpit and inserted data cables into the ports on their necks. In here, with all the sensitive equipment, we didn't dare risk a plasma bolt. Sitting, I took in the controls. I let my AI translate anything that was labeled. I knew right away I was in trouble. In addition to the fact that the controls were built for an alien, they were built for an alien much taller and wider than me. The controls I could identify weren't in intuitive places. This was going to take me a lot longer than I thought. As far as I knew, I was the only pilot among the Terrans.

Touching the throttle, Clyde's voice come from the center console. "You are not authorized to fly this vessel."

"Oh Clyde, you're in here too. I should have guessed."

"You'll never get off this planet alive. I've notified the me aboard the station. Your only hope …"

His voice trailed off as I found a data port and plugged myself in. That did the trick. As the version of Urson living in the cockpit died, my internal AI found an e-manual and translated it.

I was immersed in my work when I felt a tap on my shoulder.

"Sir," said Pace, "you're gonna want to see this."

Pace led me outside the ship. Several Porcu-bear guards in armor were lying in a row as if they were sleeping. The clerk and the two pilots were awake and kneeling on the ground. My men held rifles on them.

"What is it?"

"Please, you have to take me with you. I can fly the transport. You need me," the pilot on the left pleaded.

The one on the right said something in Erethizon my AI translated as "rotting meat unfit for food."

I hunched down on my knees. "Why would you help us?"

"I can't do it." His quills fluttered. "I can't have Urson in my head anymore. He's always there."

"Traitor!" the other pilot spat.

"No, we aren't a race. We aren't even a religion. We're that monster's slaves. Please, take me with you. I don't care if you throw me in a cell for the rest of my days. At least my mind will be my own."

The implications of his words washed over me. "I can fly that ship," I lied, "but I could use a copilot. If you can get us to the station, we'll take you with us when we leave."

The pilot's name was Zeruba. With his help we were able to get the transport in the air half an hour later.

As we were lifting off, he told me, "It's been a while since I've flown on manual. Forgive me if I'm a bit rusty."

I scanned the monitors and watched the pilot closely. "No problem. Can you answer a question for me? How long has Urson been around?"

"They put him in my head when I joined the military. Before that, he was just the deity the priests told us about. I don't know where he came from or how long he's been around."

War stood in the doorway to the cockpit. "How long until we reach the station?"

"A couple of hours," I said. "War, bolster our ranks. Find people with skills. Specifically, we need the ability to run a space station and a ship when we find one."

"Aye, aye," said War. "It will give my men something to do."

"Be ready for hostiles. Urson told me he'd warned the station before I removed him."

"He didn't," said Zeruba. "Communication with the station has been flaky for the past two weeks. Systems have been going out at random. Now they're mostly out. Comms were the first thing to go."

"Is that normal?" asked War.

"No," said the pilot, "but it's been that way ever since they took you down to Orvid."

I checked the flight path. Zeruba was good. "How many settlements are on the planet?"

"Five. Four more are under construction. Each settlement houses the leaders of a conquered world. They're kept there until Urson is happy with their reeducation, usually a couple of Terran standard years. Then he ships them back and brings more to be converted."

I grew more confident when we weren't hailed during our approach to the station. The downside was that the station wasn't the only thing up there. An Erethizon freighter was docked. It was likely our ride home. A thousand kilometers out were two Porcu-bear frigates and a battle cruiser.

"Tell me you have a plan for that," said Zeruba.

"I have a plan for that." Half of a plan. Maybe a third of a plan. Did hoping and praying count as a plan?

"We'll dock here." Zeruba pointed to a section of the station. A yellow triangle appeared in the HUD around the docking ring.

"How do we get to the control center?"

"One level up from the docks. The stairs don't have a door on that level. You have to take the lift."

"No good. The lift will have security cameras. My people will get trapped."

The pilot flexed his quills. "You're right, of course. I don't know of any other way to get there."

"Maintenance tubes?" I offered.

He clapped. "Yes, the access hatches are on every level near the floor. I don't know if they connect to the control center or if there is any security in them."

If it were me, I wouldn't connect them to the control center. That idea was out. When in doubt, give the job to the marines. War had it figured out in ten minutes.

◆ ◆ ◆

We docked. Once I assured Zeruba that I had no intention of hurting anyone, he was willing to go along with us. We met the customs agents at the lock and invited them aboard. Once they were inside and away from the station's hookups, we jacked them.

Zeruba changed clothes with one of them and Pace joined us as we crossed to the lift.

Inside the lift, Zeruba pressed the button for the control center. The panel asked him for a security code. He entered one. Nothing happened. This process was repeated twice.

I glanced at Pace as I wiped the sweat from my eyes. He appeared relaxed, with his feet planted wide and his hands on his hips. I tried to mimic his calm.

"Code?" asked a voice from the panel.

Zeruba gazed at the camera above the screen. He tapped his ear.

"Code?"

Zeruba repeated the gesture.

"Terrans aren't allowed up here," the voice insisted.

The pilot flexed his quills in frustration.

The Erethizon mumbled something my AI translated as "stupid beast," and the lift moved.

The doors opened and a uniformed Porcu-bear said, "I said …"

He didn't get any further than that, as Pace shot him with a plasma rifle. Like me, he'd hidden the bulky thing between his legs under his robes.

We sprang into the room and Pace shot the two men to the right while I picked off the one to the left. Thankfully, neither of us hit sensitive controls.

Scanning the consoles, I waited for my AI to translate the languages.

"I can't read any of this," complained Pace from across the room.

Attitude jets, environmental settings. "We're searching for emergency controls, Pace. Blue writing."

Pace examined the writing in front of him. "Why blue and not red?"

"It's cultural," I explained. "Erethizon use blue and yellow the same way we use red and green."

Zeruba bobbed his head. "You're looking for hull breach, right?"

"Yeah."

The pilot crossed next to Pace and punched a large blue button. A low whistle sounded and there was a distant clang of pressure doors. Monitor screens confirmed that the station was on lockdown.

Crossing to that console, I sat. "Thanks. This is the security position, and I can use these commands to override the doors, right?"

"Yes."

I unlocked the airlock for the transport. "Okay, let's get our people in here. We need to cut off station security. There are three levels below the docks. We need to take over the freighter and find some way to distract the warships."

"Free as many of my people as possible," Zeruba said.

On the monitor, War and his men were getting into the lift. "We're more concerned with getting away, Zeruba."

"They deserve a chance at freedom," demanded the pilot.

I pounded the workstation in frustration. "Fine, if you can find a way to do it safely."

The lift arrived and my men spilled out. "Four people to run things here. War, you take the station security center. I'm sure you remember where it is. Pace, your team takes the freighter."

There was a chorus of aye ayes.

With things mostly under control, I plugged my AI into the security station. I found Racy's worm program hard at work. As I'd expected, when they had tried to load Urson into my head, the code had infected the station. It wasn't everywhere yet, but it had the upper hand. The station AI had been fighting back, but it was a losing battle. Every node and server it lost made it weaker, less able to defend itself.

I disconnected and surrendered my seat to a villager who was familiar with station security. My AI didn't have the right protocols to interact with the Porcu-bear programs. The best it could do was identify files, read text, and see running executables.

I stepped behind the woman at the seat we'd identified as comms. Understandably, it was lit up like a Founders' Day parade.

"What are you telling them?" I asked.

She gave me a nervous smile. "The Porcu-bear equivalent of 'all circuits are busy, please try again later.'"

"Have the warships said anything?"

She huffed. "No, thank gods."

There was one screen open that looked a bit odd. "What's that?"

"Don't know," she admitted. "Something the Erethizon were viewing before we got here. From the look of it, they didn't understand it either."

"Is it coming from inside the station?"

The comm operator pressed a couple of keys. "No, local space. It's in the background static, but too weak to pinpoint. Twelve long and short notes."

"Let me hear it."

The speaker next to her station crackled and I listened to the broadcast. It went through three times before I understood the message. The room spun and I found myself on my knees.

Through the rushing in my ears I heard. "Sir! Are you okay?"

"I'm better than okay. We're saved. We have everything we need to get home."

The woman quirked an eyebrow. "It's a message?"

"Old Terran Morse code," I laughed. "It says … 'dork.'"

Chapter 32

Exodus

Using the same background radiation, I was able to contact the *Queen Nephanie*. Soon we were set up for an encrypted tight-beam.

"Mark?" asked Sara.

It was like a great load had been taken off my shoulders. "Sara, you have no idea how good it is to hear your voice."

"How do I know it's really you?" Her voice stuttered and squeaked a little, like she hoped what she was hearing was true.

Good question. How could I prove myself? "I gave you a coin, before I left the ship. It's got a picture of a sun on one side of it."

"Definitely you. I had my doubts when Dr. Martin suggested the code. Are you hurt? Are you really on the space station?"

"Yeah," I breathed a sigh of relief, "with all the Yale political prisoners. We're in control over here, but we can't leave while the escorts are sitting off our bow. Can you create a distraction?" Just hearing her voice filled me with hope. I couldn't wait to be with her again. It didn't matter anymore that she wanted us to just be friends.

"Can do. Trent and Rowdy have a plan."

◆◆◆

At the edge of the system, the space station's mass detectors picked up a ship exiting R-drive. Popping the bubble inside of a system created a large gravity footprint as the negative energy bled off. It was why we always exited R-drive outside of the system.

Scanners soon identified the mass of the object as too big to be a freighter. It had to be a battle cruiser. Though it was still too far away for a visual due to light lag, the response from the escort fleet was instant. The Porcu-bear cruiser and one of the frigates accelerated to meet the intruder.

I pumped a fist. "Yes! It will take them three days to get out there."

The tech at the scanners shook his head. "Yeah, but only a day and a half, two at the most, before they figure out it's a decoy. Maybe less, if they start wondering why it isn't moving."

"Incoming message from the cruiser," said the woman at comms. "'Finish loading the prefa, but don't let the freighter leave until we get back.' The dictionary identifies a prefa as a small Erethizon mammal similar to a lemming."

"Cheer up, friends. We're almost there."

Someone cleared his throat at the lift. War was waiting for me.

Crossing the room, I joined him. "Excuse me," I told the room, "it appears I have some details to take care of."

He pressed the button for the security level. "We have control of the freighter and full control of the station."

The lift stopped, but then started up again.

"Things like that keep happening," he continued, "but they're happening less and less. Zeruba has taken it upon himself to convert as many of his fellows as he can. The ones that are calling him a traitor are in a cargo hold. The few that have told him they want to join his crusade are in a conference room. There are about ten of them. Don't know if they're honest or not. I'm not going to trust them."

"What did you want me to see?"

We arrived at our destination and the door opened up. Pace and three marines had Werga and Yebloo tied to chairs.

I explored Yebloo's features. His head wove from side to side until his whole body began to shiver. His color went from blue to purple. Odd sounds burbled up from his fishlike mouth.

I swiveled my gaze to Werga. "Well, he knows how screwed you both are."

"You don't scare me, Terran." All of her quills stood up. "I saw the truth. Urson has shown it to me. You may have this station, but there are warships nearby. They will destroy us rather than let you go free."

"They're a bit distracted at present. It won't last long, but it'll be enough for us to get away. There are a lot of people who will pay good credits to get their hands on a Porcu-bear spy. Anubis is high on the list. Even with Yebloo to help you, we still won."

"How did you get past him?"

"Easy," I answered. "I didn't know everything. The captain of my marines was in charge of tactics after I left the ship. You never saw him, so you never knew."

Werga scoffed. "Even if you do escape, your freedom will be short-lived. Anubis is a fool. His days are finite. The Confederacy? It only cares about lining its own pockets. We will destroy them from within by exposing their corruption and lies. The Muscat are too preoccupied with their own cleverness. They will not see the true danger before it is too late."

"And the Dru?" I prompted.

"We have you to thank for that, son of Yale." Her mouth opened, showing rows of sharp teeth. "The fish have returned to the reef. Better to join the frequa you know than face a sea of unseen monsters. The Erethizon roar with the one voice of Urson."

"Where is the voice of your god now? Can't hear him?" I pressed. "I know why he has forsaken you. He fears me."

◆◆◆

"Uh oh," Pace pointed to the screen. "They're slowing down. The bears have figured out the honey pot is only tree sap."

I reached for the coin in my pocket. My brain hiccupped a little when it wasn't there. "Then it's time. Signal Nephie."

On the screen, a freighter a hundred meters longer than the frigate appeared out of nowhere. From thirty thousand kilometers out, six missiles streaked toward the Porcu-bear warship.

The frigate pivoted to return fire. This pointed the smaller vessel's aft end toward us. In naval terms, we were in the perfect position for a stern rake.

I took a breath and let it out. "Fire."

Two missiles and the station's defense cannons lashed out. Without AI targeting, the first gauss rounds went wide.

"Sorry sir," came the stressed voice of my weapons tech.

Realizing he was under attack from two directions, the Erethizon captain swung his ship vertical to the station.

The blue line indicating our shots stitched across the rear of the ship twice before it completed the maneuver.

A dozen missiles spat at Nephie and at us.

In my combat experience, I'd always either been in a fighter or mobile ship. A space station couldn't get out of the line of fire. But on the bright side, a space station is built to be a bunker.

The weapons tech activated our electronic warfare. Half a dozen of the warheads went astray. My gunner was able to shoot down three more of them. The remaining trio impacted the shields.

Atomic fire blinded us. The screen went black.

It didn't stay that way. In a few seconds it was back. Checking the status display, I saw that our shields were down 20 percent. As I watched, the percentage began ticking up again.

"Keep firing," I ordered. The weapons tech jolted in his seat and pressed the firing stud. On the screen, Nephie shot down four missiles. Then an invisible hand swatted seven more aside. They each arced in wild directions before detonating. One hit her shields, which held.

The frigate launched one more volley with similar results. Then we scored a hit amidships. The microsingularity missile crushed that section of hull. But the MSM didn't break her back. It started a chain reaction. Brief gouts of flame occurred seemingly at random along her hull. The last one blew out what must have been the bridge.

"What happened?" asked the woman at the comms.

"We may never know for sure. At a guess, we hit the ordinance locker, and the explosion followed the missile feed throughout the ship."

"Sir, look!"

On-screen, two blue dots moved toward the station.

The weapons tech slid into the scan console. "The computer identifies the new contacts as Porcu-bear battle cruisers. They're eighteen hours out."

My fist erupted in pain. I realized I'd punched the workstation. "Those, sneaky, spiky, slugging bastards. Comms, tell the *Queen Nephanie* to dock ASAP. We need to bug out now."

◆◆◆

"Are you sure you want to do this?"

Zeruba took my hand in his. "I understand this is a gesture of friendship among your people."

"It is," I admitted.

The crowd pressed past us to get into Nephie's lock, but they gave me and the Porcu-bear pilot a small circle of space.

"Along with your friendship, I accept the freedom you have given me. I am grateful that you would take me with you. However, I cannot abandon my people."

"What will you do?"

"Honor my promise to you," he offered gravely. "The station can dictate the lesson on the planet. Tomorrow's sermon will free many from Urson's paws."

"They will come for you," I pointed out.

"We will be gone. The true gods have seen fit to provide us with a ship. We'll find a new home free of the voices. Free others."

"Good luck, my friend."

His quills feathered outward in a wave and he shambled off.

"He's got quite a challenge in front of him."

I bumped an elbow into the man beside me. "And we don't, Dad?"

He put his arm around my shoulders and gave me a squeeze. "You did good, son."

"Thanks, but we're not out yet."

"You've worked a miracle. Maybe the gods will help you out with the next one." He chuckled. "You named your ship after my mother?"

"Yeah," I admitted.

"Why?"

"Would you want to get on her bad side?"

He sucked in a breath through his teeth. "I see your point."

"Sara set up quarters for you in officer country." I raised an eyebrow. "You won't have to share a hold with four hundred whiny politicians."

"Is it too much to hope that they learned a little tolerance and understanding on Orvid?"

"Yes."

He sighed. "Then I'll have to unite them around a common cause, and browbeat the opposition."

The last of the villagers hurried to the airlock. I punched my dad lightly. "Yale forever," I said and I entered the ship.

Hayden was at the hatch controls. "Lock up as soon as they get aboard and join us on the bridge."

"Aye, aye, and welcome home, sir."

While I climbed the ladders to the bridge, Pace's voice echoed up from the cargo bays. "No, there isn't another bathroom, and in here it's called the head."

In officer country, Sara was standing next to the door to my quarters. "Sir, if you'll step in here. There are a couple of things we need to take care of before we get underway." Her voice was all business, her face a mask of professionalism.

"Sure." I opened the door and stepped inside. "What—mmpf!"

The door slammed shut and her warm lips found mine. Momentary shock gone, I pressed her bodily against the door and kissed her back. My heart raced. Her hand in my hair, another on my chest. I put my arm around her waist and pulled her to me. The intensity of it surprised me. I loved this woman and never wanted to let her go.

I reached up her chest and cupped her breast. She kissed me with renewed energy. I took hold of her hair. Pulling her head to the side I nibbled and kissed my way down her neck.

Her breath came in gasps. "No. Stop."

"What?"

She grabbed my robe with both hands. Her eyes promised passion. "Right now, there's nothing I want more, but …"

"Right. Porcu-bears. Damn."

She rubbed her lips with her fingers. "About earlier."

"You changed your mind?" I suggested.

"Yeah," she panted. "I don't care. I may lose you tomorrow, but I don't want to miss today."

We took a minute to get ourselves under control. I changed into my own clothes while she watched. Once I was dressed, she took my hand in hers. I felt my coin hot in her palm. One quick kiss and we were out the door.

We entered the bridge with as much composure as I could muster. I knew that was important to Sara. Hayden looked up briefly from his console, but went right back to his work.

Mimi watched us for a moment before a sly grin crept across her face.

"How's our exit, Mimi?" I asked.

"Sir, the Porcu-bears have the acceleration advantage. Rowdy says we have moderate hull damage port side, aft. The second volley slipped through. Engines are unaffected, but stealth is compromised."

"How's the curve?" I pressed.

"We'll stay ahead of them if we leave now and nothing gets in our way."

"Nephie, do you agree?"

"Yes, Captain. Ms. Jaylen's numbers are acceptable."

I settled into my chair. "Well then, what are we hanging around here for? Sara, give Zeruba our respects. Hayden, release docking clamps. Back off dead slow when we're free."

◆◆◆

A day later, we were passing over the system's asteroid belt. The Porcu-bears were still closing. We'd be in open space and able to use the R-drive well before we'd be in their missile envelope.

"What's the word from below, Mimi?"

"Trent and the boys are keeping the civvies in line. They haven't complained about half rations yet." She pulled up a star map. "Should we stop in Cassini or New Hawaii to pick up supplies?"

"Maybe." I considered what might happen in a Terran system. Would any of the politicians break away to declare asylum? Would the Confederacy take them in? I'd have to drop them off somewhere. "Nephie, how are you handling the strain on your systems? There must be a large number of requests."

"The number of requests is within acceptable limits," intoned the AI. "But there have been repeated requests for the parts printer. Our guests are not happy that engineering has pri …"

The star field flipped ninety degrees. Alarms filled the bridge.

"Woah, Nephie," exclaimed Hayden.

"High energy laser. Evasive action required." Nephie reported calmly.

My star chart was replaced by battle displays. "Where did it come from?"

"A fourth battle cruiser." Nephie placed a targeting square around it and drew in lines where the laser was striking.

"Return fire!"

Sara appeared from the ladder and took her place at the tactical station. "Firing."

In the holo-tank, our weaving snake intersected with the base of the laser lines. They stopped coming toward us, only to be replaced by the cruiser's own bobbing snake and missile icons.

"Why aren't we using the gravity gun?" I demanded.

"Something we discovered in the last battle. Its range is short. Only useful within twelve thousand kilometers," answered Sara.

In the tank, I saw that they were twenty thousand klicks away. "Damn. Give them two volleys."

"Six fish are away," yelled Sara.

"Close with them."

"Closing," squeaked Hayden.

Gauss rounds continued to impact our shields, to little effect. Missiles homed in on us. The gravity gun caught them in a miniature black hole and they imploded.

"Second six!" roared Sara.

We spat out more of our missiles. In the tank, the cruiser battered our warheads. Three of them hit their shields. Our microsingularity missiles did significant damage to the shields, crushing sections of armor. It wasn't enough to slow them down.

"Another volley incoming." Sara and Nephie were less effective against this one, and two missiles exploded against our shields. The indicator displayed shield strength down to 34 percent. Another one struck and the number dropped to eight.

"The shields won't take another hit," warned Sara.

"Range?" I barked.

"Thirteen," trilled Sara.

"Hayden!"

"Aye, aye," he screamed.

"In range," confirmed Sara, "firing G-gun."

On the holo-tank, the hull of the cruiser deformed. Bursts of fog puffed out as atmosphere escaped. The cruiser flipped end over end, seeking to escape our invisible grasp. It gave us a perfect shot at the drive section. The engine crumpled in on itself for scant seconds. Then it simply disintegrated with the entire aft section of the ship.

I let out a breath I hadn't realized I'd been holding. "Mimi, Hayden?"

"Back on course," answered Hayden.

Mimi didn't respond.

I stared at her. "Mimi?"

"I'm sorry, sir. I've run the numbers twice." She bit her lip. "We're not going to make it."

◆◆◆

We streaked toward the edge of the system. It was a race we were going to lose, but I'd be damned if I didn't try to win. The two closest battle cruisers would reach us at about the same time. The two escort vessels we'd sent on a wild goose chase halfway around the system were doggedly chasing us. If we managed to evade the closer ships, they wouldn't be a threat. If … no, when the nearer ships caught us, there was a good chance there wouldn't be enough of us left for the other two to worry about.

"Sir?"

"Yes, Hayden?"

His brow furrowed. "Why did the Erethizon stop shooting at us with the laser?"

"The same reason why most warships don't use them," I explained. "Sure, they do damage at light speed, but they're fragile."

"Incoming message from Commander Grova."

"Which ship is the signal coming from, Nephie?"

In the holo-tank, the targeting square around the furthest cruiser flashed. He'd been on the ship assigned to escort us back to Yale.

"Accept hail, Nephie." A tone told me the connection was made. "Grova, you've come to see me off. I'm honored."

His gravelly voice responded, "Brave words, Mark Martin. My captain assures me that we will catch you before you can escape."

"The day's not over." I tried to sound confident, but even to me it sounded forced.

"Stop this madness," he chided. "You lived in a village on the surface. Were you mistreated in any way?"

"Other than being told what to think and how to behave?"

"That is the purpose of religion," Grova remarked, "to guide people to live healthy, productive, and harmonious lives."

"Most people have a choice, Grova."

"The flock needs a stern shepherd."

In the holo-tank, I saw we were minutes from action. "Terrans make lousy sheep. If you'll excuse me Grova, I have some wolves to take care of. End comm, Nephie."

"Comm ended."

"Sara, how many missiles do we have left?"

She consulted her displays. "Twenty-six."

Four volleys of six plus a bit. My crew looked at me expectantly. "Mimi, their powered envelope is thirty-three thousand klicks away. When they hit thirty-five, signal Hayden to flip us. I want the initiative. Sara, fire missiles as soon as we close the range. Hayden, get us in close, while avoiding as many hits as possible. Let Nephie help you, she may see opportunities you don't."

The seconds ticked away. In the holo-tank, red icons inched closer to the yellow sphere of our missile envelope. Just before they touched, Mimi signaled.

On screen, the star field spun.

"Fish away," called Sara.

"They're maneuvering," warned Mimi, "Slugging bitches. Slowing. They're keeping their distance."

I should have expected they'd learned their lesson from our last fight.

"They're positioning for a broadside," shouted Sara. "Twelve, no-twenty-four incoming. Rolling. They've doubled down. Forty-eight."

"Do what you can," I urged. "Hayden, forget about getting close. Evasive all the way."

Sara pulled every trick in the book. Gauss cannons created a wall of metal. She dropped our missiles in the path of theirs. The gravity guns sucked them in or knocked them off target. Eleven impacted our shields.

Alarms screamed. Smoke poured from workstations. The smell of burnt circuit boards. Lights flickered and came back on. The forward screen went to static, but the holo-tank stayed on.

"Damage report."

"Dead stick," panted Hayden.

"Rerouting," sang Nephie.

Sara slammed her fists into the console. "I'm down to two gauss cannons, one gravity gun, and two missile tubes."

Hayden's fingers danced along the controls. "Got it. We can move again."

"I've got Rowdy," said Sara. "In-system drive down to 20 percent. Shields are gone. Multiple nodes are fried. R-drive is offline. Hull …" She paled. "Cargo bay four is open to space."

Just like that, four hundred souls had died. Some would have been sucked out. Others would suffocate and freeze, their blood boiling in their veins. How many of them were people I knew?

We weren't going to win. Surrender? I'd be consigning eight hundred and fifty people to the living hell of Urson. Pretend to surrender? I could lure them in. Use the remaining gravity gun to kill one of the cruisers. The other one would kill everyone else.

"Play dead," I ordered. "Cut the drives and all visible lights. If we're going down, we're taking them with us."

Chapter 33

Firecat

IN THE HOLO-TANK, THE TWO cruisers approached. At five thousand meters they opened up with gauss cannons and shredded the remaining gravity gun.

Slugging Porcu-bears. That left only two options.

"Open comm to engineering. Rowdy, they took out the last gravity gun. Can we overload the reactor, take one of the ships with us?"

His gravelly voice sounded weary. "It would take me two hours to rig it up. After what Aasha did to the *Leo*, I wanted to make sure it couldn't happen again."

"It was a thought. Thanks old friend. Mark out." It felt like our hope was being leeched out of the hull. "Open comm to Trent."

"Captain Tren'groat is unavailable," reported Nephie. "He has been injured and is in critical condition. Dr. Martin has him in medical."

And the hits keep coming. "Open comm to War 'n Pace."

"Yes, Captain?" said War.

"Gentlemen, we're about to be boarded by two cruisers. I need you to make that as costly as possible."

"Can do," asserted Pace.

"Thanks guys. However it turns out, it's been a pleasure serving with you."

"Oorah, Captain," said War.

Orders given, it was all over but the wait. A touch on my shoulder. Placing my hand on Sara's, I kissed it. Her eyes shone. They mirrored my feelings. We'd never have the opportunity to explore what we could be. I saw understanding in those soft brown orbs.

The cruisers bracketed us and fired grappling cables. Hatches opened and Erethizon shock troops spilled out into open space, jetting toward us.

In the holo-tank, a dozen new contacts appeared, the closest only ten thousand klicks away.

Gauss rounds tore into the defenseless Porcu-bears.

Sara jumped back to the tactical station. "New contacts. One battleship, seven cruisers, four frigates. Transponders read as defense fleets from Grey, Ajax, and Butcher's World."

The Erethizon cruisers released their lines, abandoning their boarding parties to their fates.

"Hayden, spin and give us whatever thrust you can. Don't let those slugging hedgehogs aboard."

"Aye, aye!"

We corkscrewed away, putting distance between us and the Erethizon ships. Gauss cannons continued to impact their shields. At five thousand meters, the defense force cruisers opened up with missiles.

It was overkill. The Porcu-bears attempted to evade, but had little relative velocity to work with. When the glare cleared, the only thing that remained of the Erethizon were pieces of ship spiraling away in random directions.

"We're being hailed by the cruiser *Firecat*, Captain."

"Thanks, Nephie. Put them through."

The forward view screen was out, but we had audio. A familiar voice came from the overhead. *"Queen Nephanie, are you in need of assistance?"*

"Captain Kane," I responded, "your assistance is most welcome. Glad you could join the party."

"Couldn't let you have all the fun. What's the situation?"

"There should be a Porcu-bear cruiser and frigate in system. They're probably turning quill right about now." Bringing up a holo-screen, I pulled up a copy of our sensor logs and sent them to Kane. "As far as we know, they are the only remaining hostiles in system. That said, we've been jumped by hidden bogies twice now."

"They've gone vertical to the plane of the ecliptic," said Kane. "We'll give chase, but they'll be able to jump before we get to them. What about the space station?"

On screen, I saw three of her cruisers break off and give chase. She was right though: Grova would jump before she got there. "The station is in rebel hands. It's a long story. Don't fire on them."

"You promised me a reeducation camp," she pressed. "Tell me you found one."

"Five," I assured her, "all on the planet. Congratulations, you're about to become even more of a hero."

"Thanks for the bread crumbs, Martin."

"Space is a big, empty place. I'm glad you found the buoy." Then, more earnestly, "Thanks for saving my ass."

"On that score we're even. *Firecat* out."

I had to see with my own eyes how bad things were below. "Hayden, all stop. Sara, can you take over here? I want to check on Trent."

"Of course, Captain. I have the bridge."

On the way to medical, I passed by crew berthing. From there I could see down the spine. Sealing foam intruded into the passage at odd intervals. The telltale above cargo bay four glowed red. My chest tightened, and I forced myself to continue down the ladder.

Medical was full again. Sophie was by Trent's bed. She caught my eye as I approached and shook her head. Trent wasn't going to make it. That must be why she hadn't told Trent's siblings to leave. Tracy, Trey, Trippy, and Trevor were crowded around him. They looked up at me as I approached. They knew it, too.

As I reached his side, I realized the lump under the sheet that covered him was too small. Half his body was gone. A dozen or so tubes and wires were the only things keeping him with us.

His eyes fluttered open. He pulled a tube from his throat. His brothers and sister tried to stop him, but he waved them down. "Sir, I apologize." His small body was wracked with a coughing fit. He recovered a bit and spoke again. "I wasn't able to rescue the prisoners. Werga and Yebloo are dead."

I took his remaining hand in mine. "I'm sure you did everything you could to save them."

"Yes, sir." He struggled to sit up, but couldn't. He winced in pain. "Tell the queen I did my best."

"I will."

"And, Mark, it was …" he took several short breaths in a row, then let them out with a shudder, "… a pleasure serving with you."

"It was my pleasure as well."

Sophie held the breathing tube in front of him.

Trent nodded and let her put it back in his mouth.

I left Trent in the company of his family. My sister gave my hand a squeeze at the hatch. I couldn't meet her eyes. She had many more patients so I left her to her work. I walked morosely back to my cabin. I checked to make sure my father wasn't on the casualty list, and then I let myself cry.

◆ ◆ ◆

Kane was willing to give us some food and raw materials. It turned out to be a fair exchange. She only had standard parts printers on her ships and our industrial printer could make a few things she couldn't make for herself.

Grova escaped the system. It was a week to Louange or Loben, so we figured we had twice that before reinforcements arrived. Plenty of time for an evacuation.

Kane was a bit skeptical about the Porcu-bear rebels on the station. Her skepticism was somewhat relieved when they were willing to give her a tour, and even more so when they allowed her techs to examine the hardware.

Ten days later, we were mostly repaired and back in bubble space. I had been negotiating and organizing for days and felt wrung out. I was looking forward to sleep and the limited problems of my own little universe for five weeks.

Of course, that's when my father wanted to talk.

"Captain, His Majesty King George would like to speak with you."

Already in bed, I wasn't in the mood to talk. Still, he was my dad. "Thanks Nephie. Put him through, audio only."

"Hey son, can I drop by your cabin for a nightcap? You've been so busy doing captainy stuff, we haven't had any father-son time."

"Thanks Dad, but I'm already turned in. We can talk tomorrow, I promise. Nephie has my schedule."

"Yes, that AI of yours is amazing," he observed. "She asked what temperature I wanted my quarters, and what kind of tea I liked."

"Yeah, Dad. We're lucky to have her, but be careful. She'll talk your ear off about philosophy and psychology if you let her."

"Really?"

"Oh yeah." A thought occurred to me. "You should talk to her about political science. She's already read Machiavelli, Confucius, and Karl Marx. Her questions are beyond me."

"Hmmm, maybe later." My father sighed. "What I wanted to talk to you about was cargo bay four. Don't think I haven't noticed that you avoid the topic. You need to talk to someone about it."

All those dead people. My fault. One third of the refugees aboard Nephie. They had depended on me to keep them safe, and I failed them. It was hard to breathe every time my mind wandered to the memory. So cold. Suffocating. "I promise I'll talk to someone."

"No one could have done a better job than you. Not me. Not Admiral Barnes. No one. And I know how much you respected Greg Barnes."

He was right, but I couldn't bring myself to believe it. "Yeah Dad, but he wasn't here. It was me. They all died because of me. I'll get over it. I have to, but it will take time."

"Okay. Just talk to someone," he repeated. "Maybe that Sara girl, your first officer. She's smart. Good head on that one."

"Good night, Dad."

"Good night, son."

The connection closed and I stared at the ceiling. The dim light of the clock bathed the room in a soft green glow. It wouldn't be so bad if I didn't see their faces every time I closed my eyes. Frozen in horror. Desperately clinging to life. Trent in medical, half of his body torn away.

A chill swept through me, then a warm hand was placed on my chest, chasing the chills away. "Your father's right."

"About what?"

"Everything." Sara's soft eyes found mine in the half light. Her hand traveled up my chest to my neck and settled on my face. "Listen to your first officer. She knows what's best for you."

"You do, do you?" I closed my eyes again, no pain this time. Just her palm on my check. Pulling her close, I met her lips with mine. Thoughts of anything else melted away.

"Mm hmmm," she murmured as her body pressed into mine. "And right now, you need to think of something else."

"What else did you have in mind?"

In answer, she straddled my hips and lowered herself onto me. Her kisses burned away my fears. Her hands massaged out my doubts. For the next hour, my universe was Sara. My purpose: her. Through Sara, I found a way home.

About The Author

TH Leatherman is a writer from Firestone, Colorado. He enjoys science fiction, fantasy, wine making, and the Rocky Mountain lifestyle. When not busy writing his next book, he can be found hiking with his wife and two sons, or walking his rescued dogs. He graduated Summa Cum Laude from Regis University with a degree in Business Management and a minor in Psychology.

Connect with Mr. Leatherman

https://thleatherman.com/

www.facebook.com/TH-Leatherman-178966392546053/

@thleatherman on Twitter

Reviews!

Authors (especially me) love reviews. Good, bad, or indifferent tell me what you think. You can do it easily on Amazon and Goodreads, but anywhere book lovers congregate is appreciated.

www.ingramcontent.com/pod-product-compliance
Lightning Source LLC
Chambersburg PA
CBHW060933120726
47910CB00002B/312